ESCAPING *the* MERMAN

ESCAPING THE MERMAN

Cursed Mermen Book 1

Aramis Jordan

ESCAPING THE MERMAN
Copyright © 2021 Aramis Jordan

All rights reserved. The moral rights of the author have been asserted. No part of this book may be used or reproduced in any manner whatsoever without written permission except in the case of brief quotations embodied in critical articles or reviews.

This book is a work of fiction. Names, characters, businesses, organizations, places, events and incidents either are the product of the author's imagination or are used fictitiously. Any resemblance to actual persons, living or dead, events, or locales is entirely coincidental.

The person on the cover is a model and should not be connected to the characters in the book. Any resemblance is incidental.

Cover design by Fantasia Frog Designs
Edited by ClockTower Editing
Proofread by Raven Quill Editing
Book formatting by Derek Murphy @Creativindie

First KPD Edition: June 2021

*For all you slash fan fiction writers out there.
Thank you for giving me life.*

Acknowledgments

Publishing a book takes a village!

To my beta readers Kein and Lucie: thanks a million for your invaluable feedback. You are the best.

A massive thank you goes to my author friends over at the Baby Author Think Tank: Nadia, Jeanne, Hayden, B.J., Layne, J.S., Jennifer and K.D.—thank you for all your advice, support and patience with my never-ending questions.

Thank you to Shel for the gorgeous cover, Elouise for copyedits and Raven for proofreading.

I also want to thank everyone who's helped with the marketing of *Escaping the Merman*, be it through sharing social media posts, making beautiful edits, writing blog posts or any other way. I never expected any of this, and you've totally blown me away!

Thank you to all my ARC readers for taking a chance on my debut romance novel.

And last but certainly not least I want to thank my new friends over at Facebook who've enthusiastically supported the making of this book and have (im)patiently waited for its release. Thank you from the bottom of my heart for your excitement for my mermen. Your kindness is nothing short of incredible, and I am humbled by the love and support I've received.

About the Author

Aramis Jordan is a self-professed MM romance addict and has vowed to write every book they'd love to read but cannot find. A firm believer in "the steamier, the better", Aramis likes to turn up the heat in their paranormal romance novels.

Splitting their time between an office job and creative endeavors, Aramis's life is powered by breakfast cereal and chai latte. When not writing or reading, Aramis enjoys going for scenic walks while listening to obscure rock music.

About this book

Escaping the Merman is a gay romance novel depicting an intense romantic relationship between two men. It contains scenes featuring mild dubious permission and is intended for readers who are of age. *Escaping the Merman* is set in the Caribbean during colonial times.

Chapter One

Fernando

Fernando stared out at the starry night sky stretching over the endless, midnight blue ocean, the moonlight shimmering on the water's surface. It was time to go below deck and join in the alcohol-fueled revelry his friends were enjoying—as the ship's investor, he'd paid for it, after all—but it was difficult to draw himself away from the endless sea.

That was the crux of it, wasn't it? He longed to find a wife, someone to love and cherish. A woman who would understand him, a partner he could relate to, but he couldn't bring a self-respecting lady on board a ship to travel at his side to far-off destinations. He knew he was handsome, a successful bachelor who had built a name for himself among the upper-class, so there was no shortage of interested ladies. Unfortunately, he was never interested in them. They didn't share his love of seafaring adventures, of conducting business in foreign lands.

And he couldn't imagine settling down on land for good. He loved his homes in Spain and Puerto Rico, but more than that, he loved the sea. The slosh of waves against the wooden ship, the sting of a cheap drink, the camaraderie not offered among his upper-class friends on land. Time to head downstairs. He tore himself away from the view and made his way under deck to join the crew.

A drop of sweat ran down the side of Fernando's neck and caressed his collarbone before dipping under his white sailor's shirt. Absently, he tugged at the strings that held the cotton together over his chest, trying to cool himself as he entered the sweltering heat of the ship's packed mess. Twenty men were crammed into the tiny space. Some squeezed together on wooden benches, some sat on each other's laps, on empty barrels or even the floor. Laughter roared through the room and someone passed a half-empty bottle of rum to Fernando with a drunken grin as he sat down. He took a deep swig, the alcohol burning his throat as he set the bottle on the table with a heavy thud.

"And then," Darin, the first mate, said as he leaned onto the table in front of him, gaze traveling over his rapt audience, the free-flowing alcohol thickening his English accent until it was barely intelligible. "Of course, he has to fall in love with a human girl. She's all bright and pretty and unapproachable for mere mortals, but he's the god of the seas, he can have them all, right? Should be easy, right? Big god, human girl. Easy. Well, not so fast. She's in love with that prince of Atlantis! And he's a real looker!"

"Is he now?" Fernando asked.

"Oh, yes. All those Atlantean bastards are. Most gorgeous people in the world. Jealousy is eating the god alive. So he strikes Atlantis with lightning and buries the whole bloody island at the bottom of the sea."

Kristian, the ship's captain, snickered. "That makes no sense. Lightning won't sink an island in a hundred years." He shook his long blond hair and downed another drink. The man was a Swede, though Fernando didn't recall how he had ended up in the New World. Money was the likeliest reason, there was a lot to be made here.

"Doesn't have to make sense, it's a story," one of the other sailors drawled.

"Anyway, Atlantis is at the bottom of the sea, but the god's not finished yet. Oh, no. He goes and curses all the Atlanteans. Terrible curse, I tell you. He gives them fishtails." Darin paused for dramatic effect, the small loop of his single golden earring glinting in the candlelight. Kristian didn't seem to believe a word, his broad shoulders shaking with laughter. "And it gets worse! He doesn't only give them fishtails, he also curses them with eternal desire! Imagine that, they want to fuck all day but can't 'cause of that bloody fishtail."

Now Fernando was laughing too. He'd heard the old wives' tale a dozen times before, though Darin's slurred iteration had Kristian close to rolling on the floor, and Fernando wasn't far off. But behind all the laughter was the uncomfortable inkling there might be some truth to the story. Then there was also Homer's *Odyssey*, which Fernando had once read. He wondered how much of it was true.

"Well, I heard," Luis, the sinfully rich Spanish merchant, with whom Fernando had joined fleets for the trade run up to Boston and back, said, "they lure in sailors with their enigmatic song and ethereal voices. Ships burst apart when they hit the cliffs that the mermen have led them to. The men jump overboard, falling over themselves as they cannot get to the enchanted beauties on the rocks fast enough. The mermen take them away, never to be seen again. Nobody makes it out alive." Luis's voice was sober, even solemn. Like Kristian, he'd had a few drinks, but they couldn't afford to get as wasted as the crew.

The crew had stopped laughing, the mess had gone quiet. They had all listened to stories of sailors vanishing, a single one returning, telling tales of narrow escape and lost comrades.

"But first the mermen drink their cum!" Darin shouted, and now one of the men was rolling on the floor, holding his stomach, cackling, the rest of the room roistering again.

"Oh, don't you love these folks," Fernando said, slapping Luis on the shoulder.

"You got to, you got to." Luis ran his hand over his closely chopped salt and pepper hair, scratching his scalp. "Though, I enjoyed sharing this trip with a fellow Spaniard. Too many frog eaters hopping over the big pond these days. The crew loves you, you know. Sitting together with all of them, sharing food and drink. Wouldn't have done it on my own if I'm honest. But I like it. Wearing simple sailor's clothes instead of those pompous *justacorps* is just what I needed. The fashion in Spain is demanding. You're going back there soon?"

"To Spain? No, not before the summer. Boston was cold enough and Spain isn't much better this time of year." He would have shivered, at the mere thought, had he been anywhere but the heated belly of a ship in a balmy Caribbean night, his shirt drenched with sweat. "I prefer life in New Spain. Far fewer stuck-up noblemen looking down on us, no matter how broke they are and how much money we make on a single run."

"Amen to that. Life's kiss is warmer here. Got a woman in San Juan? A proper one, I mean. I know you aren't married…"

"No fiancée. You?"

"Nah, women mean trouble. I keep around ten whores, ends up being cheaper."

Fernando lifted his drink for a toast. "To cheap whores and good business." He took a sip of the well-aged rum and handed the bottle to Luis. Fernando wasn't going to tell him how he longed for love, a partner to share his life with.

"Whores and money, I'll drink to that." He turned to Fernando. "Though, you got to tell me if the stories all the San Juan whores tell are true."

"What stories?"

"Well," Luis said, glancing away and twisting the bottle on the table, "whores talk, you know. Even the pricey ones. You'd think they knew better than the girls at the harbor. But anyway, sounds like they'd pay *you* for their services if you stopped visiting them."

"Jesus Christ."

"And that's not all," Luis said, Fernando's wariness growing. "Before we left for this trip, I asked around about you. Since we hadn't worked together before, much less poured our money and resources into a single pot to hire a crew and all. Don't worry, they all praised you, payments on time, sound deals made, nobody that wouldn't recommend you. There was this one fella though—he endorsed you too—who told me this story about a friend of a friend who had trouble with his wife... in bed. Couldn't satisfy her if you're catching my drift."

Fernando dropped his head into his palm, unwilling to believe this story had made the rounds. What man would volunteer this type of information about his marriage? If Fernando had someone in his life to love, he'd cherish them. He'd make sure he would provide everything they needed himself and him alone. Not being able to and tell others about it? Unthinkable.

"Difficult lady," Luis said obliviously, "very difficult lady. Impossible to please in bed. Not her fault, of course, just not very responsive. But the husband knows your rep with the girls in San Juan. So there is this party at their house, you attend, and at the end of the night, they invite you to their bedroom, and you go to town on the wife. Show him how it's done. Neighbors recounted she screamed so loudly that they thought she was getting murdered. Body was shaking like an earthquake when you finished her off. That true?"

Luis must have been a lot more drunk than Fernando had realized. That, or a lot more shameless. Possibly both. "Not going to ruin my reputation and tell you otherwise, right?"

"Don't think your reputation is in danger."

Trouble was, the truth was worse. The husband had bet Fernando a whole doubloon he couldn't make his wife come. Fernando was confident and the lady eager. The husband was present during the whole thing, to learn and to obtain proof of the wife's orgasm for the bet. The latter was easier than most would think. When the moment approached, Fernando took the husband's hand and pressed it to her pelvis. Her powerful orgasmic contractions were undeniable. She was vocal about it too. Afterward, the husband's face contorted in a sour grimace as he handed over the doubloon while the wife's starry-eyed gaze spoke volumes of how she regretted her choice of husband.

It was insane that the couple had gone through with it. Fernando would never share his wife if he finally found the right woman. The thought alone of another man touching the one he loved soured his mood.

Nevertheless, Fernando enjoyed easy company, no strings attached. Even before he had a reputation in San Juan, Puerto Rico, he'd had plenty of success. He liked women and they liked him, his good looks opening up opportunities with the young ladies of the nobility, a social circle closed to him otherwise. Fernando loved sex, and it was easy to come by. Everyone played the good Catholic until the doors closed, the lights went out, and inhibitions flew out the window. They all wanted to screw, and Fernando took full advantage of the melting pot of the Caribbean—not only Spanish women but black, white, native, mixed-race... he didn't discriminate, they all had it coming. He started young, discovered he enjoyed giving pleasure and had gotten good at it. Too good, if stories were making the rounds.

But no matter how much he loved sex and his partner writhing in the clutches of an orgasm he alone was responsible for, he hadn't found love. While infatuation came easily to his friends, it eluded him. He—in socially acceptable ways—had courted several women briefly and in quick succession, each time pulling away after a few short weeks. It left him empty. He had turned thirty last year, prime marrying age, but the idea of proposing to a woman who didn't mean anything to him, and never would, revolted him. Maybe he just hadn't met the right person yet.

Fernando was jolted out of his thoughts when a commotion arose in the hallway outside the mess, a scream of terror, freezing everyone in place: "Pirates! Pirates!"

His head whipped around to Kristian, who stared at him wide-eyed. They jumped to their feet, burst through the door, and ran past crew, up the stairs to the deck. The scent of fresh seawater hit his nostrils and spray dampened his clothes.

"Pirates to the west!" the lookout shouted from the crow's nest.

"To the west?" Fernando asked, staring at Kristian. "How are there pirates to the west? We're supposed to—"

"I'm going to kill that navigator," Kristian said. "Where's the navigator!"

The lanky kid, barely eighteen, ran over with a map in hand, the damp wind of the sea tousling his hair. He was positively panicked, teeth clattering.

"Where are we?" Kristian asked.

"I think about fifty-five nautical miles northeast of San Juan. Fifty nautical miles north of Vieques. Just recalculated everything. Sir." Vieques. A known pirates' nest. They were way off course.

"You think?" Kristian bristled. Hiring such an inexperienced navigator had been the only mistake on an otherwise successful trip. The boy had almost run them into rocks off the coast of New England.

"How far out are they?" Fernando yelled up at the lookout.

"Half a mile or less."

Kristian cursed.

"Ship's square-rigged," the lookout yelled.

"What do we do?" Luis asked.

Dark clouds had covered the stars and shrouded the waxing gibbous of the moon. This was supposed to be their last night aboard the ship, safely approaching San Juan. Believing themselves out of danger, they'd allowed many of the crew to drink, not counting on a screw-up from the navigator. At least the kid wasn't drunk.

"I've run into my fair share of pirates over the years," Darin said, more sober than just minutes ago. By the looks of his single earring and the scar on his cheek, he might have been a pirate at one point. "We have two options. We surrender and they take our cargo, nobody gets hurt. Or we make a break for it. If they catch us, it will get ugly, painfully so. Literally. Trust me, you don't want that.

But on the other hand, we might make it with our lives and our cargo."

"Their ship is square-rigged," Kristian said, pacing. "That's not a typical pirate ship. Too slow and cumbersome. They got it recently on a raid when the boarded crew put up a fight and got slaughtered. The ship might be full of cargo, slowing it even more."

"*We* are full of cargo," Fernando said. He didn't like this one bit. This ship, this crew was his responsibility. He'd put his money in it, and he would take care of them. Kristian wanted them to run, putting everyone on board at risk. If they were boarded, they'd have to fight, something they were not prepared for. Fernando, being the son of a farmer, never shied away from manual labor aboard, hauling cargo onto the ship alongside everyone else. It got him onto the good side of the crew real fast and kept him in prime shape. He'd do all right in a fistfight—which was useless when faced with cutlass-armed opponents trained in sword fighting. Which Fernando wasn't.

He was thankful the other ships of the fleet, the ones carrying the majority of the cargo, were already safe in San Juan. He and Luis had stayed back in Boston for another week to negotiate terms for a new delivery in spring—he'd bring sugar, molasses and rum to the north and return with boat-loads of flour, livestock and lumber. His cargo was safe, but he also didn't have any back-up.

"We're on a schooner," Kristian said. "We are fast and agile and have plenty of cannons. Our draft is as shallow as it gets, we can escape or hide close to an island. The ship's called *The Haste* for a reason. The crew is well paid, trusts us and will comply with orders. This is not a situation where we have to give up our cargo." And that cargo was not only high-quality lumber, but also the gold they had earned on this trip. They'd made a killing, and Fernando hadn't risen from farm boy to one of the richest merchants of Puerto Rico by giving away what he earned. He appreciated Kristian's experience as captain. A couple of years younger than Fernando, he'd been sailing the seas for as long as him. He knew what he was doing.

"I agree with Kristian," Darin said. "That square-rigger is bulky."

"Luis?" Fernando asked.

"Fine."

Fernando took the map off the navigator and spread it on a crate. Time for him to take charge. "Hand me a lamp."

"Here."

Fernando tapped their position on the map and traced a line to a small cluster of islands east of Puerto Rico. "We're closest to the Culebra archipelago. What's there?"

"It was a pirate haven until about ten years ago," Darin said. "It was abandoned, no one's been there in years."

"Order your crew to set the sails for Culebra," Fernando told Kristian. "With the current winds, we'll reach it around dawn, and if we haven't lost the pirates by then, we can hide in shallow waters and wait for them to move on."

The pirate ship turned out to be faster than anticipated. *The Haste* cut through the sea, the pirates in pursuit, gaining two hundred yards on them over the final hours of the night. Their ship must have been empty to go this fast. Fernando chewed his lip, running the numbers in his head, how long it'd take the pirates to catch up to them and if *The Haste* could make it to Culebra.

When the first light of morning hit the horizon, the lookout shouted, "Land in sight!" Fernando, standing on the stern deck, watched as the pirates slowly changed course, turning southwest toward their nest in Vieques. They had gained another hundred yards on *The Haste* in the last hour but must have realized continuing the chase was pointless.

The main deck was buzzing with activity, Luis was chatting with Kristian and a deckhand asked loudly, "Where are we headed again?"

"Culebra," Darin said and yawned as he directed the crew's activities.

"Culebra? I heard that before."

"Yeah, used to be a pirates' nest, but they're gone."

"Oh, yes, I remember. Mermen came and—"

"What?" Luis's sharp tone had Fernando twist his head toward him as Luis stalked across the wooden floor to the deckhand. "What did you say?"

"Heard a story about mermen 'round the archipelago. That's all."

"Don't worry about it," Kristian said to Luis as Fernando took the steps down to join the others on the main deck. "Just yarn spun by old sailors."

"I have good news though," Fernando said. "The pirates turned away."

"Because they know there are mermen," Luis said.

"Horseshit," Kristian said. "They know our draft is shallow and we can hide in the archipelago."

"Dunno," the deckhand said. "I don't like it."

"Me neither," Luis said.

"In any case," Kristian said, "we've got to get there because if you haven't noticed, we're still in the pirates' line of sight, and if they see us turning away, they'll be nipping at our heels again."

"I don't think there are mermen in the archipelago," Fernando said. "And if there are, I'm sure we can resist a few men with fishtails without crashing our ship."

That pacified Luis. "Yeah, you're right. Us womanizers got nothing to worry about, right?"

Chapter Two

Arian

Arian woke when the incoming tide washed over him. His fishtail was slick with seawater, and his first thought, as every morning, was how frustratingly aroused he was. He clenched his pelvic muscles—he had them, though whether they were a blessing or a curse, he wasn't sure. It brought him no relief, but he kept tensing them instinctively. If only he had been born human, he could reach between his legs each morning and bring himself to climax. Several times a day if he wanted. Maybe that old tale of an angry god cursing the Atlanteans with fishtails was true after all.

He blinked as foam and saltwater splashed over him again, and he lifted his hand to push damp, strawberry blond strands of hair out of his face. The water crept back over him and withdrew from the beach to the sea as the early morning light kissed the sky. Arian had slept on the beach again. Not a comfortable place, but comfort wasn't exactly a staple in a merman's life.

He sat up, turned on his front and waited for the tide to return. When the next wave swept in, he pushed off the sand and into the water, working his arms hard to get as far down the beach with a single wave as possible. This was the only way to do it if he didn't want the coarse sand to grate his skin raw.

Slipping into the pleasantly warm water, he moaned. Like the sea kept rolling onto the shore, his lust came over him in waves, cresting and withdrawing, only to crest again. It had been too long since he'd had a lost sailor to play with. No matter what he did, it never brought him to completion, but if seeing them writhe and pulse with madding pleasure was what he could get, he would take it.

Arian slid deeper into the ocean, turned around and ducked under. Schools of small yellow fish passed him as he swam out of the bay. Soon he reached the group of rocks on the fringes of the Canal de Cayo Culebrita, a narrow strait separating this island from the next. When he broke through the surface, Tarlis was already there, perched on his favorite rock, the fin of his gleaming red fishtail lazily swaying in the water in an elegant arc. Zade was heaving himself out of the sea and onto a rock, muscles rippling as his dark brown, wet skin glistened in the early light. He pulled his thick, long dreadlocks back and wrung them out as Tarlis said something to him that Arian didn't hear over the sound of the ocean. He swam closer and greeted them.

"Did you sleep all right?" Tarlis asked, heavy-lidded eyes soft, his dark hair beautifully contrasting his milky white skin.

"Fine." Arian picked a rock, and he lifted himself onto it, rivulets running down the length of his body.

This was their daily morning ritual: meet at the rocks, watch the sunrise, find comfort in each other's company.

Tarlis shifted, and Arian saw the moment desire shot through him; the slight tremble in his slender arms, the white-knuckled grip on dark stone, the delicate contortion of his face, an expression Arian was displaying far too often himself. They all suffered the same fate, though there was only friendship between them. Attraction was reserved for men. Men with long, muscular legs and thick, throbbing, dripping—stop! This wasn't helping. He would endure this constant state of arousal all his life, and it was best to focus on the small joys of life and keep a positive mindset instead of getting frustrated over his lack of genitals and inability to experience pleasure the way humans did.

A sliver of the sun poked over the horizon when Finn joined them. More often than not, he was the last to arrive in the morning, liking to sleep later than the rest of them. He swam over, flicked the tip of his fishtail and waved his fin in greeting. He dove back under with a fluke, the rainbow of sunset colors of his fishtail flashing through the air.

"That's my rock," he said when he popped back up right in front of Arian.

"Not today."

Finn stuck his tongue out, but Arian ignored him. Finn would find another rock.

The sun had inched into full view when Finn, who sat behind Arian and the others at an angle, gasped loudly and Arian, whipping around, watched him fall into the water with a splash. Arian scanned the surroundings for signs of danger. There were none. When he lifted his gaze, it fell upon a ship floating through the morning fog. A narrow hull of dark wood, topped with two masts, triangular sails out front, rectangular ones in the back. Arian's heart leaped. A ship meant men.

Finn resurfaced and shook out his wavy blond mane.

Beside Arian, Zade said, "So today's a good day after all." And licked his lips.

This might not be salvation, but it was as close as it was going to get. Arian swallowed dryly, his loins throbbing, lust eating him alive as he slid into a haze. He was dimly aware that were he in a normal state of mind, he would be disgusted at what he was about to do. What *they* were going to do. But there was no normal state of mind for mermen, not with the insatiable need smoldering inside them every hour of every day.

Arian narrowed his eyes as the ship slid down the strait, closer and closer. There was no escape for the blissfully unaware men on board. Even if they saw them, it was too late. A sailboat wasn't half as fast as a merman could swim.

Oh, and there was the chest of enchanted items Zade had obtained from the sea witch in the mangroves of Puerto Rico. Finally putting them to good use would be fun. Arian clenched his inner muscles again. He could not wait.

Once the ship was within earshot, the mermen began to sing. An old melody in a language no one spoke anymore, the words tasting of wistfulness and longing. Their voices carried far across the water, and a moment later, a drove of men had appeared at the port side of the ship.

Arian's eyes wandered over the small crowd of sailors in the prime of their lives. His breath hitched when he saw *him*.

A god of a man.

His skin a deep tan, broad shoulders and a wet, white shirt that clung to his muscles like a second skin. A hint of stubble lined his jaw, and his head was a glorious mess of dark brown curls. He was wild, untamed beauty, oblivious to his attractiveness. While the other men were drooling, he was battling the sweet call of the song, fighting to get the others away from the railing. Nobody had ever put up a fight. Women and men would throw themselves at his feet wherever he went. Arian sang for him. He'd fight the others for him if he had to. No other would do. That was new—in the past Arian had been happy with any shapely young man. Not this time. Not when *he* was on the table. And how enthralling to watch his struggle, the powerful play of his muscles.

But then this splendid specimen of a man turned his head and looked at the rocks. Arian caught his gaze, and in a split second, the man's face went slack as he lost all control and surrendered to the merman's call.

Chapter Three

Fernando

The Haste sailed into the Canal de Cayo Culebrita where green islands rose out of the sea to both sides. Fernando's level of concern went from low to sky high when the ship was halfway through the strait, and the first note of an ancient melody sounded through the air. Mermen, without the shadow of a doubt. Fernando cursed. A chorus of voices so pure, so angelic, it was impossible to fight its pull. But fight he did. *Come to me.* Fog clouded his mind, and he clenched his jaw as Kristian, Luis, Darin and the rest of the crew stormed the balustrade. It cost Fernando all his willpower to not jump straight in, and instead hold his friends back in a futile attempt to save them from their doom. It was mayhem. The cook and the navigator were ready to plunge headfirst into the strait, while Darin was getting a small rowboat to let into the sea. Someone jostled Fernando, and he gripped the railing, turned to the water and looked down.

His eyes wandered to the mermen, sitting on rocks, the call of their voices stronger than ever. Fernando fought it with all his might. He would not give in to the urge to launch himself toward them. He would resist. He would—

He stopped on the most stunning creature he had ever seen. His mind went blank, and a strange compulsion took over, canceling all rational thought.

Perched on a rock was the manifestation of all things good, divine, worth fighting for. Fernando drank in every minute detail. Honey blond hair, long and lustrous. An androgynous, yet muscled body clad in golden skin. The fishtail a dizzying gradient of all shades of blue from cobalt at the trim waist over shimmering sky blue scales, to an aquamarine fin, delicately creased like draped silk. And he was looking at Fernando as if he was singing just for him.

Fernando had to have him, no matter the cost. He had to get to him before anyone else did. Darin was helpfully getting a rowboat down, and Fernando leaped over the railing and into it, followed by Kristian, Luis, Darin himself, and then a quick descent before they hit the water.

Fernando grabbed a pair of paddles and didn't even look when something—or someone—behind the boat dropped into the strait. All he cared about was the pull of that sweet voice, calling him closer with a promise of paradise and bliss. If only he were already there...

Powered by four men, the boat darted forward in the clammy air of the early morning, ever closer to the rocks. Fernando's eyes didn't leave the merman, tracking his every movement in case he'd try and get away from him. But the merman stayed on the rock, his song never ceasing.

Such beauty was out of this world, reserved for angels and divine creatures. How Fernando deserved to be in the presence of this being, he didn't know. Worries sprung up in the back of his mind, but Fernando cut them down. There was nothing to be concerned about. This was a gift from the heavens.

When the boat had almost reached the mermen, Fernando couldn't wait any longer, couldn't risk anyone else taking his prize. He jumped into the water and with a few strokes, he came face to face with the merman, who gracefully slid down the rock to greet him.

Absently, Fernando registered the area was shallow enough for him to stand, waves lapping at his chest. Up close, the merman was even more attractive. His eyes were of an intense cerulean blue and gazed up at him through thick, dark lashes, observant and unblinking. Fernando's teeth sank into his bottom lip to control his flaring desire. The merman's eyes flashed, and a pink tongue darted out to lick his peachy lips, glossing them up.

Had it not been for the water, Fernando would have dropped to his knees and worshiped him. This was how he'd wanted to feel about the ladies he courted but never did. None of them had inspired a whiff of devotion. Not like this divine creature did. Fernando wanted to speak, but no sound came out.

The merman moved so fast, Fernando's foggy mind didn't register it until he was pressed up flush against his front, the sudden touch sending shivers down his spine, the merman's scent sweet and inviting. And there was something else that had slipped past his notice until now when his erection was trapped between their bodies. There was the vague thought this was unusual, though it eluded him why it would be. And it didn't matter, not when the merman had one arm wrapped around his middle, the other hand shoved into his hair, fisting his curls. Fernando hesitated, then tugged the merman closer to him. He failed to suppress a moan as the delicious pressure against his cock intensified. But not only that, the silky skin of the merman's back had its own appeal, and he gently trailed his fingers over it.

A tangle of opaque feelings fought in Fernando's mind. On the surface, heeding the merman's call sparked the satisfaction of giving in to desire. Beneath that, a strange concern raged, though it was muffled, distant and unimportant like the screams of a prisoner in the underground dungeons of a castle, unheard on the higher levels. And at the bottom of his soul, lay a feeling Fernando had never accessed, buried so deep only the merman's call had woken it. A sense of warmth and rightness Fernando didn't understand, but it was undeniable and rang true.

This encounter was sacred.

He held the merman tighter, drowning in the blue eyes looking up at him. How could this be happening to him? How could he be worthy of it? Had he died and gone to heaven?

The merman tilted his head as if assessing the situation, but no, that's not what that was. His face came closer and only then Fernando understood, his lips parting in shock. The merman took advantage of it, taking his lower lip between his own and stroking the tip of his tongue over it. Soft, warm lips. A wet tongue. A whine caught in his throat at the deliciousness of it. Fernando's very being was pulsing. Then the merman's tender lips were fully on his, applying gentle pressure, caressing him with little movements, which drove Fernando wild. His body and soul screamed for more, and he surged, taking control of the kiss as he pushed the merman to the rock, trapping him and sliding his tongue into his hot mouth. He tasted of rain and ocean air and promises whispered in the dark. His saliva was thicker than a human's, which Fernando reveled in for reasons beyond his understanding. But it was good. So, so good. He longed to possess, to own, to mark the merman as his. Fernando ground into him, seeking friction, and the merman's lips spread into a smile.

"You like it," the merman mumbled against his mouth.

"Hmm."

The merman drove his body against his, then slipped from his grasp and dove under. Disappointment rushed through Fernando, but the merman reemerged a couple of feet away, his wet hair clinging to his shoulders.

"Come," he said, holding out his hand. For a moment, Fernando stared at the long fingers, the slender wrist. Then he placed his hand in his, the renewed contact a flash of relief. The merman's grip was firm, and with astonishing speed, he pushed forward, dragging Fernando with him.

They swam for a while, and as the lull of the song faded, resistance grew in Fernando. What was he doing? He wanted to run and, at the same time, follow the merman to the ends of the Earth.

Confused, he recalled his actions. His last clear thought had been trying to resist the song, then when he had looked at the mermen, he'd lost control. His mortification grew proportionally to the clarity of his mind. Had he really scrambled to get into a boat to launch himself into a merman's arms? Unable to stop the memories assaulting him, they rushed by in his mind's eye. Bodies pressed together. Lips. Tongues.

Oh, no. He had not—Yes, he had.

A few more strokes and they slowed to a halt. Fernando glanced up at the wide mouth of a cave the merman had dragged him to. Something was wrong. He pulled at his hand in the merman's grip.

His mind raced. The tall arch of the cave towered over them, but it wasn't deep, and he could see the end of it. At shouts from the ship, he whipped around, watching several of his friends being dragged away by more mermen. There was another rowboat filled to the brim with sailors eager for their demise. He had to take responsibility and do what was right. Anything to spare them this fate.

"Let the others go, and I will follow you willingly." He was responsible for the lives and welfare of the crew. Not legally, but the moral obligation to protect them weighed heavy on him. They ought to be safe and far away from the mermen.

"We have stopped singing. They will snap out of it soon, as you did."

"I can see them being dragged away!"

The merman tilted his head. "Just three of them, and trust me, if they're coming with my friends, they do so because they want to. The rest of the men will leave on their own when they come to themselves." He regarded the ship. "There, one of them is already swimming back."

Good, good. This way they would be safe, and he had the merman to himself—What? He shook off the insane thought, and considered following the merman into the cave. Because it would keep the crew safe, no other reason—or that's what he told himself.

"Are you coming?" the merman asked. "You do have a choice. Once we're in the cave, my rules apply, and you will obey. I'll have to tied you up, for my safety. Yes or no?"

"Yes."

Inside, it smelled of stale water and damp wood. Ledges of smooth rock a couple of yards deep lined the sides of the cave. The merman swung onto the stone and helped pull Fernando up. A rope lay along the back. Before Fernando could react, its coarse fibers scraped the skin of his wrists as the merman tied him up, his arms outstretched behind his back. Lying on the rock ledge, Fernando tugged at the rope, but it was fixed to something solid behind him.

"If you continue being difficult, I can exchange you for one of your more agreeable friends. There'll be someone else willing."

Fernando stilled immediately. He wouldn't want another sailor to be in his spot. This was his place.

"I thought so." The merman held his legs down. "It's good you're easy to read. Now keep still." He pulled Fernando to the end of the ledge, his legs hanging over. The rope around his wrists pulled taut.

Fernando's heart jump-started when the merman tied his ankles to fixed ropes far apart, spreading him wide open. "What are you doing?" The merman pulled the knots tight. Fernando was trapped. And yet... there was a curious appeal to the situation. An inkling that this could be more than it seemed.

An angry growl echoed through the cave when Kristian was dragged in by the hair by a merman with alabaster skin and waves of dark locks, hissing unintelligible threats in his ear. Despite being built like a Nordic god, Kristian was undeniably under the control of the delicate merman. He also wasn't putting up a real fight, his half-hearted attempts to get away more for saving face than anything else.

Fernando's merman came up between his spread knees and stroked his thigh. At the sight of him between his legs, a feeling dangerously close to lust, rose deep inside his belly.

Splashing noises continued to fill the cave long after Kristian and Tarlis disappeared into the shadows. The sound of ripping fabric tore through the air. Fernando told himself Kristian had snapped the ropes that surely held him too, unwilling to entertain other possibilities. Kristian did not reappear.

Luis and Darin's handlers were friendlier when they entered the cave. A blond merman was all but wrapped around Darin as they swam in, and Luis had his face buried in the crook of the neck of a black merman.

"What do you want? I'll make it easy for you if you tell me, and we can come to an agreement." Fernando had led business negotiations from Boston to Havana to Madrid and he was good at it. He understood people and culture, knew how to close a deal. He was a better man now, but in his youth when money had been short, he sold boatloads of horseshoes to people without horses and a year's worth of fish to people living on an island. If he could get the merman to talk, reveal what he wanted, he could gain leverage. Negotiate. Turn this to his advantage. He had suspicions of what was going to happen. After all, the stories about mermen luring in sailors had proven true. There were two reasons why he'd get tied up and he didn't think he was going to get gutted alive.

"I won't hurt you. None of you will get hurt, I promise," the merman said.

"Why would I believe you." A statement, not a question. Bait for information.

"You know the stories they tell about us."

"The ones where nobody makes it back alive?"

"No." The merman licked his lips. "You will like it."

Fernando trembled when the merman pulled himself up on the ledge by grabbing onto his knees, gliding over him. They lined up perfectly, the place where the merman's crotch would have been hovering over Fernando's, who gasped when he came to rest on it. He stared up at the gorgeous creature. Fernando had held many beauties in his arms, but never one so devastating. Not a single imperfection, not the slightest blemish. More attractive than any woman. Helpless and laid open, Fernando was inexplicably aroused. Had his hands been free, he wouldn't have pushed the merman away but pulled him closer. Touched the soft skin, the silky hair. Kissed those peachy lips, the crook of his neck. Why hadn't Fernando visited a few whores up north? Then he wouldn't be this ridiculously turned on by a merman. He was sex-starved. That was the only possible explanation for his arousal.

He turned his face to the side and focused on the far wall of the cave. Hands seized his shirt, and the forceful rip of wet fabric hit him as the cotton gave way. He knew where this was going. Exhilaration and panic flooded him. Fernando yanked at the ropes, muscles bulging. The restraints held.

"Stop fighting it."

"Then stop undressing me."

"If you don't want this..." the merman ripped Fernando's breeches to shreds and cool air enveloped his naked legs, his hips, his cock, "...then why are you hard?"

Fernando panted, eyes shut, heat creeping into his face. Why indeed.

A gentle hand cupped his face as if in apology. "What's your name?" the merman whispered, so close that soft breath brushed Fernando's skin.

"Fernando."

"Fernando," the merman said, testing out the word. "I'm Arian." Warm lips laid a chaste kiss on his cheek.

An onslaught of strange emotions flushed through Fernando, which intensified when Arian lay down next to him. The merman shifted to align their bodies and a moan between pain and pleasure puffed hot against Fernando's ear. Fernando turned, bringing them nose to nose, no more than an inch separating them, and regarded him carefully. Arian's pupils were blown, a faint blush gracing his cheeks.

"I need it badly," Arian said, keeping his voice low so it wouldn't echo through the cave. "Otherwise, I wouldn't do it. It won't hurt, that's a promise. I'll make it good for you." He trailed his fingers over Fernando's cheek, along his neck and down his chest. "In fact, the more you enjoy it, the more I'll enjoy it too."

Should he put up a fight? No, he would accept this and find a way out.

Arian's hand traveled across his tightly clenched abs and further down. "I'd let you go if you were crying, kicking and screaming. But you're not. Tell me you don't want me to touch you and I won't."

Fernando's skin tingled wherever Arian's hands went. "Don't stop."

He held his breath and braced for the moment Arian's long fingers would curl around his cock. Except they didn't, and Arian took his hand away entirely. Fernando was relieved. Definitely relieved, not disappointed.

A self-satisfied smirk graced Arian's lips. "Your cock just twitched."

"No, it didn't."

"Hmm, if you say so. I'll let you pretend for a while longer. As long as you're still able to."

Then Arian was on him, kissing him. It was different now that Fernando was no longer under the spell of the song. Clearer. It wasn't like kissing a woman; Arian's body was hard where a female's would have been soft and rounded. Fernando didn't return the kiss, but neither did he fight it, knowing full well it would lead nowhere. Arian's lips were full and silky, brushing over his own gently.

"Not much fun kissing a dead fish," Arian said.

He moved to Fernando's neck, licking his pulse point. Pleasure shot through him, and he inhaled sharply when Arian covered the area with his mouth and sucked. Hard. Fernando wriggled in his restraints. He refused to feel anything. This was the aftereffect of the spell, he told himself over and over like a mantra, even though deep down, he knew better.

Arian trailed the tip of his tongue down his body, curving around to work on a nipple. Fernando went stiff as a ramrod when Arian's tongue flicked it. Heat pooled in his stomach and further south as if an invisible cord connected his pecs to his throbbing cock. He focused his mind elsewhere, on memories of summer days in Spain, but everything blurred as Arian licked and sucked, only letting go when his nipple had gone hard, finishing the job by blowing cool air on it. An involuntary shiver raced over Fernando's skin. Satisfied with his work, Arian turned to his other nipple, this time looking Fernando in the eye as his tongue darted out to flick the pink nub. Fernando's cock grew impossibly harder.

A wanton groan that sounded suspiciously like Darin echoed off the walls.

"Your friends are enjoying themselves," Arian said. "You should relax too."

Like hell he would. He brought up images of the most disgusting things he could think of, willing his dick down. Since the merman didn't have a cock, there'd be no penetration. All he could do was give him a blowjob, and if Fernando grew soft, Arian would give up, wouldn't he?

His dick had other ideas when Arian gently bit his erect nipple. Surely it wasn't precum that was beading on his glans. Arian planted kisses down his stomach, each one lighting fire in Fernando's blood. He hissed as his stomach tightened. Excitement bubbled up, and he gave in to it for the briefest moment as it rushed through his body.

Arian slipped between his legs, and Fernando steeled himself for the inevitable. Since his dick wasn't cooperating, and a mouth was a mouth, he imagined a woman was going to suck him off. A woman with strawberry blond hair and an incredibly deep, blue gaze. Eyes shut, Fernando waited for that first lick, for lips closing around his tip applying just the right amount of pressure.

It never came.

Instead, his cheeks were pulled apart, and he shouted in shock. On instinct, he clenched his hole tightly, but there was no intrusion, just a slick tongue lapping at his entrance. Fuck, that felt good. He tossed his head back and bit his bottom lip, unwilling to let any sounds slip out. Arian flattened his tongue against his hole and gave it a few broad strokes. Fernando dug blunt fingernails into the palms of his hands. He didn't find men attractive. But stroke by stroke, the tension seeped out of him until Arian's tongue was drawing little circles around him. Fernando didn't moan, though a restrained puff forced its way out as he sagged back against the rock surface. He'd pay the harlots gold to do this to him once he got back to San Juan. If he got back. The edge of fear lingered, but it was unimportant and far away. Arian wasn't going to hurt him. Fernando let go, his sole focus on the wet caress around his most private place.

Arian's tongue pushed inside. Fernando bit down hard on his lip to keep from crying out in pleasure, but no pain was sharp enough to distract him from the wet piece of heaven in his anus. It was too much, too intimate, having another person, another man, slide into his most private orifice. And he was helpless, enjoying it. Unbelievable Arian was tonguing him there, his movements full of care and affection as if Arian accepted, no, wanted every part of him, even the darkest. No one had ever touched Fernando there and never before had he felt so exposed. In and out, in and out. His muscles loosened under Arian's ministrations, relaxation coaxed out of him. Ironclad self-control kept him from moaning like a whore. He had never experienced such tender affection. Arian pushed his tongue in as deep as possible, then withdrew. Fernando whimpered at the loss.

"That didn't hurt, now, did it?" Arian didn't wait for an answer. "And it's only going to get better." No, it hadn't hurt, though it was distressing how good he felt under Arian's hands, lips and tongue. Especially that tongue.

Fernando watched Arian lick his own finger, first the tip, followed by the whole digit. So that was next. Kissing Arian had taught him that mermen saliva was different from humans', thicker... the digit would slide in nicely. Fernando's heart beat fast. He had counted on penetration being out of the question, yet the merman had already invaded his body with his tongue, and his finger was next. What else did he have in store for him?

With the lightest touch, Arian circled and tapped his entrance. "How does it feel?" He kept stroking it for a while, Fernando's insides undulating. When his pleasure spiked, Arian pushed in the tiniest bit, causing Fernando to bite down hard. "Better than you thought it would? I bet it feels fantastic, opening up for me." It did. God, it did. "Having something slide into you. You don't know what I'd give to have someone do this to me." The finger pushed in deeper. "Invade my body, touch me in all those hidden places, taking me to ecstasy. You're not there yet. But you will be." All the way inside. Fernando panted. Arian's words stirred an urge deep inside of him, an urge to take and be taken. What was going on with him? He didn't think of men like that, not ever.

After a moment of letting him adjust, Arian began to finger him lightly, pushing in and out in an unhurried rhythm. "This is just the beginning." He kept the movement going for a while, then pulled out, slicked up a second finger and placed both of them at his entrance. "You will have to cooperate. I told you I wouldn't hurt you, but you need to do your part." He tapped his digits against Fernando's twitching sphincter. "Push out for me." Fernando stared at him. He would do no such thing. "It will make it easier." Arian rubbed the pads of his fingers over him. "Please."

Fernando exhaled and pushed out against Arian's wet fingers. They pressed into him despite his body's noticeable resistance.

Arian's gaze never left his as he slowly entered his hole through that tight ring of muscle. He was laying Fernando's soul wide open for him to see, all the while stripping away his inhibitions.

"You're doing well," Arian said.

The intrusion felt incredible, though it was far too personal. Fernando wriggled in his restraint, but it only caused him to shift forward, seating himself fully onto Arian's fingers.

The sudden fullness forced the air from his lungs. It didn't hurt. A strange sensation of too full yet not enough held him suspended. "Fuck, you're squeezing so hard around me. Wish I had a cock to slide into you." For a long moment, Arian didn't move, granting him a moment to adjust. Then he picked up a lazy rhythm. "Don't worry, I'll stretch you properly before we go further." Further? Were mermen shapeshifters? Was this going to make Arian turn? Would he fuck him?

It didn't fit with what he'd heard. No, Arian was going somewhere else.

With two fingers inside him, Fernando was sweating, and he struggled for control. And he wasn't the only one, judging by the tight grip Arian had on his thigh. He hadn't noticed before, but tremors raced through Arian, causing him to shake. Was he that turned on?

Arian followed his gaze to his shaking hand. "Yes, this is what you do to me," he said. "I'm always aroused, but this is something else. You are something else."

In and out, in and out. Then a twist and Arian's fingers scissored his pulsing inner walls apart. Fernando's control was slipping fast. His breath hitched while Arian probed him, his digits running along his insides as if searching for something. When they found their target, Fernando saw stars. What was that? His groin was burning up with desire. "Here we are," Arian said, sounding far away, as blinding pleasure coursed through Fernando. "That's your prostate. It's a part of your body that takes you to ecstasy when someone penetrates you. And I'll use it to milk every last drop of cum out of you." Arian rubbed sweet circles around that sensitive spot but never touching it again. Fernando groaned in frustration. A thick pearl of precum welled up at his slit. A war raged inside him as his desperation to be touched *there* grew. To have his cock inside a hot mouth. He didn't want to want it, yet he did so badly. He needed it. Torn between begging Arian to rub his fingertips over his prostate and wishing him to hell, that pearl of precum was about to spill over.

"I think we're ready," Arian said—Ready? Ready for what?—and removed his fingers. Fernando was about to scream in frustration when Arian leaned forward, licking the precum off his slit, strangely careful not to touch Fernando more than necessary. He nearly died of pleasure, nonetheless, at the wet touch of Arian's tongue along the tip of his glans. Arian's lustful groan spoke of trembling need.

Arian disappeared from his sight, and Fernando sank back. His eyes had long adjusted to the darkness, but only now that he couldn't see Arian, he took in what was going on around him in the cave. Luis was across from him, tied to the opposite wall, a dark-skinned merman getting busy between his legs. Further in, Darin was making out like a teenager with a shaggy blond merman. He didn't give the impression of being overly concerned with their current situation, and was the polar opposite of Kristian, who was letting out huffs in a dark corner as the brunet *beau* worked him over.

With flaming cheeks, Fernando turned away. The next moment Arian was back, holding a dark blue object in his hand. Two loops on one end, a phallic shape on the other. Aquamarine specks littered its surface, and it oddly pulsed in the dim light of the cave.

"What is that?" Fernando asked, alarm bells ringing in his head.

"One of the enchanted artifacts we got from the sea witch." Arian licked over the phallic form.

"Of course there is a sea witch." It looked suspicious. "Is that thing alive?"

"No," Arian said and laughed.

"Then why is it vibrating?"

"Wouldn't you like to know."

Fernando clenched his jaw as Arian took it deep into his mouth, then pulled it out slowly. Mesmerized, Fernando reacted too late when Arian pushed the first loop over his cock, letting it constrict around his base. "Oh, shit." It was a snug fit. Fernando hadn't thought he could get any harder, but he was being proven wrong fast as blood pumped into his dick, giving him an iron erection. Bulging veins throbbed in time with his heartbeat, and the head took on an angry purple color.

Arian placed the second ring around his balls. It pulled them away from his body, leaving them suspended. He would never come with that thing on.

The wriggling, blunt end came to rest against his twitching entrance.

"Push out."

"You're not putting that in me."

Arian raised an eyebrow. "That's the best part. We asked the sea witch to design these for maximum pleasure. You'll lose your mind."

"And you don't see how that might concern me?"

"It's not like our song." Arian pushed the slick end against him. "Open up for me." A tremor went through Arian, hips rolling, eyelids fluttering. "I need you."

Fernando's body reacted before his mind did, pushing out as the tip of the plug dipped inside him. It was bigger than Arian's fingers, stretching his hole wide, but lubed up in merman spit, it slid in smoothly. The sensation was strange, but it wasn't painful. Arian worked the plug into him, opening him, filling him to the brim. The toy went impossibly deep, then moved on its own accord as it wiggled in him, sending gentle vibrations into his groin that rippled over his whole body.

And the smirk on Arian's face told him this wasn't all. He placed his hand over where the toy vibrated against Fernando's perineum, and the damn thing started to rhythmically contract and relax. Fernando threw his head back. "Fuck!" And then there was that thick bump on the toy. Every time the plug contracted and expanded, it plunged into his swollen prostate.

All clear thought evaporated. The only thing that mattered, existed, was the cruel bump massaging itself firmly into his oversensitive bundle of nerves, causing him to throb and twitch around the toy. His hips jerked, his pulse quickened. He needed to come. He needed to come now. The urge to shoot his load had never been so overwhelming. As if in answer, the first ring constricted tighter around his engorged cock. The second pulled his balls away from his body. They hung swollen and heavy in the air as a cool finger traced them. *Contraction.* Pleasure radiating through him. *Contraction.* Lust urging him to bury himself in a tight hole. *Contraction.* Everything pulled taut. *Contraction.* He writhed as pleasure ripped at him, yet he couldn't fucking come.

The plug grew inside him, swelling to reach deeper, to spread him wider and the pressure on his prostate increased again when it was all but impossible.

Firm hands held his hips down, though Fernando didn't stop bucking. "You don't even know how gorgeous you are," Arian said.

More precum welled up, and Fernando caught Arian watching it with a hungry expression on his face. The merman licked his lips, greedily eyeing the droplet as it grew. What was he doing? He was supposed to blow him, for crying out loud. The pressure in his balls was unbearable.

Precum kept gathering on his cockhead until a thick bead spilled over, dripping down the underside of his dick. Arian lapped it up, running his tongue from the base of his cock along the bulging veins to the engorged head. Fernando lost his mind as Arian tongued his slit, drinking up every last bit of his precum.

His clenched fists shook, and he growled when Arian pulled back.

"Aren't you supposed to blow me?" Fernando grunted. "I need to fucking come."

"And you will. Eventually."

Precum beaded anew and Arian let it swell before he bent down to close his lips over Fernando's slit and sucked it up. Tingles shot through him like fireworks. The combination of Arian and the toy was wreaking havoc on him.

"I can't take this." His cock pulsed angrily in agreement.

Arian tilted his head and dragged his flattened tongue over Fernando's glans at a maddeningly slow pace.

"If you have to do this, at least do it properly," Fernando gruffed.

"But I am. You're delicious. Though, your balls aren't heavy enough yet." Arian traced a single finger over them, then cupped them in his hands, weighing them. "Not by a long shot."

Fernando gasped at the gentle handling of his full, oversensitive nads. "I disagree," he forced out.

"When you come, I want you to be gushing." Arian continued fondling his sack. "And for that, you need to produce more sperm. The toy helps with that." No kidding. It plunged back into his prostate. "Plus, I like seeing you naked, sweaty and desperate. It would be a shame to put an end to this too soon."

Fernando gave up and sank back, letting himself get carried away by the ceaseless lust and mounting pressure. The toy contracted relentlessly, keeping him suspended on the verge of orgasm but never taking him over it, the firm grip of the ring around the base of his cock denying him.

Arian kept lapping at him for hours. Fernando didn't care anymore. His body floated in rhythmic pleasure so unbearable he screamed for more.

His head pounded and his lips were cracked when finally Arian eased away. "We need to go and get fresh water for you and the others." His warm hand stroked Fernando's leg. "I don't want you to dry up, so we'll need to make sure you stay hydrated."

"Where are we going?" Fernando croaked.

"Not you and me. Just us mermen. Don't worry, I'll be back soon, and then you can drink. Your throat must be parched."

It was.

Arian touched the plug and the contractions slowed to a lazy pulse. Then he pushed out into the water, and together with the other mermen, he swam out of the cave. The moment they were out of sight, Fernando shuffled back on the rock. His hands raked over the rugged surface behind him, searching for a particularly rough spot to grate his bonds on. A muffled moan sounded through the cave. Luis? Fernando wasn't sure.

"Try to find an edge to cut the ropes on," Fernando told the others. Something rustled, maybe Kristian trying to move.

Wedged between two rocks, Fernando found a loose object—a seashell. The top ridge made for a ragged blade. With one hand, Fernando sawed at the rope binding his arms to the rock behind him. The seashell was a rudimentary tool, but the rope was old and frayed quickly. If he managed to free himself, he could cut the others loose. They had a chance. He worked the rope, though with the toy pulsing inside his hole and against his taint, it was hard to focus, and he made slow progress. Back and forth he sawed until the rope was thin enough to rip it. One hard tug and Fernando was free.

He sat up to bow down and cut his feet free, but the sudden movement pressed the plug against his prostate. Fernando gasped for air as a surge of throbbing need flushed first through his groin, then his entire body, leaving him trembling. He cursed and moved to take the toy off, only to find he couldn't. It had glued itself to his skin, and he couldn't get as much as a finger between his taint and the glossy blue material. When he tried to pull the plug out of his ass, something in there sucked itself to his pleasure point, wrecking him with ecstasy. He couldn't focus like that, much less escape. With harsh, fast jerks, he fisted his cock to tear an orgasm from himself. It was the only way he'd be able to think clearly. But as he touched himself, the cock ring constricted more and more. With growing terror, he realized that the thing wouldn't let him come. Arian had mentioned it was enchanted, and Fernando believed it. Nothing natural could ruin a man like this. Carefully, as not to shift the plug, he leaned forward to cut his feet free.

As soon as the ropes came off, he glided into the water and waded across the cave. In the far corner, Kristian had freed himself and was helping Darin, who lay on the ledge with glassy eyes and jerking hips. Both of them were wearing toys and so was Luis, who appeared out of it. Fernando averted his gaze from his friend's exposed crotch as he cut his ropes. They were thicker than the ones that had held him, and sawing through them took a while. When they finally fell off, the mermen had been gone so long, Fernando worried their return was imminent.

Darin regained some of his composure by the time Kristian helped him into the water. Luis was coming around too, and with Fernando's help, made it off the rock ledge. They pointedly avoided talking, self-conscious with the plugs stuck inside them, pleasuring their insides. Kristian's face was red in mortification, but other than that, he moved with practiced indifference. Fernando gritted his teeth as the plug moved with every single one of his strokes in the water, brushing over his most sensitive spot. When they came out of the cave, the sunlight was so blinding that Fernando had to squint.

"Let's try and find the rowboat we came in on, with any luck it's still floating around somewhere between the islands," he said.

"If the crew didn't take it," Luis panted out. He didn't look good, sweat running down his face, the lines on his skin deeper than the night before. Luis was Fernando's senior by at least ten years, and the intensity of the last hours had taken its toll on him.

"I'm sure they would have left it behind for us, in case we got a chance to escape," Kristian said.

Fernando swam ahead into the strait. Where would the mermen have gone for fresh water? Likely to one of the larger islands. Fernando and his friends would have to get away from those while keeping a lookout for the boat. That was his only hope. If the boat was gone, there was no way they could escape.

With powerful strokes, he swam toward the rocks the mermen had been sitting on when he first spotted them. If he was lucky, the boat was there. But as he got closer, the boat was nowhere to be seen. Had the crew taken it with them after all? Had the tide swept it out to sea?

Strong arms wrapped around him. "Don't go," Arian whispered in his ear.

Fernando turned in his arms. The sexual frustration and his annoyance at the failed escape had him on edge. But it was odd—he should feel devastated Arian had caught him. Instead, he was... relieved? Fernando didn't understand himself anymore.

Arian tilted his head. Completely wet, his hair was a couple of shades darker and slicked back on his head. "Will you come back to the cave?"

Fernando searched Arian's blue gaze. "Don't punish the others for trying to escape. If you take it out on someone, let it be me. I cut the ropes."

Arian cupped his cheek and gave him a peck on the lips. "I won't hurt you and neither will my friends hurt yours. Have you still not understood? None of this is about pain."

When they returned to the cave, the merman didn't tie them up with ropes. They put them in iron shackles. And for reasons Fernando didn't understand, he and the other men agreed to it.

Chapter Four

Arian

Being in Fernando's presence was nothing short of ecstatic. Ever since Arian had allured the sun-kissed sailor to get off the boat and into his arms, he had been in a haze. When lust took over, Arian lost all control. His consciousness, his whole being shifted its center from his head to his groin.

Lust crippled him as his hands closed the shackles around Fernando's wrists. Arian's body had long taken charge of his actions. It was as if he was dying of thirst, withering like a flower in the desert, and Fernando was cool rain dripping onto his tongue. It wouldn't satisfy him, though, in his desperation, he would never stop trying to drink from the sky. He had taken away sailors in the past, reveled in their exploding pleasure. These encounters were few and far between, and it had been a long time. He relished being close to this man with hard muscles and a sharp mind. Lying on top of Fernando was paradise. Arian traced invisible patterns on his skin as he kissed his chest.

Fernando's attempted escape was impressive. Despite the distractions of the toy lodged inside him, he had been able to gather his wits enough to find a tool to cut the ropes with and swim away from the island. That display of willpower alone set off tingles on his skin.

"Let me know if you need more to drink." He'd let Fernando drink a good amount before he shackled him up. The last thing he wanted was dehydration ruining the fun.

The cave filled with moans and the slap of skin on skin. One of the other mermen must have been grinding hard against his captive. Tarlis was too calm for that, but Zade easily lost it.

Arian ran a hand down Fernando's side, who let out a soft hum. That was new. Arian repeated the motion, but Fernando kept quiet.

"Tell me what you like," Arian said. "Show me what you enjoy and I will make you feel good."

"I like women."

Ignoring his statement, Arian pushed up and kissed him, exerting gentle pressure. To his surprise, Fernando kissed him back. His lips opened under his and allowed Arian to slide his tongue into his mouth. Arian teased it over Fernando's, who responded in kind. Their tongues tangled together, stroking and licking. Fernando tasted fresh, yet earthy, of strength and gentleness.

"Change of mind?" Arian asked.

"No, I just don't want you to be kissing a dead fish. If that makes the rounds, I can forget about the ladies." He hesitated. "And I take pride in making my partners feel good."

Arian kissed him again but kept it brief and superficial. He didn't want to push his luck. Instead, he licked a wet trail down Fernando's body. Dipping between his spread legs, he planted kisses on his inner thigh, ever closer to his entrance, which closed around the plug buried deep inside his anus. Arian's arms encircled Fernando's thighs where they met his hips and held him down as he licked the puckered skin. His only reward was a slight tremor. Fernando's self-control was ironclad. He hadn't as much as moaned when Arian had licked and fingered him earlier. Even with the toy massaging his most sensitive spot, he stayed quiet except for little gasps here and there. Arian lived for those. But he would get Fernando to the point where he was lost to the throes of passion. Where he'd groan and pant and beg for more. For release.

How long would Arian be able to keep him suspended in ecstasy?

Arian clenched his pelvic muscles in a futile attempt to get relief.

The toy moved inside Fernando in a slow and steady rhythm. Too slow to force true despair. Arian laid his hand on it where it rested against Fernando's taint and focused on the dark blue plug, imagining it moving faster, deeper, harder. The enchantment responded, and the toy began to work Fernando with vigor. A rare groan spilled from his lips, but it was the small reactions of his body that gave his arousal away. The quickening of the pulse. Tremors running through his thighs. His cock twitching. A cock that was out of this world. Long, thick and veiny with a broad head. To have it inside him... Arian couldn't go there. It wasn't possible for him.

He fixed his gaze on the beading precum. With every subtle throb of Fernando's cock, more was pushed out of his slit. The smell of his arousal drove Arian wild, yet he waited until it had formed a full, gorgeous pearl, then licked it up. The sweet flavor exploded on his taste buds, sending him to heaven.

"Is this another not-blowjob?" Fernando was breathless.

"Afraid so."

A grunt.

"Feeling good?" Arian asked.

Fernando's mouth didn't answer, but his jerking hips did. Arian trembled when the next spike of lust hit him.

Soon, Fernando was sweating and shaking, his cock oozing precum. Arian lapped at the rivulets dripping down. This is where he belonged: between a man's spread thighs, worshiping his cock. He was created for it. A creature like him was unworthy of love, but pleasure, he could give in abundance. Tracing bulging veins with the tip of his tongue gave him purpose, especially when it caused Fernando to gasp.

He licked and teased him for hours. Every time another drop of precum pearled off the tip, Arian closed his eager lips around it, kissing and licking the liquid off, all the while he clenched his inner muscles in desperate lust, which grew with Fernando's restlessness. Arian's groin screamed for release, for an orgasm that would send him flying. It would never happen. Fernando's cock against his mouth, his only hole, was all he would ever have, all he was worthy of. And he would revel in it.

Chapter Five

Fernando

Obscene noises bounced off the walls of the cave. Luis was moaning non-stop. Fernando had lost count of how many times Darin had shouted his release, a litany of, "Yes... please... harder... deeper... don't stop... oh, god... I'm your fucking whore," falling off his lips. It was astonishing what young age allowed you to do. Kristian was quieter, only the occasional grunt came from his corner.

Fernando was on the verge of begging. The plug undulated against his prostate to the point where he was silently sobbing with pleasure. Desire was eating him alive. He needed release, and he needed it now. Arian's lips and tongue only ever touched his cock to lick his precum off.

By now, he could have come from the pulsations against his prostate alone a dozen times over, had it not been for the vice grip of the cock ring around his base and the second loop that prevented his balls from hiking up to his body to shoot his load all over his abs, over Arian's pretty face.

Arian was tonguing his rim. The wet slide where skin met plug made Fernando's toes curl. Arian's tongue pressed against the puckered skin, then wriggled its way in, next to the pulsing plug. It had Fernando's hole singing while his cock throbbed in agony. He had been toyed with all day, and unlike Darin, he hadn't been allowed to climax over and over. He hadn't come at all, no matter how desperate he was for it.

Arian licked inside him, then trailed his hot tongue up his taint and for the first time, let it travel over Fernando's swollen balls. Fernando fought the groan that threatened to escape his lips. He had no interest in this. Whatever Arian was doing, only caused a superficial, physical reaction. There was no smoldering heat in his belly when he looked at him, taking in his beauty. No fluttering stomach when Arian kissed him and he responded to his amazing lips. Definitely not.

He gave in to Arian's delicate licks across his nads and shuddered as Arian's tongue stroked them again and again. The groans he could suppress, but the trembling in his groin was impossible to hide.

"You like this, don't you?" Arian asked.

"Yes." Fernando swallowed, searching for words as the plug ceaselessly rubbed over his sweet spot. "Very much."

"I could take your balls in my mouth."

That would mean placing an incredible amount of trust in Arian. But then again, Fernando was already tied up with his legs spread wide open. "You could."

Arian placed a tender kiss on his sack. "Tell me if it gets too much, I don't want to hurt you." And with that, he took one of Fernando's balls into his mouth. The vulnerability of placing the most sensitive part of his body in Arian's control screwed with Fernando's mind. His heart beat out of his chest. There was the danger of teeth. But also, wet heat. The tentative movement of a tongue. The smallest bit of suction. Despite having him chained up, Arian was gentle with him, showering him in heady sensations. Just when the pressure increased, Arian let his testicle glide out of his mouth and moved to tend to the other one. He was perfect. And the tenderness with which Arian's lips and tongue surrounded him made Fernando's head spin.

Here he was, captive of an insatiable merman, yielding to his caress. His life, his lust, in someone else's hands. Someone else's mouth. What would Arian's ministrations on another part of his body feel like? When he wasn't kissing off precum, licking his balls, but taking Fernando's cock into his mouth... He forbade himself the thought.

Another lap of his tongue, and then Arian's mouth was gone. Fernando tried and failed not to regret the loss of it. He needed Arian. Needed, not wanted. Needed his mouth on his cock to finally take off the pressure. Fernando's hole twitched around the plug at the thought of Arian sucking him off.

Fingers traced his slick balls. Arian cupped them in his hand and rolled them. "Nice and heavy." He brushed Fernando's taint as he touched the toy. The vibration slowed down but intensified to a powerful contraction around his prostate in time with his heartbeat. The plug grew wider, gloriously pushing his inner walls apart. Blood pounded in Fernando's ears as his body pulsed in a singular rhythm.

Arian's hand stayed on Fernando's balls as he leaned forward to mouth his cockhead. His blue gaze held Fernando's, and he pulled his bottom lip over the frenulum while tonguing the slit. He played with him, licking and teasing until Fernando couldn't take it anymore, pressure mounting in his balls.

"I need to come," Fernando panted. "Need to come so hard."

"You want to come for me?"

Arian let his pink tongue circle the corona of his glans, never breaking eye contact. God, his face was perfect.

"Yes. Please."

Another circle around his cockhead.

"Then come."

He swallowed Fernando's cock whole in one swift downward motion. Fernando throbbed in the delicious wet heat engulfing him, his balls tightening in Arian's hand.

He had been teetering on the edge of climax for hours. Now there was the delicious pressure of Arian's tongue against his underside. The tight embrace of his lips. Arian's hand rolling his balls. The slow, bombastic pulse of the plug against his pleasure point. But it was Arian looking at him, Arian staring into his very soul that had him within a hairsbreadth of orgasm.

Arian bobbed his head, fast and purposeful. Oh, yes. Fernando's balls climbed toward the loop that kept them away from his body. The cock ring pulsed angrily as Fernando tumbled toward his climax. Arian's tongue licked and swirled, those perfect lips stretched all around him. But it was the cock ring that wouldn't let him come.

"Take the ring off."

Arian must have not heard him as he made no move to get rid of it and kept sucking him off.

"Take it off, I can't come with it constricting me."

Arian lifted off his cock. "No. You will come like this."

"I can't. Not with the ring on."

"You will come despite it," Arian said. "If you crave it badly enough, you will come. I want you so desperate for orgasm nothing can hold you back. Not even magic." His plump lips brushed Fernando's engorged, sensitive glans with every word. "I want you to overcome what's holding you back. I want you to look at me and fucking explode into contractions, splashing your cum against my lips because when I pleasure you, nothing else matters. I am your pleasure. I have wound you up for hours so when I tell you to come, you do, all else be damned."

With Arian's lips brushing his cockhead, his tongue playing with his frenulum, and his blue eyes never leaving his, a cord in Fernando's groin pulled tight from his sack to his stomach. Nothing in his entire life had felt so good. Let him fly so high. His balls slapped against his body, pressing toward the malicious ring trying to hold him back. Trying to keep his orgasm at bay. Trying and failing. His balls pulled taut. His prostate swelled toward the pulsing plug hammering it. His cock straightened against Arian's full lips and a keen need raced from his spine into his balls and his cock, breaking through the ring at the base as it pushed its way up.

"Come," Arian said.

Fernando exploded against his parted lips. Orgasmic contractions tore his insides apart. White ropes of hot cum splashed Arian's face, his hair. He wrapped his lips around Fernando's hard, twitching cock and took him home into the heat of his mouth. His cum gushed onto Arian's tongue and down his throat, filling him. With satisfaction, Fernando watched him swallow it all, Adam's apple bobbing. He moaned as his muscles pumped and pumped in never-ending ecstasy. And when he slowed, the combination of plug, tongue and Arian's hand around his balls massaged another wave out of him until his release slowed to a trickle.

Fernando's vision and hearing faded for a second, and he dropped back on the rock. When he came to it moments later, Arian was easing off his cock, drinking up the last drops of cum as Fernando's cock slipped from his mouth. As he pulled back, a thin white string of cum hung in the air between them, connecting his bottom lip to Fernando's glans. He leaned forward one last time, gathering it on his tongue. Then he licked his lips and cleaned Fernando's cum off his face with his finger. Which he licked too.

"I hope you take it as a compliment when I say you put every whore to shame."

Arian pushed himself up and onto Fernando until their faces were mere inches apart. "Oh, I do." He stalled in hesitation, and Fernando surged up to kiss him. His tongue invaded Arian's mouth, and he tasted his essence, salty and rich. He couldn't believe such a beautiful creature not only let himself be drenched in his cum but craved it. Arian pressed him back down, and Fernando let him take over as they kissed lazily. Bliss thrummed through his veins.

"I've never come this hard," he said against Arian's lips.

"I'd be surprised if you had."

"Yeah. That was out of this world." Fernando deepened the kiss, stroking Arian's tongue with his own. He couldn't get enough of his own taste mixed with Arian's. Eventually, bone-deep fatigue enveloped Fernando, and the kiss slowed to a halt.

"Have some more to drink," Arian said as he pulled off. He held Fernando's head up, massaging his scalp, while he fed him the waterskin. Fernando drank in greedy gulps, the cool liquid soothing his parched throat.

"You're going to take that off now?" he asked, pointing his chin toward the toy.

"No. I need you to be ready for more tomorrow."

"It's still massaging my prostate."

"I sure hope so."

"You're unbelievable." Tired and sated, Fernando lay back. "Fine."

"I'll take some of the shackles off so you sleep better. Your arms and one foot." Metal clinked against metal as Arian unlocked the chains around his wrists. "I trust you won't run away."

Fernando pulled his freed arms in front of him and winced as blood rushed back into them. He stretched them carefully to loosen his sore muscles. "Not if I get to come again like that tomorrow." He paused. His post-orgasm mind wasn't functional. "What I mean is, I can't run away with a chain around my foot."

"Sure thing, Mister I-Don't-Like-Men."

Fernando snorted. "You made me."

"Made you what? Come like a geyser?" Arian turned to look at him as he unchained one of his feet.

"That too. Now leave me alone," Fernando said as he pulled Arian to his chest, curling around his slim frame. Hair tickled his nose, but he didn't care. It was the rock digging into his side that bothered him. Having grown up on a farm, he was no stranger to roughing it, but this bothered him. "Do you usually sleep here?" He disliked the idea of Arian laying on the hard rock all night.

"Here or on the beach."

"That's not comfortable." At least the beach would be softer than this, though not by much.

"Being a merman is supposed to be a curse. I don't think anyone cares if we are uncomfortable."

Fernando rolled on his back and pulled a surprised Arian on top of him. He wrapped one arm around his waist and petted his soft hair with tender strokes. Arian sighed, his shoulders relaxing.

"There," Fernando said. "Now go to sleep."

Arian was out in seconds flat while Fernando lay there, contemplating his life choices with the rock poking into his back and a plug vibrating in his ass. He wouldn't sleep like this, he was sure, but soon, exhaustion took its toll and his mind drifted away, the dull splash of the waves lapping against stone lulling him to sleep.

The next day, Fernando woke with a stiff back and a bad case of morning wood poking into Arian's stomach. He was resting on top of him, awake and stroking his thumb over Fernando's side. There was an urge to kiss the top of his head, to run his fingers through Arian's hair, but he suppressed it. Having snuggled all night with his captor was bad enough.

Loud moans came from the opposite side of the cave where the black merman was already—or still—playing with Luis. Further in, Darin and the blond merman were wrapped up in each other. No sign of Kristian, but since Tarlis was gone as well, Fernando doubted he had escaped.

"I need to get back into the water. My fishtail is getting too dry," Arian said against his chest. "And you, my friend, need food."

Fernando's stomach rumbled as if in response as he pushed up on his elbows and watched Arian glide into the water. Arian removed the one remaining shackle around his foot, and Fernando stretched his legs. Then he followed Arian, hissing when with every movement the plug pushed against his insides. He had grown sensitive overnight, his hole responding eagerly to the smallest movement of the toy.

Arian led him outside and around the coast of the island to a rocky beach. The sun was high in the sky, it wasn't quite midday, but Fernando had slept longer than he normally did. He was an early riser, up with the first birds singing in the garden of his house in San Juan. He'd light a candle in the dim light of the early hours and work at his desk, planning trade runs and going over his finances while he waited for the rest of the world to wake to meet them for business lunches and, later, evening balls.

Kristian and Tarlis were already at the beach. Kristian was wearing a disgruntled expression—his hands were tied behind his back and his erection, sustained by the unforgiving cock ring, jutted out angrily—as Tarlis fed him a plantain. The way Tarlis held the long, curved fruit, looking up at Kristian with bedroom eyes was so obscene, Fernando had to turn away.

Arian found a spot at a rock pool where he could dangle his fishtail in the water while Fernando sat on land. Tarlis tossed Arian an orange, which he peeled, and then he pushed a slice to Fernando's lips, who took it out of his hand and ate it. There was no way he'd let Arian feed him. The orange slice smelled of Spanish orchards and home, the taste sweet and a tad sour, delicious and refreshing. Arian gave him the rest of the orange and let him eat in peace while he asked Tarlis for more fruit.

Chewing the pulp, Fernando considered his options. Trying to run was out of the question. But if they played along with the mermen for a while, they would grow tired of Fernando and his friends, and opportunities to get away would arise aplenty. What were the mermen's intentions? Did they plan to keep them indefinitely? Or screw with them for a while, and then let them go? Did they even know themselves?

When would he be missed in San Juan? The majority of his fleet had left with boatloads of cargo while he and Luis had stayed in Boston for further negotiations. It could be another week before anyone would think anything of his delay. Before then *The Haste* would arrive in San Juan and report what happened. Would there be a search party? No. Too many pirates in the area, and no one would launch themselves into an archipelago full of mermen. Fernando and his friends were on their own.

Arian peeled another orange and handed it to Fernando.

"You're not eating?"

"We don't have much fruit, and I can eat raw fish," Arian said.

"Humans can eat raw fish."

"Oh? I didn't know. I will catch some for us later."

"You only eat seafood?"

"No, we can eat most things humans do. Except for meat, it doesn't agree with us."

Fernando nodded, and his gaze fell on Arian's fishtail. The fin swayed gracefully in the water, sunlight catching on the smooth wet scales further up. How would Arian…?

He must have been staring because Arian caught him and raised an eyebrow. Fernando averted his gaze.

"You can ask," Arian said with a nonchalance that had Fernando wonder if it was an act. "We can have the fishtail conversation. I'll spare you having to ask and just tell you my digestive tract ends with the belly button." His cheeks flushed. "And no, we don't like to be touched there. That's about as sexy as sticking something up your nostril."

Fernando frowned. He might as well ask instead of wondering all day since Arian was offering. "How do you…?"

"Have sex? Didn't I show you yesterday? I'll have to repeat yesterday's lesson to make sure you don't forget."

"No, I mean, how do you get off? Did you come yesterday?" Fernando didn't think so, but he had been so out of it that he might have missed it. That'd be no good.

"No."

Fernando ate another slice of orange, contemplating. "So, what makes you come?"

"I can't. The curse, the fishtail… we don't get to come."

So, the story about the curse was true, at least part of it. It bothered Fernando. His partner's pleasure had always been of paramount importance to him. "But you want to."

"You don't know how badly."

Fernando leaned down and placed a chaste kiss on his lips.

Showing Arian pity wouldn't go over well, and he stirred the conversation away from the topic. "Is your fishtail sensitive to touch?"

"No. I have feeling in it but not as much as elsewhere. The scales are comparable in sense of touch to thick skin... like on your elbows. There is sensation, but it's muted."

"Would you let me touch it?"

"You're asking? I tied you up and touched your most private areas. You are at liberty to put your hands on me wherever and whenever you like."

"Am I?"

Fernando pushed himself off the rocks and arced feet first into the water. It was less than knee-deep but a pleasantly cool contrast to the hot stones in the sun. He sank down until he was in up to his chest. The movement shifted the plug inside him just the right way, and gentle nudges stimulated his prostate. Arian moved in with a flick of his fishtail and crowded him against the edge, settling between his legs.

"Touch it," Arian whispered as he kissed his cheek.

Fernando placed his hands on Arian's waist and ran his fingers down his sides. The transition from velvety skin to scales was smooth, and the shiny, rounded plates were soft and slick in the water. Arian sighed and pressed in tight, aligned their bodies and pushed against Fernando, who moaned at the contact. He regretted the slip immediately. He couldn't let this get out of control like yesterday. Plus, Kristian sat well within earshot, less than thirty yards away.

"You do like to be touched," Fernando said. "Even if it doesn't get you what you want."

From Arian's hips, he ran his hands around and down until he palmed his butt. It didn't have the separate cheeks of a human one, but the round bump was definitely an ass.

"Hmm. And you like touching me more than you want to admit."

Fernando considered his words. He didn't mind men sleeping with each other, it happened plenty at sea. Crossing the Atlantic, there were no women for weeks, and more often than not, sailors ended up in each other's arms at night. Even though he had never engaged in it, it was impossible not to notice it the next morning when some men could barely walk or sat virtually on top of each other in the mess. Fernando had no problem with it, he just wasn't interested in partaking in it.

"I'm not into men."

"Your cock disagrees," Arian said and ground into his raging erection. "Besides, no man has ever been able to resist a merman."

"Sounds plausible," Fernando said and released his butt. No need to further encourage him.

Arian ran his fingers through Fernando's short curls. "It's a good thing. Otherwise, I'd have no one to play with. And that's the only small relief that I get." His thumb traced Fernando's bottom lip. "I'm aroused every second of every day. I want to fuck and get fucked and come so hard, but my body doesn't allow it. I want to feel pleasure, but with a fishtail, I can't be touched where I need it."

"So that's what the plug is all about. Is it punishment because we can orgasm, but you can't?" Fernando asked, keeping his voice gentle and free of accusations.

"Punishment? No, not at all. The opposite. I want to watch a man's arousal, see it grow and expand to the point where it is as bad as mine. And then let him explode, let him come so hard he can't breathe, so hard he loses his mind. That's what I want for myself, but I can't have it. So I live through you."

Fernando gave a slow nod. How would he deal with it if his arousal yesterday hadn't ended, if he had never come? He would be moments away from losing his mind. Whenever he was stressed with work and incompetent business partners, and no willing lady was nearby, he went to the whores and fucked his frustration into a willing hole. Climaxing relaxed him, especially when he got the whore to lose it first, and then came in her clenching grip. Not being able to orgasm while being constantly aroused was the epitome of frustration. Having to spend your entire life like that was cruel beyond imagination. Considering that, Arian had shown enormous restraint. In his shoes, Fernando would have humped to death everything he saw.

The next words tumbled out before his brain could stop him. Blame it on the plug that relentlessly stroked him, it made it impossible to focus on anything else. "I want to make you feel better."

"You already do," Arian said, and took his face in his hands to kiss him.

Fernando gave in to those soft lips, parting his own. He met Arian's tongue and stroked it, gentle yet firm, conveying the pleasure he'd like to give him. Pleasing his partners had always been important to him but never as desperately as now. He took pride in making sure his partners had the time of their life. When someone didn't, he wouldn't let it go until he had rocked their world. Unable to do anything about it, Arian's ache preoccupied him. He wanted to soothe it, take the edge off the all-consuming lust.

Arian's hands wandered from his face, over his neck, and down to his chest where he toyed with his nipples, running his fingertips over them, then rubbing them more firmly before pinching the nubs between his fingers and thumbs. Fernando's cock twitched with interest, and he kissed him harder, wordlessly admitting his desire. Heat ignited in his groin and burned through his entire body, turning every fiber of his being to molten lava. How did Arian make him feel this way?

Arian pulled back a couple of inches, and Fernando chased his lips. He tangled one hand in Arian's golden hair and rested the other on his hip, pulling him close. He groaned when Arian took his bottom lip between his teeth, fingers playing with his hardened nipples.

"We should stop. We can't do this again."

"But you don't want to stop, do you?" Arian asked. No answer.

"Sit on the edge." He grabbed Fernando at the waist and helped him push up onto the stones on the lip of the shallow rock pool.

Feet in the water, Fernando braced his wet hands on the hot, smooth rock surface behind him, leaning back. That shifted the plug a little deeper, the angle even better. Fernando's head fell back.

Through half-closed lids, he watched Arian. Seeing him push up between his legs was a sight to behold. A young god of slender proportions. Firm, well-defined muscles shaped his body.

Arian leeched his mouth onto one of Fernando's nipples, lips and tongue sucking at the hard nub. As if connected by an invisible cord, the sensations shot straight into Fernando's cock. He had been hard before, the cock ring never allowing him to soften, but now he was made of steel. Arian's hand found his other nipple, pulling Fernando's hips flush against his front with the other arm. Twisting, licking and carefully biting his nipples, Arian's ministrations fueled his arousal. The air was heavy with the scent of keen need as precum welled up.

Arian let go of his nipples and pressed a firm kiss to his sternum. "I want to see you come undone. I want to see you lose your mind."

He reached between Fernando's legs and touched the toy. The plug inside his anus responded, and the bump that had been stroking his pleasure point turned into a sucker. It attached itself to his prostate, embracing the little bundle of nerves, massaging it with heavy vibrations that had Fernando almost coming off the rock, had Arian not been holding him down. He didn't know up from down as he eagerly squeezed and throbbed around the plug.

His mind a fog of lust, there was no coherent thought. Just more, harder, deeper, please touch me. Had he said that out loud? No idea. Control forgotten, Fernando rutted Arian's abdomen, smearing precum over it. Fernando let the groan building inside of him escape. After last night, he was past pretending he didn't like what Arian did to him. Hell, he was past caring if Kristian was still around and heard him lose it. No one had ever made him feel this good. All he wanted was to explode against Arian, cover him with his cum, mark him as his for the world to see.

Having had the plug inside of him all night and all morning, Fernando was ready to come. The cock ring constricted around his base, starving off his impending orgasm. But when the pleasure was great enough, when Arian had wound him up to the point where his body could not be denied by anything, he would erupt no matter what. And surely Arian wouldn't deny him so long again.

He rocked his hips but couldn't move much with Arian holding him down. With effort, he leaned forward and stroked Arian's hair, his silky skin. It wasn't fair that only he experienced pleasure. His hands found Arian's nipples. Rubbing his fingertips over them a few times, Arian whimpered. "So good."

"Yeah? You feel it all the way to your groin, don't you?"

"Yes," Arian mumbled, mouthing his throat. "I'm clenching up inside so hard for you."

"Fuck," Fernando panted. "Me too. All around that plug you put inside me."

He twisted Arian's nipples, smoothed his hands down his sides and pressed him to his body. They rocked together, and he buried his face in the crook of Arian's neck, inhaling his scent of seawater, ocean breeze and something so sweet and dark that he couldn't resist running his tongue over his skin, seeking out his pulse point. Arian's breathing hitched as Fernando kissed and sucked at his neck. He wrapped his arms tightly around Fernando, shuddering with waves of lust.

Arian writhed against him. "You feel amazing. Wish I could fuck you." He pulled back, and disappointment zinged through Fernando. It was wiped away by Arian's next sentence. "Can't wait to taste you." With a twist, he slipped from Fernando's hands and slid down his body. "Lie down and pull your feet up."

He closed his eyes to the bright sun and sank back, opening his legs wide. Expecting Arian to kitten lick at his beading precum, he jerked when blunt teeth sank into his thigh, inches from his crotch.

The adrenalin rush put his senses on high alert. With Arian, he better expect the unexpected. Arian kissed the bite mark and trailed his tongue to his hole.

Worried about more use of teeth, Fernando tensed up. But there was only that sweet, wet tongue against his pucker. Unbelievable Arian was doing that again. The soft, warm rush of indulgence spread in Fernando, and he reached to pet Arian's hair. "You're so good to me."

As if in response, Arian edged his tongue into the rim of his loosening hole, next to the plug. The gentle stretch relaxed Fernando. Arian massaged the inside of his entrance and it sent him floating on cloud nine. His body cared for and accepted on the deepest level, he gave himself over to the feeling. The withdrawal came too soon, but before he could protest, the slicked-up pad of a finger pushed against him. By now, he knew what to do. He pushed out carefully as not to disturb the toy, the tender sucking on his prostate far too pleasurable to risk losing it. The finger wriggled in, just the first knuckle, and Fernando arched his back when small movements stroked him from the inside.

"I like having you in me."

The stretch was intense, just short of painful. Arian soothed the dull ache by running his tongue over Fernando's rim. Caught between finger and tongue, his ring of muscle slackened, allowing Arian to push in another knuckle. More caresses to his inner walls. How good that finger would feel rubbing his prostate... Then it was gone, and Fernando clenched sadly around the plug, wanting Arian back.

"Look at you, all eager for me," Arian said. "And your balls are filling up too. So worth it to have you plugged up all night."

Blood shot into Fernando's face. Good thing he had his eyes shut, no way he could face Arian when he talked like that, no matter how many people Fernando had slept with. "As I said, you put every whore to shame."

Arian laughed softly. "Your nads are getting nice and heavy."

He cupped Fernando's balls and weighed them in his hand. "It's going to be amazing when you come."

Fernando couldn't suppress a shudder. When would he finally come? His prostate was under constant stimulation, and Arian running his bawdy mouth brought him closer to the brink. Arian's hand worked his balls, applying the tiniest amount of pressure in a tentative squeeze. Fernando's heartbeat picked up. Arian was holding his most sensitive body part in his hand, possessing so much power over him.

"Tell me if I hurt you," Arian said. He eased off, and Fernando gasped as tingles rushed into his balls. Arian repeated the motion, squeezing a little more until Fernando warned him to stop, but he was already releasing the pressure. Arian kept tightening and loosening his grasp in an unhurried rhythm. Something was building inside Fernando. With every squeeze and release, his balls grew heavier, his cock more eager to shoot his load.

"You like having me at your mercy, don't you?" Fernando said.

"I like watching you surrender." Squeeze and release. "I wish I could surrender to you."

Fernando nearly came then and there, were it not for the cock ring and the loop around his balls tightening angrily and pushing his nads away from his body—all the while the plug was pleasuring his prostate. The toy was a two-faced bastard.

Arian gave him one last squeeze, then let him go and moved to Fernando's taint, placing a finger on either side of the toy's neck connecting the rings to the plug. "I'm going to press here," Arian said. "It will feel... strange. Just let it happen, there's nothing to worry about."

Arian pushed down and moved his spread fingers over Fernando's perineum. His pelvic floor tensed, and when Arian pressed the right spot, the sudden need to pee flooded him. "That feels like... like I need to—"

"Trust me, you don't. That's just your prostate. It will pass."

"How do you know this?" Fernando asked, sinking a canine

tooth into his bottom lip. He had plenty of sexual experience, more than Arian, who looked no older than twenty, but he hadn't even known this particular pleasure point existed.

"Why I know more than the whores you slept with? Tell me, Fernando, do they care about how much cum you sputter? No. They want you to get off. They may be whores, but they aren't whores for your cum." *Unlike me.*

The unspoken sentence hung between them as the pressure inside Fernando increased with every passing moment.

"Focus on the feeling," Arian said. "The toy's showing your prostate a good time?"

"Y-Yes." The plug's sucker ceaselessly vibrated against him from the inside, while Arian pushed toward him from between his spread legs. Precum dripped down his length, and Arian dove in. At the first contact with his tongue, Fernando's toes curled, and he cried out in pleasure when Arian rolled his tongue up his shaft over and over.

"Do you want to go insane?" Arian asked with a self-satisfied smirk.

He didn't wait for an answer but placed a hand on Fernando's abdomen between his belly button and straining cock and gently pressed down. When he started rubbing in firm circles, Fernando's eyes rolled back.

"I'm stimulating your prostate from all sides now," Arian said. "You will lose your mind any second."

Fernando already had. With pressure applied from everywhere, his swollen bundle of nerves had nowhere to go. His mind was clouded with lust, unable to focus on anything but the pleasure center deep in his core as it was surrounded by Arian's ministrations. *He* was surrounded by Arian. Arian, who had reduced him to an engorged, oversensitive gland. Arian, who had him pulsing with desire. Arian, who was massaging his very soul to orgasm. A deep need for connection bloomed inside Fernando. He couldn't bear this intensity if it meant nothing.

"Kiss me," he rasped and pushed up slowly, careful not to dislodge Arian's hands taking him to heaven.

Arian rose to meet him. Lips brushed together, but as pressure mounted, Fernando needed more. He needed to own the man pleasuring him into oblivion. He caught Arian's bottom lip between his teeth and bit down gently. The kiss turned wild. Arian's mouth was coy, inching back every now and then, but Fernando conquered him, pushing his tongue in, taking possession of him. All the while, Arian's hands never stopped applying pressure. Fernando's prostate was singing. He grunted, and Arian pushed him back down.

"I'm going to milk you."

Fernando frowned, but only seconds later, he understood what Arian meant when his groin seized. It was no orgasm, though intense nonetheless, and Fernando watched in astonishment as milky fluid spilled out of his slit and drenched his cock. Arian was there immediately, taking him home into his mouth and licking it all off with sweeping twirls of his tongue.

It was too much. The plug vibrating inside him. Arian's fingers pressing against his taint. His hand pushing down on his abdomen. And his hot, wet mouth all over his cock.

Everything inside Fernando pulled taut. His balls climbed to his body despite the ring trying to hold them back. His cock twitched inside Arian's mouth, ready to shoot his load down that glorious throat.

Arian pulled off, and the cock ring tightened painfully. "Don't you dare come."

Fernando gaped at him, unblinking, unbelieving Arian would do this to him. Yet he was dying to obey. Despite Arian's hands bearing down on him. He gritted his teeth and stared Arian down.

Everything pulsed with need. His inner muscles strained in an effort to hold back. Hot white liquid flowed from his cockhead and leaked down his shaft. Arian was back on him, licking it all off as Fernando clenched his jaw and balled his fists.

"You'll be the death of me."

Arian looked up, licking his lips. "I will drain you until there is nothing left, you can count on that."

Fernando's legs shook violently as more prostate fluid trickled out of him. Spilling without orgasming grew more unbearable by the second.

"Will I even be able to come after this?"

"Oh, yes. All your sperm is still here," Arian said, trailing a single finger over Fernando's engorged balls. "You're producing more by the minute."

He pressed down, and Fernando's prostate palpitated, pushing out more liquid which Arian greedily swallowed. Fernando was gone. Lost to Arian's rhythm of pressing into him, massaging him, Fernando was moaning like a whore or ten.

"Fuck, yeah… make me spill it. Make me spill it for you."

"Do you want to come?"

"Fuck, yes."

"You want to come for me?"

"Yes. P-Please. I need to."

Arian pushed down one more time, a last trickle seeping out of Fernando's cockhead. He took it with the tip of his tongue, closing his eyes as if to savor the taste. "You are delicious. Glad we did this."

Fernando's blood was boiling with hunger.

Arian reached out and touched the plug. Fernando keened when the sucker let go of his prostate, stopped vibrating and wriggled out of his hole. And while it did what Arian wanted it to do, it clung to Fernando longer than necessary, sending little pulses here and there as if it had a life of its own and wanted to continue wreaking havoc on him. But the plug was retreating, and Fernando raged at the sudden loss. He had never been this empty.

"What are you doing?" he demanded. "Why is it—"

"I'm glad you enjoyed my toy," Arian said. "But you're not coming with the plug inside you." Fernando was about to protest when he added, "Your hole belongs to me. You will come with my tongue or my fingers inside you, not that dead thing. I want to be the one who makes your muscles contract. Nevertheless, the toy can be useful…"

The toy pulled up further and shrunk until it was a solid shape resting on Fernando's taint. Still vibrating. Still pushing into his prostate from the outside. Still those annoying rings holding back his climax. His cock twitched, all but ready to finally, finally come.

"Then fuck me," Fernando said. He arched his back when a wet tongue gathered the precum leaking from his cock.

"Soon."

He leaned down and placed his lips over Fernando's pucker, kissing it. His tongue circled his entrance. With the plug removed, it was free to roam all over him, and Fernando sighed at the soft wetness. His stretched hole accepted it as it pushed inside. Arian massaged him, dipping in as deep as possible, making his inner walls throb. He could have Arian eat him out all day.

Too soon, Arian pulled away but only to replace his tongue with two wet fingers. They rubbed over Fernando's entrance, then pulled the surrounding skin taut, opening him up from the outside.

"You should see yourself," Arian said. "Opening up so easily."

His fingers plunged inside Fernando without warning.

"Yes!" Fernando shouted.

This time Arian didn't toy with him. His fingers pushed in deep, probing him. Fernando searched his gaze, and when Arian responded, he held it. Arian looked wrecked, hair messy, cheeks pink, lips red and plump. Like he was the one getting toyed with. In a way, he was, Fernando mused.

Arian crooked his digits and hit his prostate. Fernando cried out at the jolt of pleasure. Having fingers massage him was different from the plug. The plug was rigid, the surface smooth. Arian's fingers were lissome and soft, and every move expressed emotion—need, want, lust and deeper ones Fernando was too afraid to contemplate.

Arian placed his other hand back on Fernando's belly, rubbing him. The triple stimulation back in place, he had Fernando's prostate surrounded, and his gaze held a promise: this time he was going to take the fortress.

Fernando's mouth hung open, his breathing came in fits and starts. Those fingers pounding the core of his very being, like they were making love to his soul, drove him to ecstasy. There were no thoughts, only all-encompassing warmth. There was nothing he wouldn't do for Arian if only he let him come. Arian's fingers switched from prodding to lightly running up and down his gland. Fernando's cheeks were wet, though that barely registered, his entire focus on the caress in his most private place.

"Do you feel good?"

"Y-Yes," Fernando sobbed.

Arian's eyelids fluttered over dilated pupils. "Watching you makes me feel so good."

The pads of his fingers drew sweet circles inside Fernando.

"That's it," Fernando panted. "Just like that. Keep going. Don't stop."

Arian licked his lips, and his face contorted in arousal. "Fuck, you're sexy." His voice broke. "You're going to come untouched. I want you to come with the ring, fighting your orgasm, and I'm not even going to stroke your cock."

"Then make me."

Arian shivered, his body undulating. "You need to come dry."

Fingers nudged his core, again and again. "Yes, yes, yes, yes. Don't stop." More pressure. "F-Feels so good." The rings tightened. "You're gonna make me come. You're making me fucking come so hard." Arian's hand pressing down on him. The toy vibrating against his perineum. Crooked fingers dragging over him. "Y-You're incredib—"

Fernando's muscles locked. He hung suspended in blindness. Then his prostate spasmed. His insides broke into rapid contractions as his untouched cock jerked in a dry release. Wave after wave of bone-deep orgasmic tremors raced through him. One more push of Arian's fingers, then he pulled them out.

There was no post-orgasmic relaxation. Fernando's aching balls and straining cock screamed for attention. He leaned forward and kissed Arian, rough and demanding. Losing himself in the kiss, Fernando snapped back to attention when three fingers pushed into him. His crotch tingled in anticipation, cock twitching, balls hiking up to his body. He was ready to blow.

Arian laid his hand back on Fernando's stomach and ran his tongue over his bulbous cockhead in a broad sweep.

"You know, mermen can hold their breath for ages," Arian said casually, licking up and down his shaft.

"Show me."

Arian placed a kiss on his frenulum. Then he took Fernando into the wet heat of his mouth, all the while looking up at him through those long, dark lashes. He hollowed his cheeks and his tongue massaged Fernando's underside as he pushed his head down and took him deeper and deeper. Fernando was about to burst by the time his cock hit the back of Arian's throat.

"Fuck, yeah."

He shook when Arian kept pushing. There was resistance. Arian paid it no mind, and then something gave way. Fernando slid in further until he was balls deep inside Arian, cock lodged in his throat, blocking his airway. Arian's tongue swirled, and he swallowed, his throat closing all around Fernando's thick mushroom head. It was devastating.

Arian bobbed his head, sucking him. Fernando's cock slid up and down through the silky wet heat of his throat. It was too much. No whore on either side of the Atlantic could suck like that.

A litany of groans and curses fell from his lips as Arian worked him. His hand sank into Arian's hair, not to hold him down, not to force his head—Arian was doing that all by himself—but to stroke him, to show him affection while he gave him ecstasy.

With Arian's hand pressing on his abdomen, the plug vibrating against his prostate from the outside, Arian's fingers nailing it with firm thrusts from the inside and his cock sank deep into that continuously swallowing throat, an insatiable monster built inside Fernando. His entire being existed only in his surrounded prostate, his swollen, heavy balls and his throbbing cock dripping down Arian's throat. He couldn't take any more. His groin pulled tight as his balls and cock tingled.

The toy's heavy pulse against his taint amplified, Arian's hand pressed his abdomen and the tingling intensified. It spread from his groin to his butt and into his thighs. It crawled up his stomach and chest. It rushed up his spine and over his scalp, shot into his arms and down to his toes. Arian's fingers hammered his prostate, he swallowed harder around his cock, closing his throat around his glans. Fernando's body vibrated. It tightened until it was so taut, the slightest movement would set him off. He was on a hair-trigger. Arian bore down all around him.

Fernando erupted into orgasmic convulsions. His body, his entire being spasmed in pure white rapture as he came down Arian's throat, cock jerking with a vengeance. He screamed his release, every muscle in him contracting, over and over and over again, never stopping, taking him higher and higher. His entire body was coming. Euphoria flooded his veins, his inner muscles convulsing ever harder as he shot more cum down the wet heaven of Arian's throat. Those fingers inside him never ceasing their penetration until with one final, world-shattering explosion, Fernando collapsed. Darkness surrounded him, and his body sank into blissful inertia.

The sun was beating down on him when he regained his vision. Arian had pulled his feet into the rock pool to cool him. He glided on top of Fernando, his wet lower half providing further relief from the heat.

Fernando cupped the back of his head and pulled him down to place kisses on his cheek, his nose, his mouth. A goofy smile spread across his lips as he looked into deep blue eyes gleaming with happiness, his body limp and relaxed. After the best orgasm of his life, he was flying on an insane high. Arian kissed him leisurely and Fernando kissed him back, soul singing with affection.

"How long was I out?" Fernando asked.

"Just a few moments," Arian said, cheeks flushed. "You look blissed-out."

"So do you," Fernando said, but then he stopped himself, and his brow creased. "How do you feel though?"

"Good. Better than before." Arian looked away.

He wasn't satisfied. Of course not. The muscles of his abdomen were tense and so were his shoulders. It wasn't right. Fernando had come harder than ever before, and his partner hadn't climaxed at all. He was completely fucked out and in post-orgasmic paradise while Arian was clenching up his inner muscles in desperate attempts to provide relief for himself. Guilt crept over Fernando. He always made sure his partners came at least once, if not two or three times before he did. And here was Arian, his fin jerking in subliminal agitation.

If only he could return the favor and make Arian feel as incredible as he did. Though… had Arian been a human man, Fernando would have never ended up in his arms. He was attracted to women. There was no hidden interest in hard cocks and bearded faces.

Arian's kisses enticed him, nonetheless. It was all just circumstantial though. The heat was probably getting to him too.

When he got back to San Juan—an inconsequential and far away place—he would sleep with plenty of women. Round breasts and hips instead of lean, hard muscle. At least he'd still get to run his hands through long hair.

Maybe he shouldn't worry so much about whether or not Arian found release in his arms. He never would. Sure, he had made women come where other men had failed, but that was different. There had been ways to stimulate them, get them close enough to the edge so he could take them over at the right moment. He would never be able to stimulate Arian like that. Right?

Chapter Six

Arian

Shortly after Arian had let him come, Fernando's expression darkened. He seemed lost in thought, probably regretting everything that had happened between them. Luring Fernando in with his song had been selfish. It had sprung from Arian's compulsion to have someone experience intense sexual pleasure in his presence when he was being all but denied it.

Fernando had to hate him. Arian should've never lured him in. In fact, he should have never lured any man in. He had done it before, captured them and toyed with them for a while, and when they grew tired, he had let them go. It would have been best had he not joined the mermen of the Culebra archipelago and instead sought out a remote island, away from all human habitation to live far from temptation.

Because he would always give in to temptation. Like an unquenched thirst, his never-ending lust drove all his decisions, his mind clouded and incapable of rational thought. He was acutely aware of his selfishness. When it came to men, Arian went for what he wanted—their orgasm. They never complained, well, not after offering up initial resistance for show. Had anyone put up an actual fight, he would have let them go immediately. Forcing himself on someone that truly didn't desire him was not his style. Plus, he got nothing out of it. He wanted them moaning and shouting in pleasure, not crying and screaming in terror.

Fernando didn't have a choice when Arian sang to get him off the ship. The effect of the song had faded by the time they had reached the cave. But how good would it have felt if Fernando had come to him on his own free will? Regrets, regrets.

Arian had to put an end to this. He would keep Fernando around until the other mermen were through with their captives, and then they'd all let them go. And Arian would never sing again. There wouldn't be a man after Fernando. None of the ones that had come before could hold a candle to him and no one would after.

In the late afternoon, Fernando decided they should get coconuts for the group. Arian argued they would be hard to crack open, but Fernando gave a good-natured laugh. "You just have to smash them hard enough against some rocks a couple of times," he said.

Arian showed him to a beach where the palm trees grew close to the shoreline, their trunks stretching their necks out above the water. They swam up to the beach where Fernando walked out of the sea.

"I wish I could help you," Arian said as Fernando headed across the sand, looking for coconuts.

"Don't worry about it. I'm always glad to get exercise." Fernando picked up a coconut and eyed it. "So you don't eat coconut a lot?"

"As I said, I find them hard to open."

Fernando walked up and down the beach, piling up his findings in one spot. Arian loved watching him. To his surprise, Fernando had quickly gotten used to walking around naked after Arian had shredded his clothes. He didn't seem to notice his nudity as he strutted around the beach. Fernando was free of shame, and why wouldn't he be, he had the body of a god after all. The muscles in his buttocks and legs worked as he walked, bulging and rippling under his olive skin. Impossible to look away from. It had Arian all but drooling over him.

When Fernando turned his head, he caught him staring. Arian flushed and averted his eyes. At least he didn't say anything about Arian gawking at him. Why was he being shy now? It wasn't like he hadn't seen Fernando naked before. Heck, Fernando probably still felt him in his ass. Everything inside Arian throbbed with need.

"So where are you from?" Arian asked to break the silence and shift his attention elsewhere. As if that was possible.

"Funny you ask *after* sleeping with me."

"Better late than never."

"I live in a country house in San Juan, Puerto Rico, but I was born in Spain. That's across the Atlantic."

Arian nodded. He had heard of the people that had come from the Old World to conquer the continents to the west. "So you are a conqueror?"

Fernando laughed, but Arian wasn't sure why. "I'm a merchant."

"You look like one though."

"Like a merchant?" Fernando asked as he added another coconut to the pile.

"Like a conqueror."

It was hard to see with Fernando's brown skin, but a faint pink crept into his cheeks.

"Where are you from? Where were you born?" Fernando asked, clearly hoping to stir the conversation away from Arian pining for him. Fernando didn't want him, and Arian would do best if he kept himself in check.

"In a giant clam at the bottom of the sea of course."

Fernando blinked rapidly. "Really?"

"Asexual reproduction."

"Oh, I see," Fernando said, took one of the coconuts and set it among a group of smaller rocks, pointy end up.

Arian's eyes nearly popped out of his head when Fernando picked up a rock that should have been too heavy for anyone to lift, and dropped it straight onto the coconut. He did that a few times, and once the outer husk was breaking up, Fernando turned the coconut over and dropped the rock onto it one more time, causing the fibers on the other side to bust too. Muscles straining, he repeated the process with the other coconuts. His sheer physical strength was beyond impressive. If Fernando had wanted to escape, he would be long gone. So why was he still here? Perhaps the weaker of his friends would slow down the escape too much. Or he was afraid Arian would sing and force him to stay. Which, of course, Arian would never do, but Fernando didn't know that. For Arian had told him the opposite.

When all the husks were cracked open, Fernando sat down on the beach with his feet in the outgoing tide to remove the outer shells of the coconuts. Arian swam right up to him and sat beside him. Fernando smelled of man and work and endless nights. Arian cleared his throat. "Tell me about Spain."

"What would you like to know?" Fernando said, and wiped the sweat off his forehead.

"I don't know... what was living there like? What did you do?"

"I grew up on a farm outside Malaga," Fernando said, and a faraway look crossed his face. "Started working when I was old enough to walk. Fed the animals, helped with the harvest and the like. I was lucky to have a slew of younger siblings, the twins born just a year after me. It meant there were enough hands to help on the farm, and I was allowed to go to school. That changed everything."

Fernando picked up a coconut and peeled the husk off. "Let me help you," Arian said, took another one and tore at the outer shell. It looked easier when Fernando did it. "What changed?"

"I did well in school. Well enough for my parents to later sell part of their land and send me to university when I was older. I studied in Seville for a few years. Life there was different. I was suddenly able to mix in circles that otherwise would have been closed to me. Make friends. There were galas and parties and evening balls, and we attended them all. Between studying and partying, I worked for a carpenter. I was good with my hands and better with my head, and soon I was doing his books, and then the books of everyone in the street. It was a good way to make money. When I came back to Malaga four years later, I had set myself up. Gold in my pockets, I became co-owner of a ship trading between Spain and the New World."

"So that's how you got to the Caribbean," Arian said, husking another coconut. "Do you like it?"

"I love it. People here don't care that I'm a farmer's son. It doesn't matter. I make good money trading between New Spain, New England and the Old World, and that's good enough to be part of polite society here. Not that I care about it, I'm not a wig wearer. But it makes business easy. Though, it's not about the money. I like building something, you know? Making connections with people from different parts of the world. I even enjoy doing the damn books."

A crab walked across the beach, its legs leaving tiny footprints in the wet sand, soon to be washed away again.

"Your life sounds wonderful," Arian said.

Fernando turned to him, eyebrows lifted. "You think so?"

Arian nodded. "You do so many different things that aren't watching the sunrise and catching fish every day."

"Those are beautiful things."

"They are," Arian said, looking out to sea, "and I know many people would love to laze on the beach all day, every day. I just wish there was more to my life. Something that I can work on, create. Something that goes somewhere."

"Like a project."

"Exactly. I do what I do every day, but ultimately, it leads nowhere. I do get the occasional distraction," Arian said and kissed Fernando's shoulder, "but other than that, life is the same over and over again. There is no future. And when I try to work toward something... I can't do it."

"Why not?" Fernando asked.

"Because I can't think straight. I can't concentrate. Imagine you tried to do your books or whatever while someone was teasing your cock."

"Now that's an image."

"Yes, but it never stops. It goes nowhere. There's no relief for me," Arian said and tossed the final husk aside.

Fernando brushed his knuckles over Arian's cheek, making him shiver at the contact.

"You have no idea what you do to me," Arian said.

"I don't know if it makes you feel better, but you confuse me too."

"How so?"

Fernando leaned in close and tucked a loose strand of Arian's hair behind his ear. "You make me want to do this," he said, and pressed a kiss to the corner of his mouth.

Arian couldn't let Fernando push him; otherwise, he'd end up rolling on top of him and nail him into the sand with the thrusts of his hips. Fernando had said himself that he was confused. "Tell me about your house in San Juan," Arian said to steer the conversation back into safer territory.

"It's on the fringes of town, down a wide road lined with trees to either side."

"You're a rich man, you said."

"And you're a blunt one."

"I bet your house is big," Arian said amused. "Do you have a wife that takes care of it when you are away for so long?"

"I never married."

"No? I'd think women would fall over themselves for you. So you do everything by yourself?"

"Well, yes, except the slaves and—"

"You have slaves?" Arian said, voice ringing with appalment. Impossible that an upright person like Fernando would own slaves. Arian had seen the ships that came from Africa, full of human cargo packed so tightly that many didn't survive the journey. He had heard their cries in the bellies of ships as he swam past them.

Fernando's brow furrowed, and he was quiet for a long time as if only in response to Arian's shock he realized something about having slaves was wrong. "I do," he finally said. "It's not like up north, though. They are treated with respect."

"If you say so."

"I would never mistreat a slave. Never."

A thousand thoughts swam through Arian's head. He wanted to believe him. Did this change his perception of Fernando? "Have you slept with a slave of yours?"

Fernando ran a hand through his curls, his mind going a mile a minute. "I have. Though, I would never force myself on a woman, slave or not."

"I'm sure you wouldn't. And looking at you, I doubt they wouldn't have liked you in their bed," Arian mused. "But if she is your slave, can she say no?"

"Of course she can."

"There's your blind spot. You might never want to beat her, but does she know that? She would have heard stories of masters who never raised a hand to their slaves until one refused him. Not all men take rejection lightly."

"Many take rejection as an insult."

"In the end, you slept with them when they couldn't risk saying no." Arian paused. "Maybe you and I are not so different after all."

"How do you mean?"

"I chained you up and touched you."

"That's different," Fernando said.

And he was right. What he had done to Fernando was much worse than whatever he could have done. Nobody in their right mind wouldn't want Fernando. But a merman? Fernando was just waiting for an opportunity to get away from him.

Wordlessly, Fernando got up and collected the husked coconuts. With their outer shells gone, they were smaller and easier to carry.

Arian gathered the other half.

"Can you swim with those?" Fernando asked. "I can walk back in shallow water and carry them, but you…"

"It's not a problem."

Fernando cast a glance at the outgoing tide that had retreated from the beach. "Let me carry you back into the water," he said, and was about to put the coconuts down when Arian told him not to worry about it.

"Go ahead," Arian said. "I'll be right behind you."

He waited until Fernando had turned around and was walking away. Then Arian shuffled across the grating sand toward the water. He was raw by the time he reached the waves.

Chapter Seven

Fernando

The sun was setting when they got back to the cave. Its warm rays danced upon the water and illuminated the rugged walls. The black merman, Zade, as Arian had told Fernando, was dry humping Luis, who kept on moaning no matter who was around. Shame had gone out the window long ago. Darin and Finn were putting their heads together, smiling as they quietly talked in their corner. Kristian was the only one who got the shackles again. Occasionally, he gave them an unmotivated tug.

Finn had caught them all some fish, and Fernando cracked the coconuts open and shared them around.

"This is not bad," Darin said with a wide grin, one arm wrapped around Finn's shoulders. "I get to come all day, there's no work, and we get food."

"Except we're being held captive," Kristian growled, rattling his chains for emphasis. He earned a smack to the thigh from Tarlis for that.

Fernando felt Arian's gaze on him. Arian had to wonder how he felt about the situation. The truth was he didn't know. He had taken an unexpected liking to the merman, but it was all circumstantial. Were they both men and had met in San Juan, Fernando wouldn't have given a second thought. Or would he? He picked up a coconut half and drank its water.

Darin shared the fish around, and Fernando picked out a couple for himself and Arian while Tarlis gave them a skeptical look.

"For god's sake, feed me some fish," Kristian snarled.

Darin snickered, trying too late to swallow the sound.

Tarlis picked a fish, scaled and gutted it with deft fingers. He washed his hands and offered a piece to Kristian, who took it in his mouth and licked the tips of Tarlis's fingers clean. Interesting.

By the time night fell, Luis and Zade were the only ones that hadn't eaten, too busy otherwise. The others had left them a couple of coconuts and some fish so they could get sustenance whenever they... finished.

Their sounds continued to fill the cave and soon others joined them. What would Arian do to him tonight? The rings around his cock and balls had been looser after Arian had finished him off, and now with groans echoing through the cave, he waited for his move. He had been thinking of ways to pleasure Arian. Being the only recipient of it was unfair, and there was more he could do than Arian thought.

"You're going to tie me up for the night?" Fernando asked, but Arian shook his head. "Then come here," Fernando said, and heaved Arian on top of him. He was past questioning why he wanted Arian to touch him. It was what it was and all due to the situation.

He took Arian's head between his hands and pulled him down for a kiss. Massaging his scalp under his soft hair, he pressed his lips to Arian's. Arian opened for him, and he pushed his tongue in, tasting him. It sent him flying, the tangling of their tongues building a comfortable, mellow lust in him. This was how it should be, something buried deep inside told him.

Arian broke the kiss and placed a chaste one on his cheek, then another on his chest. As he slid down further, Fernando made a sound of protest, wanting Arian up here with him so he could take care of him. Arian glanced up at him. "Don't worry," he said. Worry about what? It was hard to think because Arian had placed his hand over the toy and... And it came off. Arian laid it aside, Fernando tracking his movements. What else did he have in store?

But Arian moved back up onto the rock ledge and lay down beside Fernando. Turning his back to him. Fernando paused, staring at his back, confusion mounting. Had he done something wrong? Said something he shouldn't have? Perhaps he had unknowingly offended him. He was accustomed to dealing with people from different countries and societies, but he was, of course, unfamiliar with merman culture. Fernando racked his brain for what he might have done to upset Arian, but nothing came to mind. Instinct told him to reach out and pull Arian to his chest, though it could make matters worse. Instead, he stared at his back, the elegant lines of his shoulder blades and his hips where bronze skin met dark blue scales. Better to wait for the morning and try to sort things out between them. It took Fernando a long time to drift off to sleep.

The next morning, he woke with a raging erection. Fernando pressed the heel of his hand on it to relieve the pressure, and he let out a soft moan. At a scraping noise next to him, he opened his eyes and blinked away the sleep. Arian had turned toward him, zeroing in on his cock, licking his lips, eyelids fluttering and pupils dilated. All his tells on full display.

The things Fernando wanted to do to him... He stretched, back sore from another night of sleeping on hard stone, but also presenting his body in invitation. He should have pulled Arian in last night and let him sleep on top of him, he couldn't stand the thought of Arian being as uncomfortable as him.

"Tomorrow, we're sleeping on the beach," Fernando said, taking Arian in from his gorgeous bed-hair to his long, elegant fishtail. Sleeping on sand wouldn't be better by much, but anything was an improvement from the cold, hard rock. He could make a thin mat by weaving together the leaves of a coconut tree. And when he departed from the island, he would leave it with Arian so he had something a little softer to sleep on.

Arian dragged his gaze up his body, lips tight. "Good idea," he said. "It will be more comfortable for you on the sand."

Something about his word choice bugged Fernando, but before the thought fully formed in his mind, Arian slid into the water. Fernando rubbed his temples, willing down his frustrated cock before following Arian. He could take care of his needs himself, and maybe he should, but he wanted to feel the burning desire Arian endured. As his cock throbbed with need, he reminded himself that this was Arian's life every moment of every day. If Arian lived with it, Fernando could deal with it for a few hours.

On the way out of the cave, he passed Luis and Zade, going at it like rabbits. Did these two ever stop? Luis must be nothing but coming dry by now. Well, at least he was coming.

The day was warm and sunny. While Arian pointedly avoided looking at Fernando's cock, he was happy to be around him and do other things. Maybe Fernando hadn't offended him after all, and Arian had simply lost interest.

It was fine with Fernando if Arian wasn't interested anymore. Completely fine. Fernando wasn't interested in men, and his strange desires would pass the minute he set foot in San Juan, surrounded by women wherever he looked. He would never touch a slave again after the eye-opening conversation he'd had the day before, but willing women were aplenty in the whorehouses and the homes of the nobility alike. Though it would be difficult to find one with a tan as deep and mouth-watering as Arian's. The ladies stayed indoors far too often, avoiding the sun darkening their skin.

Under the bright blue sky of the late morning, Arian taught him how to catch fish with his bare hands in waist-deep water. His wet skin was glistening in the sun, droplets pearling off his torso.

"You," Arian said, "will need to stand very still and let the fish come near you. There are two ways to go about it. Either you let your hand hang into the water and wait until a fish swims into your palm, or you watch the surface, and when a fish is close you shoot forward and snatch it."

"How do you do it?"

"Dead man's float. Then when a fish comes close, I grab it. Since I don't have legs to stand on."

"You mean since you can hold your breath for a long time." He wasn't going to let Arian talk himself down.

"Let me show you how I catch them."

Arian dove under, buoying at surface level, his blond hair swirling around his shoulders. His body went lax. Fernando drank his form in, his narrow hips, the elegance of his azure fishtail. A school of fish danced past Arian, close to him as if he was one of their own. They flew past the slender length of his arm and faster than Fernando could track the move, he ripped a fish out of the water.

Fernando could watch Arian resurfacing all day—rivulets ran down his body, kissing every inch of him. His cock rose, throbbing with renewed need in the balmy water. A storm of images assaulted him. Pressing Arian against the rocks. Conquering his mouth. Shoving—No. This had to stop.

"You try," Arian said, oblivious to the chaos in Fernando's mind.

"Sure," Fernando said absently and stood still, waves lapping at his stomach. It was impossible to focus on the task at hand when his cock was begging for attention and Arian so close. Fish skidded past. Fernando's hand shot forward. He was fast but not fast enough. The fish scattered.

"Sometimes I lie on the rocks to snatch them," Arian said, nodding towards the rocky shore a couple of hundred yards away, "because I can't stand in the water to give me the leverage to use my arms for a quick grab. And underwater, I'm too slow." He looked at Fernando as if weighing his options. "Can you hold me up above the surface while I show you how to do it?"

Arian didn't wait for his answer, and before Fernando could tell him this wasn't a good idea, he was in his arms. Fernando's erection pressed into him, and he stiffened. Something flickered across his face, but then it was gone, and he turned.

"Hold me around the middle," Arian said, and Fernando tightened his arms around his hips and waist. Arian was light in the water, and he made it easier by wrapping the end of his fishtail around Fernando's leg. "Watch."

Arian pulled his hair to one side, baring his neck. Fernando was tall enough to peer over his shoulder, but his eyes kept trekking back to the delicate curve where Arian's neck met his shoulder. His erection was pressing into Arian's butt, and he quivered against him. Fernando wanted to press a kiss to his neck, but after Arian's lack of interest the night before and again in the morning, he was restraining himself. The situation downstairs was bad enough.

"Sink down a bit," Arian said.

Fernando did and Arian tensed, his fingertips hovering above the water. Fish flew past them. Arian's arm jerked, and before Fernando knew what happened, he held a writhing yellowtail snapper in his hand. Arian tossed it in the net they had brought and slid out of Fernando's hold.

As it turned out, Arian was nimble, hauling fish out of the water with ease while Fernando took a long time to make his first catch. He kept his arms underwater, letting a myriad of squirrelfish get close until one was virtually in his hand, slipping along his palm and all he had to do was grab it. With pride, he showed it to Arian and added it to their growing catch.

"You're learning quickly," Arian said but Fernando waved it away. Compared to Arian, he was terrible. "No, I mean it."

"If I ever get any good at this, it's only because I had a great teacher," Fernando said, and winked.

"You know there's a lot more you could teach me than vice versa, right?"

"I'm not sure how useful bookkeeping skills and negotiating the price of lumber would be to you."

"You could teach me how to read," Arian said, and somehow held another fish in his hand. Of course Arian couldn't read. Lots of people couldn't. He should teach him if there was an opportunity. "Or you could read to me, I'd like that too."

Fernando contemplated the idea. "I wish I had something to read to you. Homer's *Odyssey* would be perfect."

"How so?"

"Odysseus is a man sailing home after a long war, and his ship passes the land of the sirens, whose enchanted song had been the death of many. He orders his men to stuff their ears with wax and tie him to the mast so he can hear the sirens' song but won't jump into the water and die."

"I'd love for you to read me that," Arian said. "Although, it does sound like this story makes mermen look bad."

"You did lure me in with your song."

"Yet you are alive."

And he was having a good time.

They brought their catch on land, and in exchange for the new skill, Fernando built the mermen coconut leaf mats. He wove the leaves together while he told Arian what he remembered of the *Odyssey* from start to finish.

"I love stories," Arian said later, lying on the wet sand, drawing patterns in it. "They give me new things to think about. Thank you for telling it to me."

Every day was the same for Arian. Fishing and swimming and seeing the occasional ship pass. There would be many more after— Fernando stopped himself. What happened after he left and the next ship came was none of his business. Yet the mere idea left a sour taste on his tongue.

"Then tomorrow, I'll tell you the *Iliad*," Fernando said, finishing the last mat. "I think you might like it even better."

"What's it about?"

"A ten-year-long war, a great siege and Achilles, the best warrior of the Greeks, who joins a man in his quest to get his wife back after she ran away with another. That's the frame of the story if you will. But it's also about Achilles and his undying love for

Patroclus, a prince and soldier in his army." The palm trees overhead rustled in the wind.

Arian's face lit up. "So it's a love story?"

"Not quite," Fernando said, and put the final mat aside.

"Thank you for making those. Sincerely. It will make my nights and my friends' easier. Tell me another story tomorrow. Then I'll show you how I catch bigger fish. For now, I want you to meet my other friends," Arian said and placed a hand on Fernando's ankle.

"There are more of you here?"

"Well, yes," Arian said. "But they're not what I'm talking about. These friends are different. I think you'll like them better than us. Come with me."

Like the day before, Arian refused Fernando's help getting back into the sea. He made it look easy, though the sand had to be rough on his skin.

Fernando followed him around a peninsula and into a bay, the water too deep for him to stand. Sometimes, he would lose Arian, who swam ahead with his greater speed, staying underwater for long stretches as he preferred to dive when he swam. But then his head would pop back up again, and he would turn around and throw a bright smile at Fernando.

When Arian was underwater once again, and longer than Fernando liked, a dark shadow, thick and long approached. A shark? Fernando's heart jump-started into action. Where was Arian? He jerked his head left and right, scanning the surface. No Arian. Could Arian outswim a shark? He was fast, but so were sharks.

He had to keep calm. No splashing, no sudden movements, that much he had learned after many years aboard ships. Better to get a weapon, look for Arian, help him if he was in danger. Fernando sucked air into his lungs. If he dove deep enough, he could pick up a stone from the seafloor and use it as a weapon. If it wasn't too deep down. Impossible to tell from the surface. Sharks were less likely to attack when you were on eye level with them or below them instead of floating at the surface.

Fernando pushed down and was greeted by the adorable nose of a manatee. Relief washed over him, and he laughed at his overreaction, air bubbling out of his mouth. Looking like the lovechild of a friendly walrus and an overweight dolphin, the manatee was the most gentle creature the seas had birthed. In the crystal clear water, it swam up to Fernando, regarding him with curiosity through small, round eyes.

And then Arian was suddenly there too. Golden hair fanning out around his head, his sky blue fishtail a bright contrast to the elephant gray of the manatee. He swam past it and charged Fernando. Fernando kicked back and flattened himself into the water. Then Arian was on top of him, holding him and rolling them over, around and around until his head was spinning.

His lungs burned with the need for air, but Arian already knew, and with a few strong strokes of his fishtail, they broke through the surface and into the bright sunlight.

Fernando gulped down air, relieving the pressure. Arian let him go and pushed back, fishtail lifting into the air in a graceful arc. He dipped under, headfirst, completing the loop underwater before surfacing chest to chest with Fernando. Warmth settled in his stomach. Arian tipped his head back and raised his face to the sky. Beauty incarnate.

"So, you've met Stubby," Arian said after a long moment.

"Not a very flattering name for your friend."

"He doesn't know."

Fernando chuckled. Arian's directness was refreshing. He trod in the water to stay afloat, watching out to not kick the animal.

"You're ready to dive back under?" Arian asked. "Rosie and Scar are coming."

Instead of answering, Fernando took a deep breath, then dipped underwater. And indeed, a couple more manatees had followed the first, drifting toward them. One had a broad scar along its nose, while the other one's thick gray skin had a pinkish undertone.

Rosie floated between him and Arian, but Scar swam right up to Fernando and gave his chest a curious nudge with its flat snout, bristles rubbing his skin. Fernando reached out and petted the thick hide. Scar held still, trusting and eager for affection. Then it turned and presented Fernando its side, asking for more. Fernando obliged, running his hand over the rough skin. The animal was calm under his touch, moving slowly through the water.

He came up for air regularly while Arian stayed underwater, only resurfacing once. Sometimes, the manatees came back up with him. Fernando wouldn't have guessed they needed air more often than Arian.

Back underwater, Scar took a particular liking to him. It swam up to him and did barrel rolls, then held still, underside up. Was it asking for a belly rub? Fernando reached out and petted Scar's stomach. The manatee didn't move, enjoying the affection.

More manatees came to join the group. Arian swam over to Fernando, wrapping an arm around his shoulders as he pointed at the approaching group, his movements fast with excitement. And that's when Fernando saw it: the group had two calves with them. They were miniatures of the adults, the rounded noses even cuter than those of the grown ups. He pulled Arian tighter to him at the sight of the little family, ignoring the growing urge to come back up for air.

After a while, the manatees grew restless and dispersed. And when Fernando surfaced from the sea, he saw why. This time it wasn't a false alarm. The distinctive fin of a shark poked out of the sea.

Fear flooded him. A split second before he dove back under to get Arian, the merman emerged from the depths, eyes wide. He had noticed the shark too.

Arian pulled him tight. "Take a deep breath," he said, "I'm going to propel us forward to the shore.

"What about the manatees?"

"They'll swim into shallow waters by themselves. They will be fine. Ready?"

"Yes."

Fernando had barely closed his mouth when Arian grabbed him and pushed them toward the island with incredible strength.

They zapped through the water, approaching the shore at record speed. But the shark was faster. Yards from the beach it snapped at Arian's fishtail, missing by a handbreadth.

Fernando kicked out, hitting the shark in the gills. His feet touched the floor. The water was shallow enough to stand. Arian was thrashing. Fernando picked him up and held him close as he gunned for the beach with all his strength.

The water slowed him down, but after the kick to gills, the shark had enough and didn't attack again.

"I liked your other friends better," Fernando said.

"I'm not friends with sharks."

"He seemed to like you a lot. Chased you all across the bay."

Arian snorted as Fernando bridal carried him on land. "You can put me back in the water. The shark won't come there, it's too shallow."

"No."

"No? Don't be ridiculous."

"I'm going to carry you back."

"All the way to the other side?" Arian asked with raised eyebrows as Fernando marched up the beach.

"Precisely." He wasn't going to endanger Arian by putting him in a position where the shark could get him.

Fernando was glad for every single time he had helped loading the ships with barrels and lumber and chests. Despite his slim form, Arian was heavy, the long fishtail adding weight to his body. Fernando didn't care. He would have carried Arian a hundred miles if it meant he was safe.

Chapter Eight

Arian

Arian wrapped his arms around Fernando's neck and clung to him. If Fernando insisted on playing his hero, he wouldn't complain. He rested his face on Fernando's strong, muscular shoulder. His skin was smooth, and he smelled of seawater and man. Swoon.

How much he'd like to kiss that tanned skin, run his tongue over it, take his nipple between his fingers until it hardened. But no. He'd vowed to not touch Fernando. He wasn't here of his own free will, and Arian better respected him and his wishes.

They'd had a fun day together, nonetheless, fishing and telling stories and swimming with the manatees, shark or no shark. During all of which Fernando had been stark naked. It left Arian throbbing with need. He clenched his inner muscles in a slow rhythm, like a compulsion. There was no relief to be found in it.

The night before, Fernando had pulled him in for a kiss, but Arian was all too aware he had only done it to make the situation easier. He must have thought Arian was about to touch him again and kissed him to take control over what was happening. Sleeping away from Fernando had been unpleasant, and not just because he did make for an excellent mattress. Arian would choose to sleep on him over the rocks if it was an option. It wasn't. Tonight, they'd get to sleep on Fernando's coconut leaf mats for the first time. He hoped he'd expressed enough gratitude for them. They were life-changing, swapping out hard rock and scratchy sand for soft leaves.

Arian's shoulders sagged at the thought of sleeping another night next to Fernando without touching him. He had noticed Fernando's morning wood and tried and failed not to stare at his body. It was an ordinary thing humans experienced in the morning, a physical reaction, which had nothing to do with him. They sometimes got erections for no reason. Like when Arian showed Fernando how to fish earlier in the day. That hadn't been sexy at all, at least not for Fernando. Arian had enjoyed the sight of Fernando's wet body glistening in the sun. And that hard cock pressing into him. It had cost him all his restraint not to have his hands all over and inside Fernando right then and there. He wanted to pleasure him, drive him wild. But it wasn't the right thing to do, and although Fernando might have gone along with it, it would have been another mistake. He would stay away from him.

Fernando's kindness was a double-edged sword. Arian appreciated that he tried to make him comfortable throughout the day, but Fernando didn't know how it made Arian want to do things to him, things he wouldn't accept.

The sun was setting when they reached the others on the side of the island where a freshwater creek ran out of the depths of the island's jungle, dissecting the beach before it flowed into the sea.

Zade was *still* on top of the oldest one of the humans—Luis, as Fernando had told him.

Finn and Tarlis were sitting in the creek, positively drooling over their men—Finn doing so more obviously than Tarlis, who kept his nonchalant expression intact. Darin was preparing a fire pit next to the creek while Kristian strutted around collecting wood and kindling.

Fish lay on flat stones next to the pit, ready to get cooked over the fire. It was going to be a perfect night at the beach.

Fernando sat Arian down in the creek and joined Kristian in getting more wood. The water of the creek was cool, pleasant in the warm wind of the late afternoon and the heat of the setting sun, which never let up, keeping the Caribbean warm throughout the night year-round.

"How has your day been?" Tarlis asked, lips and eyebrows pulling up suggestively.

"Good, though not in the way you think. I can't believe they are still going at it," Arian said, pointing his chin at Zade further up the beach, whose head had disappeared between Luis's legs.

"They're like rabbits," Darin said, looking up at them through his bangs.

"What's a rabbit?" Arian asked.

"Some kind of animal. Small, furry, cute. Likes carrots."

"One that fucks all day, apparently," Finn said. "They did take a break this afternoon though."

"Not for long," Tarlis said with a long-suffering expression on his face.

"He's going to wear him out," Arian said.

"If he hasn't already," Tarlis said. "If the man's cock is still up, it's only thanks to the toy."

Arian peeked up. Indeed, Darin and Kristian were both still wearing their toys. Darin was more than happy to have Finn play with him all day, and while Kristian was grumpy, Tarlis's slender hand was firm enough to handle the large blond man. But Kristian was placid now, walking between the edge of the jungle and the fire pit, carrying food and chatting with Fernando.

Arian couldn't help fixating on the toned, dark body of the man that had carried him halfway around the island to make sure the shark wouldn't get him. He had tried to tell him the shark couldn't swim all the way to the beach, where Arian was able to move in shallow waters but not the shark. Fernando heard none of it and carried Arian the entire way.

Fernando's muscles bulged and rippled with every move. It made Arian feel things. He clenched up hard inside, taking in every detail of Fernando's form. Those lush curls, the sweat pearling down his torso and that thick, long cock between his legs. Arian tore his gaze away.

The men filled the pit with kindling and built over it with wood until they had erected a triangular structure. Kristian rubbed two pieces of wood together until one smoked and used it to light the kindling. He stuck the burning bundle into the fire pit where it lit the rest. Soon the flames were dancing, and the men skewered the fish on sticks to cook it.

Fernando sat down between fire and creek, feet planted in the water next to Arian. It was no deeper than his ankles, but it was enough to keep Arian's fishtail wet and comfortable.

Fernando leaned in close and gave a subtle nod toward Kristian and Darin. "Have you seen their faces?" he whispered. "They look blissed-out." Blissed out with plugs buried deep inside them and cock rings keeping them erect.

Of all things Arian had expected Fernando to say, this wasn't it. Was he hinting at something? But no, of course not. Fernando turned away, adjusting the fish over the fire. Arian had to stop his wishful thinking, misinterpreting everything Fernando said.

Though, it was true. They did look blissed-out, their hips giving little jolts here and there when the plugs moved and hit them just right. Arian stole a surreptitious glance at his friends. Finn's gaze was fixed on Darin as if in trance, his fin jerking nervously in the water. Tarlis's face was stoic on the surface, but he too was twitchy with sexual frustration, and Kristian better sat down next to him soon, lest Tarlis's patience ran out.

Smoke filled the air as the fish cooked, tickling Arian's nostrils. Soon it was ready to eat.

"You're coming to get your dinner?" Kristian shouted across the beach at Luis and Zade, but only a grunt came in response.

They ate without them, keeping a few fish aside for them; they would be ravenous later. Chatter resounded around the fireplace, but Fernando kept quiet. While Arian hadn't pegged him as someone who was constantly vying for attention, he had expected

Fernando to be more talkative. Instead, he was deep in thought, turning over the skewers from time to time, handing Arian pieces of cooked fish on a leaf but barely partaking in the unfolding conversations.

They finished the food, and the chit-chat died down. Fernando scooted closer, the fire in his back casting him in shadows. Before Arian could stop himself, he laid a wet hand on Fernando's arm. Fernando broke out on goosebumps because the water was cold. Well, not that cold. More lukewarm than anything. Arian licked his lips as his breath quickened. He searched Fernando's gaze in the fading light, but he couldn't see properly and so he leaned in.

Fernando's lips met his tentatively. Arian froze in shock. He hadn't expected that because why would Fernando go for a kiss when Arian had left him alone all day, keeping his hands to himself? Mostly. Arian's jaw slackened in surprise, and his lips parted. Then Fernando's tongue was there, stroking over his, eliciting a soft moan made of the repressed lust of the day, bubbling under the surface. He couldn't hold back anymore. The How and Why no longer important, Arian slipped between Fernando's legs and pressed up against him, kissing him back with all he had, putting his longing, his despair, in every brush of his lips, in every stroke of his tongue. He wanted Fernando with every fiber of his being. He burned for this man, who was as strong as he was kind, as intelligent as he was humble.

When Fernando pulled back, Arian reached up and tangled a hand in his curls as if to tell him not to go. Fernando mirrored the gesture, burying his fingers in Arian's damp strands.

"And I thought you weren't interested anymore," Fernando mused. "Good thing I tested that theory."

"I'm as interested as it gets."

"Hmm. I have another theory."

Arian leaned in and brushed his response over Fernando's lips. "And what is that?"

"I've been thinking a lot."

"I noticed. And?" Arian pressed.

"I'd have to show you, I don't want to make promises I can't keep."

"Then show me."

"Let's get away from the others."

This time, Arian didn't protest when Fernando picked him up and carried him away. Fernando took him along the beach and around the next corner where the sand gave way to a rocky shore, starting with pebbles, which grew into stones and rocks rounded by the waves. A bird shrieked in the trees. Arian turned his head. And there it was, the little rowboat Fernando and his friends had come in on. It had been washed onto the island by the tide and sat on the beach under the hanging leaves of the trees. Arian looked up at Fernando, surprise written all over his face. He hadn't known either. So he hadn't come here for the boat. But now that he knew where it was, it changed everything. He would leave.

Fernando turned away from the beach and walked them into the water, ignoring the boat. He let Arian down once they were in to their hips.

"Your boat is here," Arian said, leaning back on a rock, propping himself up on his elbows.

"I don't care if there's a boat," Fernando told him, crowding him against the smooth stone.

"You're testing a theory."

"Yes."

"And you're not going to tell me."

"I'm an ambitious man," Fernando said in his ear, erection pressing into Arian's stomach. "I didn't build a trade empire from scratch by giving up when there are obstacles. Nobody has ever left my bed unsatisfied."

"We're not in your bed."

"I'm not giving myself an out because of semantics."

Fernando's lips wandered from his ear down to his pulse point. Arian let his head fall to the side, baring his neck. As Fernando sucked it, Arian's body relaxed, and he let himself be trapped against the rock and pulled him close. Fernando's chest rumbled in approval, and he sucked harder. It had Arian writhing, demanding more.

Fernando slipped a hand between them, running it down Arian's chest and stomach until it came to rest on his lower abdomen, applying gentle pressure.

"You said you can clench these muscles."

"You remember that?"

"Show me."

Arian pulled an incredulous face but tensed up.

"Again."

He clenched his pelvic muscles hard, wanting Fernando to feel it. Having his hand there spiked Arian's arousal. Something buried deep inside his core wanted to be touched, pleasured.

"Good, you're strong," Fernando said, pulling back. A pleased smile spread across his face as if this was especially great news.

Then he was back to kissing him. Fernando made him chase the kiss, kindling his lust. Every time Fernando drew back, possessiveness sparked in Arian, and he pursued him, crushing their lips together, a hand in his curls, pulling him close. His teeth grazed Fernando's bottom lip, tugging at it. Fernando's hands wandered over his body, from his hips to his waist and up to his chest where they found his nipples. Soft finger pads rubbed them, and Arian sighed against his mouth. His nipples hardened, and when the twist came, it went straight to Arian's groin. He was trembling with arousal, his shaking fingers curling into Fernando's hair.

"I know how to rile you up, and you'll do what I tell you to. So, you are going to breathe deeply," Fernando said as he pulled back and laid his hand back on Arian's groin. "All the way to down here. And while you do that, I want you to clench up hard for me and hold it." A rough twist at his nipple. Arian gasped. "Then when you breathe out, you let go and get all nice and loose," Fernando said as he leaned in to whisper in his ear, "and moan like you are my fucking whore." Blood rushed into Arian's cheeks. He hadn't known this side of Fernando. Where was he going with this?

Fernando took his earlobe between his lips, between his teeth. And bit down. Arian yelped. "Will you be good?"

"Y-Yes?"

This time, the twist to his nipple was brutal. Fernando's hips thrust him against the rocks, his teeth sank into his neck. "Yes! I will!" Bossy Fernando was something else... It spoke to a dark place in Arian's mind, and he no longer sought to be in control.

"Then do as I say."

He moved back and looked at Arian expectantly. Arian closed his eyes, focusing on his breath. It streamed into his lungs, deeper and deeper, and he clenched his pelvic floor hard, making sure Fernando felt it against his hand. He held the contraction for as long as he could. When he breathed out, he let go, relaxed his muscles and the moan came by itself as Fernando's mouth was back on his pulse point, tracing his tongue over the bite mark he'd left there.

With the next breath, heat and awareness flooded into Arian's groin, fanned by Fernando's mouth and hands on him. He wanted Fernando to hear his moans, loud and shameless. Desire pooled in his core, growing with every breath. Tingles rushed over his skin and settled in his belly, and then Fernando's mouth was on his nipple, tongue circling the hard nub while his hand worked the other. As if connected by an invisible cord, it pulled at Arian's loins in the most pleasurable ways.

His moan came out strained, and he gasped as his core tightened. "What-What are you doing?"

"Winding you up."

Another gasp escaped Arian at the next tug of his nipple. It earned him Fernando's hand closing around his throat, his hips nailing him to the rock. "You'll breathe as I told you to breathe."

Arian's eyes widened, pulse hammering against Fernando's

grip. He wanted to be good. Wanted to do whatever Fernando asked for. He nodded, and Fernando let up, tracing his bottom lip with his thumb. He stroked his cheek, then cupped the back of his head and pulled him in for a scorching kiss. Arian was burning up with need, yearning for nothing but Fernando and more, more, more of what he was giving him.

Fernando let him go, pressed a kiss to his neck and sank down to take his nipple back in his mouth.

Arian went dizzy. His focus was scattered between his breathing, Fernando touching his nipples and the growing tension in his core. He breathed out and moaned at the flick of Fernando's tongue at his erect nub, falling into a slow rhythm.

His breathing took him higher and higher. Pressure built, and he clenched his inner muscles. Fernando hauled him up and a sharp smack hit his butt. Arian's inner muscles shifted as if realigning themselves. The next contraction was involuntary. His head fell forward, onto Fernando's shoulder. "Do that again."

"Don't hold back," Fernando said.

The following slaps hit him harder and harder, and he bit his groan into the crook of Fernando's neck, wrapping his arms around his shoulders. His breathing turned erratic, but he tensed and relaxed his muscles in time with it. Every time his breath reached its deepest point, his pelvic floor suspended in tension, Fernando struck his butt. His cock pressed into Arian's groin, trapped between them.

With every hit, every breath, he moaned louder. Urgency rose in his middle, and he rutted Fernando, seeking friction. Another involuntary contraction. Something in his loins responded to each smack, swelling and straining at the attention it got. Fernando drove him back against the rock wall and ground into him. When Arian looked up, Fernando's pupils were dilated, sweaty curls clung to his forehead, the rest of his hair a disheveled, sexy mess. Fernando let loose a sound between a growl and a moan, and only now did Arian see how turned on he was.

"Can you come like this?" Arian asked, stealing a glance at his engorged cock between them, the mushroom head leaking precum onto their skin.

A deep, throaty laugh broke out of Fernando. "Can *you* come like this?"

Realization dawned on Arian. Fernando wouldn't try and... It wasn't possible. But here he was, pushed against the stone, Fernando rubbing into his lower abdomen, trapping something between rock and man, something that relished the pressure digging into him from both sides. Something connected to the nipples Fernando relentlessly toyed with. Something that pulsed with every breath, every contraction.

Fernando rocked his hips harder, eliciting a string of helpless sounds and incoherent pleas.

"Fuck... yes... please don't stop."

"Keep breathing and clenching up for me," Fernando said in his ear, licking the shell. "I want you to squeeze so hard I can feel it against my cock."

Had Arian needed any more motivation, this was it. He tightened his inner muscles with all his strength as Fernando thrust into him. Almost there. He required more pressure. His hands dropped and rounded the globes of Fernando's butt, and he pulled him closer yet. The force of it emptied Arian's mind.

He had wanted to come his entire life but never this badly. Nothing compared to Fernando rutting against him, playing with his nipples, panting into his ear. His scent in Arian's nostrils, his warm skin under his fingertips. Arian was teetering on the edge, inner muscles straining, ready to explode.

It was Fernando who did this to him. No one else had taken him to this place where his mind blanked from pleasure, where all he longed for was to belong to someone and fall apart with them.

They ground together, Arian panting and moaning and clenching. With every passing minute, his need to come grew. Fernando, Fernando, Fernando. Arian stared up at him, everything inside him pulling taut like a bow about to snap. He raked his hands through Fernando's dark locks, clawing at him. His conqueror.

"Make me," Arian ground out. "Please, make me come."

"The moment you do, I'm gonna explode all over you."

"Oh, fuck."

"Can feel you tightening down there."

"I swear," Arian said, and looked up into Fernando's eyes, putting all his desire in every word he bit out, "if you make me come, I will serve you for the rest of my life. I will be yours to do with as you please. There will be nothing I won't do for you."

Fernando caught him in a violent kiss, teeth clashing, tongues fighting for dominance. Combined with the constant thrust of his hips, it set all of Arian on fire. He needed to come, needed to come right now. And if anyone could make him, it was Fernando.

"Relax your inner muscles," Fernando growled.

Arian obeyed instinctively, he let go—only to find he couldn't. His pelvic floor locked. For a moment, time kept still as he gazed up at Fernando. He wanted to worship him like a king.

"Let go and come for me. *Now*."

Arian gaped at Fernando and forced his muscles to open up, relaxing them despite their urge to strain. He broke through the resistance, and his jaw dropped, never breaking eye contact.

A lifetime of pent-up sexual frustration erupted in violent contractions. They tore through his groin and ripped through his body. They hammered into Fernando's cock pressing into him. Fernando's cum splashed his stomach, his chest, as Arian spasmed in never-ending convulsions, body shaking. Goosebumps raced over his skin. Blood pounded in his ears. Wave after wave of deep, satisfying, heavy contractions pulsed through him.

"I love you, I love you, I love you," Arian panted between convulsions, shivering at the ceaseless pleasuring throb. "Only you. You are everything. I'm yours. I love you." He sobbed the last words, only for his body to cramp and relax again in the most delicious way.

Arian sagged against Fernando when the contractions slowed

to a steady beat. Fernando wrapped his arms around him and held him tight until the last tremors ebbed away, stroking his hair. Arian's heart took a while to slow down. He played with the soft hair of Fernando's nape, breathing in his dark, masculine scent. Fernando kissed his head, and in turn, Arian mouthed his neck, slow and lazy. Drunk on happiness, he smiled into Fernando's skin. He sighed in bone-deep contentment, tired and sated, but for the first time, his thoughts were clear, his mind no longer shrouded by lust.

"I was wrong about you," Arian said. "I thought you were a conqueror. But you are the god of sex, who has come to deliver me from my curse."

Fernando chuckled. "Glad you found it satisfying."

"Oh, more than that. It was life-changing. It's even better than how they make it out to be. I loved it," Arian said, blushing at what else he had told Fernando when his climax had rolled through him.

"I loved it too," Fernando said, hugging Arian tighter.

"Good."

"Hmm. I finally did my part. I wasn't too rough on you?"

"You were perfect."

Arian reached up and met him in a gentle kiss, the need to connect overwhelming. His heart sang as their mouths slid together. He never wanted to be apart from him. Because he had meant what he said. He would follow Fernando to the ends of the Earth.

They stayed in the tender embrace for a long time until Fernando mumbled something about getting cold. He picked up Arian and carried him back to the beach fire. Arian rested his head on Fernando's shoulder. They would sleep next to the fire, wrapped up in each other on one of the new mats, dreaming of what had passed between them.

They reached the sand beach where the fire had died down but not yet gone out. Fernando headed toward it. Then a groan that screamed of pain, not pleasure, ripped the perfect night apart.

Chapter Nine

Fernando

It was Luis. Fernando set Arian down at the waterline and sprinted over. Luis was doubled over, clutching at his chest, gasping for air. Zade had wrapped an arm around his shoulders, comforting him.

"What's wrong with him?" Fernando asked, coming to a halt and dropping to his knees in the wet sand next to them.

"I don't know," Zade said. "We were..."

"Don't even tell me."

Luis was sweating profusely. In the distance, Arian was calling Kristian and Darin. They had been too busy to notice something was wrong with Luis. Fernando cursed.

"Luis?" Fernando asked but only got pained groans in answer.

Luis's eyes were half shut, his face a grimace of pain.

Fernando looked up at Zade. It was clear what had happened. Zade had exhausted Luis. They had been going at it for days. And while someone as young as Darin could take it, it had proven too much for Luis.

"What happened?" Kristian asked as he rushed over with Darin.

"I—I don't know... I..." Zade stammered.

"For god's sake, get away from him," Kristian said, and Zade flinched back before Kristian could push him.

Luis tipped to the side. He had lost consciousness. Darin held him up to keep him from falling into the sand.

"He needs a doctor," Fernando said.

"There is no doctor..." Zade said.

"We know there is no doctor on this godforsaken island," Kristian barked, causing Zade to back away further. "I knew this would happen! I knew it! This is where it leads. You lure in sailors. You have your fun with us for a few days, and then when it gets too much, our hearts give in. That's where the stories come from. That's why everyone warns you of mermen."

Zade's mouth opened, but no words came out. His otherwise proud posture crumbled.

What had Luis said the night before they ran into the mermen? *Nobody makes it out alive.* Fernando's body felt too tight. Every horror story about mermen was true. Fernando turned, and his gaze caught Arian, who had come over in the shallow water. All color had drained from his face.

Darin sat there, frozen. "Tell me this is the first time this has happened," he said, voice shaking.

Zade looked away, fiddling with a seashell he'd picked up. And Fernando understood. This had happened before. He clawed his fingers into the sand, fists shaking. It didn't matter whether back then it had been Zade or Tarlis or even Arian. But this was not the first time. Arian. Fernando stared at him. Arian should have told him. Why hadn't he? Fernando would have never let it go this far had he known.

Darin shifted to keep Luis up and winced. Kristian whipped around and stared at him, then jumped to his feet. "Tarlis!" he snarled. "Tarlis!" He stalked over to the merman.

Fernando looked between Darin and Kristian. Of course. They still had those cursed toys attached to them. And Kristian was getting his removed, even if he had to beat Tarlis into doing it.

"Take it off!" Fernando said to Arian, motioning his head toward Darin's crotch. The idea of Arian near another man's genitals irritated him. Only because of the damage he could cause as they had all learned.

"It's Finn's. He needs to—"

"Then get him."

Arian nodded, eyes wide.

The next minute, he'd fetched Finn and the toy came off. Fernando took Luis off Darin and propped him up against his shoulder, petting his friend's neck. Finn and Darin didn't talk, avoiding each other's gaze. Nevertheless, surreptitious glances flew between them, both looking away quickly every time. Whatever had happened between those two was over.

Betrayal. Shock and betrayal. It poisoned his thoughts. He should have known better than to trust the mermen. Arian could have said something. He hadn't. Because mermen were inherently selfish. Weren't they? They only cared for their pleasure, consequences be damned. Fernando had thought Arian better than that. How had he been so blind?

Two forces tore Fernando's mind apart. They had to leave, bring Luis to the next doctor, get to safety, away from the mermen. The irrational part of him wanted to stay. He laughed at his stupidity. Stay and what? Live with a merman? He must be losing his mind. Especially now that he knew where this led. No, his life was in San Juan and on the ships that sailed between the continents.

Kristian returned, though Tarlis was nowhere to be seen. Hopefully, Kristian hadn't broken his neck in his rage.

"I'm so sorry," Zade said, eyes wet. "This wasn't meant to happen. I didn't—"

"Stow it!" Kristian snapped, the veins of his neck bulging, hands balled into fists.

This wasn't going anywhere, and they had more important things to do than play the blame game.

"There's a boat," Fernando said, looking Arian in the eye.

"A boat?" Kristian asked, perking up.

"The rowboat we came over on. I discovered it before we came back to the beach. It's been washed ashore," Fernando said, never taking his gaze off Arian. "We're going to carry Luis to it, and then we leave. You will not stop us."

"Of course not—" Arian said.

"Oh, you little—" Kristian said.

"Kristian!" Fernando said. "There's no need." Nobody talked to Arian like that. No matter what had gone wrong, Kristian had no right.

Kristian snorted.

"Puerto Rico isn't far," Fernando said. "Twenty miles true east. There's a small coastal town right on the Eastern shore of Puerto Rico. They'll have a doctor. If we row all night, we can make it." He paused to think. "Are there other mermen around Culebra?"

"There are," Arian said, "but they're easy to avoid. I'll show you where they live."

He drew a map of the archipelago in the sand, pointing out the different areas mermen frequented. And Arian was right, if you knew where they were, the mermen were easy to go around.

"And it's night," Arian said. "They will be sleeping anyway. Stick to the northeastern coast of Culebra and you won't run into them. I could accompany you to make sure no one—"

"No," Fernando bit out before he could agree to this insanity. Part of him roared in protest. Arian swallowed hard. He was trying to help, keep them safe, but every minute Fernando spent in his presence was a risk. Of what, he wasn't going to admit. "We will go alone."

"Look," Arian said, "I'm sorry for your friend. Zade didn't mean any harm. It was an accident."

"You're going to call it an accident too, if Kristian strangles Tarlis? Zade was grinding on Luis for days. I should have stopped this madness yesterday. To be honest, I don't care if it was an accident. It happened. And now Luis might die. We are leaving and that's it."

Arian's shoulders heaved, and his face contorted in pain. Then he backed away.

Fernando's heart screamed. Arian shouldn't feel like this, not because of him, not because of the things he said. But why would Fernando still care? Either way, he did.

Arian slipped into the water, Fernando tracking his every move, burning his features into his memory. They wouldn't see each other again, but Fernando would never forget him. Despite everything, he had enjoyed being with Arian. It had been so different from the meaningless encounters with uninspiring ladies he'd had. He felt something. And it lingered, didn't allow itself to be washed away, circumstances be damned. Arian looked up at him one last time, their eyes locking for a painful heartbeat, then he dove under. He was gone.

Fernando blinked rapidly. Got to his feet. "Let's get out of here," he said, his voice flat and strange to his own ears.

Zade regarded them, regret written all over his face as they gathered up Luis. Had Darin and Finn said goodbye? Did Kristian even look at Tarlis as they passed him leaving the beach? Fernando didn't know, nor could he get himself to care. He was wrapped up in a bubble of pain. His body was numb to the strain of carrying Luis as the world turned dull and gray.

He had liked Arian. More than he cared to admit. He still liked him despite the fact he was holding the motionless body of his friend. But leaving was his only option. Even if nothing had happened to Luis, what would he have done? He couldn't stay on this island. He had a life, a business to get back to, work he loved. There was no reason to stay. Well, one reason. But not anymore. It was over. Or that's what he told himself. Why did it bother him? He should be glad he was getting away. Glad like the times when he had been entertained by a woman and then got to leave. He never stuck around long enough for breakfast. Yet, he wanted to have breakfast with Arian every day for the rest—No. He wasn't going there. They were done, and he was moving on. Or he would, eventually.

The rough rocks of the beach were a welcome distraction from the stabbing pain in his chest. They reached the boat, pulled it out into the sea and placed Luis in it. In silence, they picked up the paddles and started rowing. Fernando forbade himself to think of what had happened among the rocks of the beach less than an hour ago. Or that this was the boat he had taken to get to Arian days ago. How fitting that it was the same one carrying him away.

Stoically, he focused on the water ahead when they passed the beach they had spent the evening at. He didn't turn when the boat floated past the rock Arian had sat on that fateful morning.

The bright light of the full moon reflected on the water, illuminating their journey. Fernando should be glad that it was such a calm night. But part of him wanted it to be dark and stormy, wind and waves drowning his pain in the endless sea.

They kept their distance from Culebra's northern shores until they hit the tip of the long peninsula sticking out from the island. And there, hidden in a bay, lay *The Haste*. With their surgeon on board. Relief flooded Fernando.

With renewed vigor, they rowed toward it. The sails of *The Haste* were tied back. The crew had been waiting for them. Help for Luis was near.

"Hey! Hey!" Darin shouted when they were within earshot, waving a paddle.

But the crew was already letting down another rowboat to come and get them. The lookout had spotted them.

For the first time in days, Fernando consciously acknowledged the fact he was naked. Never mind. He had clothes on board to change into.

The other boat darted toward them, setting off waves in its fast approach. The navigator was among the men on it, that stupid little kid. Fernando had never been so glad to see him. And the ship's doctor, one of the best traveling surgeons money could hire.

"You're alive!" the navigator said.

"Barely," Kristian said. "Take Luis. We don't know what's wrong with him. Collapsed on the beach, clutching at his chest."

"His heart," the surgeon said.

"Will he be okay?" Darin asked.

"Can't tell like this," the surgeon said. "I will do my best."

They got Luis onto the ship, and the surgeon took over.

"Sticking around and waiting for us was incredibly stupid," Fernando said to the navigator. "You could have been lured in by another group of mermen and there would be more casualties. Look at the shape Luis is in. But I'm glad you did stick around, for his sake."

Chapter Ten

Arian

Arian hated himself. How could he have been so stupid? How could he have not seen the signs? Luis was older than the other men. Zade had gone insane with him. Arian should've never let that happen. And now, Fernando was gone. He was gone, and he hated Arian. Rightfully so.

Arian stayed underwater for a long time. When the rowboat passed, everything inside him pleaded with him to resurface, to see Fernando once more, steal a last glance. But he couldn't bear the thought of how Fernando would look at him. So he stayed until the boat was gone. His chest hurt, his lungs screamed for air. Yet he stayed. When he couldn't stand it anymore, he came up, gulping down air.

And then his gaze fell on Zade, sitting at the beach where the men had left him, being comforted by Finn. White-hot rage flooded Arian, and with a few harsh strokes, he was at the beach.

"What did you do!" Arian spat.

"I didn't—"

"Why did you have to go this far? The man is dead by now. What were you thinking? Why did you not pay attention to how he was coping? You know better than this!"

Zade shrank back further in Finn's arms.

"Arian..." Finn started.

"No! Zade should have been more careful. He's killed a person."

"He didn't do it on purpose."

"I don't care! And neither do Luis's friends!"

"Arian, stop. Can't you see he's distraught?" Finn said, holding a shaking Zade. "You're not going to make it better by yelling. Your man is gone, and so is mine. Zade's is dead. Please, just stop."

Arian was about to let loose another spate of anger and pain when Zade sobbed loudly. It caused Arian to swallow his next outburst, but his nostrils flared. This wasn't finished.

A wet hand settled on his shoulder. Tarlis.

"Arian, come," he said, and pulled him with him to the other side of the beach where the creek ran into the sea.

Being angry with Zade allowed Arian to focus on something other than the gaping wound in his soul. He didn't want to let go of it, didn't want to feel the pain. For it was unbearable.

They sat in the mouth of the creek, looking out at the moonlit sea. It was horrendously peaceful. Arian hated it.

"I'm hurting too," Tarlis admitted. "And so is Zade, worse than any of us."

"I doubt it. If he cared, he would've been more careful." Arian picked up a stone from the stream bed and tossed it as far as his wrath would take it.

"You know how he is. He gets carried away. And whether you believe it or not, it does matter that he didn't do it on purpose. It was an accident. Nobody wanted this to happen, least of all Zade."

"I'm just so angry," Arian said. Because anger was the easier emotion.

"Perhaps Luis had health problems," Tarlis said, running his fin over the surface of the water. "Some humans have fragile hearts, and while Luis is far from old, he isn't young either. Remember that it could have happened to him anywhere."

"It was Zade that didn't stop for days."

"There's nothing I can say to make your pain go away. Or mine, for that matter."

"You liked Kristian."

"He does look like a Norse god."

"He has the temper of one too," Arian said.

In the pale light of the moon, the faint blush that crept up Tarlis's face was almost invisible, but it was there. "He is thunder and storm."

And Tarlis was drifting snow, as beautiful as he was calm, cold even. Except that behind the cool front lay a warm heart.

"You have taken to him," Arian said.

"Of course I have, but it doesn't matter. He didn't feel the same. He's not the same as Fernando."

"Fernando doesn't like me. Certainly not anymore."

"Feelings aren't washed away that easily. But what does it change?" Tarlis said. "Even if it had ended differently, neither of us had a future with those men. It was over before it started. A brief distraction."

Arian shook his head. "It changed everything for me."

"How so?" Tarlis asked.

Arian had said too much. He wouldn't tell Tarlis what had happened earlier. It would be cruel to wave Fernando's gift in his face when it was something he would never experience.

"He's a special person," Arian said instead. Better to evade. He didn't want to think about it. Now that he knew what it was like. What it felt like to reach the highest peak of lust and tumble down into ecstasy. It was too painful that it'd be a one-time experience. One he'd treasure forever.

They sat in the creek all night and talked. Tarlis wasn't one to share how he'd experienced the last few days and his feelings, though conversing with him was calming.

When the first light of morning kissed the sky, Arian could no longer keep his eyes open. He wasn't worthy of sleeping on Fernando's mat, but it would make him feel close to him, so he did anyway. He lay down on the green mat, running his hands over the leaves Fernando had woven together. If he closed his eyes, he could see his fingers working as he told him the *Odyssey*. He'd never hear the other story Fernando had mentioned. The sad one about war and the tragic love of two men.

Sleep never came despite his exhaustion. Arian silently sobbed, fighting to not let a sound past his lips, lest the others found out how distressed he was. He pressed a fist to his mouth as he shook and shivered out of control.

What he had shared with Fernando was *more*. More than a few fun days together. More than the ecstasy of sex. It was a connection. Fernando had come from nothing and carved himself a place in the world. He had grown up in a place that looked down on him, and for that, he had left it behind. How could Arian not admire such courage, such determination? He had taken his life into his own hands and molded it until it had taken a form he loved.

Now he was gone. Arian was never going to see him again. Besides, even if, Fernando wouldn't forgive him for not holding back Zade in his haze of lust. Arian bit the inside of his cheek to feel anything other than the agony tearing him apart from the inside.

He was hopeless, pathetic. Had confessed how he felt about Fernando at the point of climax when his words couldn't be taken seriously. How embarrassing. Besides, his feelings would never be returned. Fernando could have any woman, any man he wanted wherever he went. One look at him and they tripped over their feet to lie at his. And that was before they knew the kindness of his heart, the sharpness of his mind. He truly was better off without Arian.

By the time the sun was up, his head hammered with dehydration and lack of sleep. None of his friends had gone back to the rocks in the strait this morning to watch the sunrise, the memory of the ship's arrival too fresh in everyone's mind.

Arian stayed on the mat throughout the morning, not even crawling into the sea when his fishtail grew dry and coarse. It was Finn that brought him water and fish. Arian gulped down the water faster than he should, and even then, his body demanded more. But one look at the fish and he was sick to his stomach.

"You've got to eat," Finn said.

"I don't want to."

"Just have a little bit."

Never had a yellowtail snapper looked more unappealing. He had caught some with Fernando. With a scrunched-up face, he peeled off a bite-sized piece. But when he held it to his mouth, his throat closed up, his body revolting at the thought of eating.

"I can't," he said, and put the fish back down. "I just can't. I'll only throw it up if I force it and that's not going to make things better."

Arian's lack of appetite continued. He ate a bite here and there, but never more than a mouthful. Silence and time to reflect were his worst enemies. Everything reminded him of Fernando. The rocks at the beach where he fed him oranges. The manatees in the bay they swam with. The coconuts on the palm trees Fernando had husked. Fernando was everywhere. Talking to his friends proved to be no help, their own pain too fresh. So he swam over to the south coast of Culebra and spent his days with the mermen colony there. His misfortune unbeknownst to them, light conversation came easy, and it distracted him throughout the day. Although, he had to grit his teeth now and then to fend off the tears that threatened to spill whenever a stupid thought, a memory of Fernando crossed his mind.

At night, he returned to Culebrita to sleep on Fernando's mat, closing his eyes and pretending he was there, he'd only have to reach out and he would be touching his smooth, warm skin.

Arian was going out of his mind. The days passed, yet his pain remained, so present it canceled out the lust that had returned to his loins. He couldn't let it be. As if he had found water in the desert only for it to be taken away. What he'd had was not enough. They'd never had an opportunity to explore their connection. All he had gotten with Fernando was a glimpse at what could be.

His mind churned. What if, what if, what if.

What if he refused things to end here? What if he pushed? Fernando never gave up. When circumstances didn't suit him, he worked until they did. He didn't give up.

One morning, he couldn't stand it any longer and swam back out to the rocks to watch the rising sun. It would be painful, but better to confront the memories than to run away from them. If he allowed his grief to run its course, it'd pass more quickly.

Zade was already there. Arian hadn't expected to see him. They hadn't talked much since that night and stayed out of each other's sight wherever possible. The sudden proximity was uncomfortable, but Arian would bear it. Zade's shoulders were hunched, his body turned away from Arian.

They sat in silence, watching the sun peek over the horizon and paint the sky in hues of pink and orange.

Arian had been harsh with Zade. That night, his pain had overwritten everything else, including his concern for his friend. How would Arian have felt if he'd killed Fernando in the first couple of days, when he had been toying with him, winding him up tighter and tighter? He would have been inconsolable. And chances were, that was how Zade felt. Inconsolable. Arian had been a real dick about it because of how Zade's actions affected him. He'd been angry as Zade had cost him Fernando, not thinking about Zade's price being steeper.

He wanted to say something, apologize, but for the longest time, he didn't. The sun was up when Zade shifted away from Arian, ready to get back in the water.

"I'm sorry," Arian said before Zade slipped away. "I wasn't thinking. Said things I shouldn't have, and I'm sorry for that."

He could tell Zade that it had been because of his grief, that he hadn't been able to think of anything except the pain in his heart, but it would sound like an excuse. Fernando wasn't the kind of person who made excuses, and Arian shouldn't be either. So he let his apology hang there without justification.

Zade turned toward him, a startled expression on his face. "It's okay. I know you're hurting."

"Still, I was harsh and inconsiderate. I'm sorry it took me so long to see that."

Zade nodded slowly, full of apprehension as if afraid Arian would jump him and tear him apart, never mind Zade was of a bigger and stronger build, muscular where Arian was slim.

"I didn't see much of you and Fernando," Zade confessed, "but Tarlis told me you got close."

"You could say that. He meant something to me. Still does. Always will."

"That bad?"

"Yeah."

"I liked Luis," Zade said. "Wish we had taken the time to talk. I was completely out of it. He was there, in my arms and watching him ebb and flow in lust switched my head off. I wish I had paid closer attention to the signs. Sorry if what I did caused you pain."

"No, I'm sorry. Fernando would've left sooner or later, it was inevitable. The timing was the biggest shock, it was so sudden. I'd thought we'd have many more days together until I would no longer be able to hold him."

Zade's fingers traced the rough edges of his rock. "I feel bad for Luis's family. Maybe I have robbed a wife of her husband, children of their father. I don't even know that about him. As I said, we didn't talk much." His face contorted in regret.

"He probably wasn't married. The sailor types often aren't."

Zade shrugged. "Then he had parents, siblings, friends. I wronged them. And I've been thinking a lot about how to make amends. It's not right for me to sit here and continue my life when someone else might be grieving more than I can imagine."

"There's little you can do."

"I know. Just wish I could do something." Zade paused for a moment, thinking. "Humans value gold, don't they? I still have a pouch full of it tucked away somewhere. If I could get it to his family… But I don't know where he lives."

"That's unfortunate."

"Let's go back and catch fish," Zade said as he slid into the water, wanting out of the conversation. "Finn says you haven't been eating."

"I have, just not much."

"Then come," Zade said, and swam over.

"You go ahead, I'll be there soon. I need a moment to think." Because the seed of a *very* bad idea had been planted in his head.

Chapter Eleven

Fernando

Fernando sat at his desk. He had meant to finish a letter to his brother in Spain with instructions to prepare for a trade run across the Atlantic in summer and purchase enough manufactured goods to fill a ship. Instead, he found himself turning over a seashell in his hand.

It wasn't even from the Culebra archipelago, just a piece he had picked up on a beach near San Juan months ago. Yet it captivated his attention. Like anything that reminded him of the sea. Of Arian.

On the one hand, he had experienced how dangerous it was to get near mermen. Luis was alive, but not well. Worried about his friend, Fernando had visited him in his house in the center of town on a couple of occasions since their return. The doctors said he would recover. Not completely and his heart would always be weak, but they were optimistic about his return to normal life.

On the other hand, Fernando had met an incredible person. For the first time, he had found someone keen to talk about the stories he loved, who listened eagerly. If only he'd had the time to teach Arian how to read. They could've had endless conversations discussing Homer and Shakespeare. Even Plato and Aristotle.

And there was that spark. A spark he had never experienced before. It made him want to jump into the next boat and get to

Arian, all else be damned. Which was, of course, not an option. He didn't want to share Luis's fate. But Arian was not like that. Well, maybe a little, considering how the first couple of days on the island had gone.

The memory made him rock-hard in his breeches. It wasn't easy to admit, but he'd let himself be tied up by Arian again. Or he could tie up Arian... But no, better not to think about that.

He glanced back at the letter he was supposed to finish. What would it be like to go sailing again? If he set his sails for Europe, he'd pass north of the Culebra archipelago. It would cost him everything not to jump into a rowboat and gun for the place he wanted to be. No, not the place. The person he wanted to be with.

A knock on the door of his study had him looking up. "Come in."

Ayah entered, carrying a tray with his morning tea and a stack of letters. "Good morning, *Señor*. I trust you slept well?"

She set the tray down on his desk, her cotton dress shifting over her plump figure with every move as she handed him the tea. Ayah was one of the new servants Fernando had employed after he freed his slaves. He had hoped some would stay as his employees, but they had all wanted to make their fortune elsewhere. Good for them.

For a woman in her fifties, Ayah was swift, a quick learner, albeit a bit motherly.

"I see Isabella has written to you again," she said, handing him the letters. "A nice lady, if I may say so."

"Thank you, Ayah," he said, accepting the stack of mail. "That will be all." He wasn't going to discuss his love life with his servants. To his shame, he had been short with them, finding himself irritable for no reason.

Ayah gave him a slight bow and exited the room as he opened the letters.

A note from a business partner in Hispaniola about an opportunity to share in a trade run to Africa, which he would decline. He had never been interested in bringing slaves to the New

World, and after seeing Arian's reaction to the fact he'd had slaves of his own, he abhorred the idea.

A letter from his lawyer about a property purchase he had considered. He'd get back to him.

And of course, Isabella's letter. He had forgotten all about her while he was up in Boston. They had met twice before he'd left, but like all the women before her, she hadn't left a lasting impression. Now that he was back, she was eager to meet up. After he'd been too preoccupied to respond to her first letter a couple of days ago, she'd sent another one. Fernando sighed. He should reply, even if it was out of politeness rather than interest. His eyes traveled from her letter to his pen and onto the seashell.

He had experienced something short and precious with Arian. But the stories sailors told about mermen had proven to be true. More or less. Luis was ill, but he wasn't dead. And Arian wasn't like that, at least most of the time. Though, he did get the right amount of wild and heated when things went further.

Fernando got up from his desk and opened the door to his garden. Any distraction to get his head out of the gutter and away from thoughts of Arian.

His new gardener, a young Englishman, was watering the roses. When he spotted Fernando, he waved and smiled, showing off his crooked teeth. Yet when the sun fell onto his ginger hair it took on a golden hue and—No. Jesus Christ. His gardener didn't look like Arian, a far cry from the merman's beauty.

Fernando put his face in his hand and shook his head. His mind wasn't kind to him, taking him back to Arian at every turn. He should give up trying not to think of him, pointless as it was. Arian's face popped into his head wherever he went, whatever he did. When he lay down at night and sleep refused to come for hours, he wondered if it would be different had he held Arian in his arms. He'd run his fingers through his hair and plant kisses on his head, his face, his whole body.

Except it couldn't be. Mermen were dangerous, and Arian was

no exception. Fernando better thought of what happened to Luis. And none of it mattered anyway. He was never going to see Arian again. It was over. Nothing but a bittersweet memory.

It would be for the best if he wrote to Isabella and arranged to see her.

Chapter Twelve

Arian

The conversation with Zade replayed itself in Arian's head long after Zade had left him at the rocks and gone to catch fish. Zade was right, trying to make amends with Luis's family was the noble thing to do. They all had a part in the tragic accident. Yes, Zade should've been more careful, but Arian, too, ought to have paid more attention. Helped Zade break out of his haze. He wasn't going to shy away from his responsibility.

While Zade had no clue where to find Luis's family, Arian had an idea where Fernando lived. He'd said he had a house in San Juan. Arian had a rough description of where. *It's on the fringes of town, down a wide road lined with trees to either side.* Not much to go by but it was better than nothing. And Fernando was rich, meaning people knew who he was and more importantly, where he lived.

But Arian couldn't swim to San Juan, hand the gold to a stranger at the port with instructions to whom they needed to give it to. Because for starters, the whole port would empty if there was as much as a whiff of a rumor that a merman was coming. And if there wasn't, they'd run the minute he arrived. Apart from that, he couldn't give the gold to a random stranger. Zade was right, the coins were of inexplicable value to humans and anyone given the gold would, in all likelihood, keep it to themselves, never to be seen again.

Which left one option: make a deal with the proverbial devil. It would cost him dearly, but it was the only way.

If he could see Fernando one last time, he'd apologize. Arian's heart beat faster at the thought of being in Fernando's presence. Just one more time. He'd give everything for that. Considering the possibility filled him with hope and joy, which was idiotic because nothing more would come from it. But seeing him would soothe the pain for a few minutes. It'd be worse afterward, but what did he care about that. It was the moment of being near him, exchanging a few words, that mattered. It was all he wanted. An opportunity to apologize and do his part in making things right with Luis's family. It was the least he could do.

How long would Fernando be in San Juan for? How soon was he going to depart on his next voyage? If Arian wanted to do this, he had to do it now. He should leave today.

Fernando wouldn't be happy to see him, but at least Arian would do his part in making amends.

"You're insane," Tarlis said when Arian told him of his plans over breakfast.

"It's the only way." Arian picked up a small fish and swallowed it whole. He couldn't stomach a full meal, but his appetite had returned enough for him to eat a little.

"First of all, you don't know if you'll see him. If you find his house."

"I'm sure I will."

Tarlis shot him a skeptical look. "Secondly, you need to rid yourself of the illusion that it will change anything. I'm sorry to say, there is no future for you and Fernando."

"I'm aware. Heck, he might not want to see me. It's a risk I'll take. Trust me, I've gone over this in my head often enough."

Tarlis took his hand. "You don't know the price you'll be asked to pay. You might get to San Juan and be asked for something you cannot give."

"There's nothing I wouldn't give up."

"Don't take this lightly," Tarlis said, squeezing his hand. "You have no idea what it will cost you. A lot if you ask me. Too much. And even if it's something you're willing to do, you might come to regret it. You may never return to Culebrita, and I won't see you again."

"You're being dramatic."

"I'm being realistic. Be careful."

"You know I've already decided."

"That doesn't change the fact it's a horrible idea."

There was nothing left to say after that. If Arian wanted a shot at seeing Fernando, he had to leave now. When Zade returned to the island later that morning, Arian told him of his plan. Zade listened quietly, nodding along. He agreed to it with enough reluctance to be polite but not enough to convince Arian he'd rather go himself. No, Zade had been to that mangrove forest before and asked for a small service, which hadn't cost him the world. What Arian wanted was a request of another magnitude. Zade gave him his pouch of gold, avoiding eye contact. Then he described the route Arian would have to take, his face growing darker with every word.

Afterward, it was farewell. Arian liked the archipelago, he loved his friends and saying goodbye, not knowing if and when he would return, was hard.

"You could have at least gone yourself," Tarlis told Zade.

"No," Arian said. "He's already paying the price in gold."

"Which is worthless to us," Tarlis said. "You're the one that will truly pay."

"Let it go," Finn said. "He's made up his mind. And we all know it's not about the gold."

"That's not true," Arian said.

"Whatever," Finn said, and pulled him in for a hug. "Be careful. Come back to us."

Arian hugged Zade and even Tarlis, briefly. Then he was off.

The swim to Puerto Rico was long and monotonous. It gave

him too much time to think as he drifted underwater, surrounded by nothing except the clear blue sea, the ground too far down to be visible. He swam faster than a human could have, but the journey stretched, nonetheless. Time gave room to his doubts, his fear. What if he paid a price so high it destroyed any future he may have, and then Fernando wasn't there, or worse, refused to see him? It ate away at him in the endless blue, though it didn't erode his determination.

He swam all afternoon and spent the night on the beach of a tiny island off the coast of Puerto Rico. His mind stayed busy long after his body had come to rest on the sand, but eventually, exhaustion won and he passed out under the stars, dreams of Fernando and nightmares of failure haunting him alike.

Night after night of staying awake with his thoughts had taken its toll, and Arian only woke when the sun was halfway up the sky. Disoriented, he looked around, not recognizing his surroundings before it all came back to him. He was on his way to Puerto Rico. And he had slept late, wasting hours. What if Fernando was leaving as he sat here, loading his ship with cargo going wherever. Arian cursed. The coast of Puerto Rico was long, and he first had to find the mangrove forest, then San Juan.

Zade had given him a good description of where to look, and after swimming near the Puerto Rican northern coast for a few hours, he spotted a dream catcher hanging from the drooping branch of a mangrove. Here, the trees parted and gave way to a natural channel. It resembled a tunnel with the trees forming a dense ceiling made of branches and leaves. The water was green and murky, and Arian regarded it with suspicion. Zade hadn't mentioned any crocodiles, but that didn't mean there weren't any. They thrived in the shallower waters.

One way to find out. Arian pushed forward and into the pathway between the mangroves. The mangrove forest was a curious place. Unlike the jungle and other forests found on land, it consisted of trees growing in brackish water. Their roots stuck out of the channel, twisting like snakes, raising the trunks above the surface. The water tasted different than out at sea, stale and old with only a hint of salt.

Arian followed the tunnel till its end, only for it to split off into two and the junction had no markers. Hadn't Zade mentioned a triple spiral carved into a mangrove trunk? He scanned the trees, but none of them were marked. In the end, he picked a path at random, hoping for the best.

The mangrove forest was a labyrinth. Arian alternated left and right turns whenever a channel branched off to avoid getting lost. It led him to a dead-end, and he had to go back, try a different path. He did his best committing his turns to memory, though it was useless, and soon he had no idea how to get out of the forest.

He wasted hours, concern mounting. What if he could neither find his destination nor his way back out? Then, finally, an intersection bore another marker, a five-pointed star. Arian followed it, but there were more turns after and no marks to be seen.

It was getting dark when a channel gave way to a wider pond. The putrid smell of dead wood filled the air. Fog wafted over the basin and there, built on stilts under mangrove branches sagging under their lush green weight, stood the crooked shack of the sea witch.

A boat was tied to the rotting wooden pier with a fraying rope. Dim candlelight illuminated the small windows of the hut. And as Zade had described it to Arian's disbelieving ears, there was indeed a staircase under the house, leading up from the water.

Mosquitoes buzzed around Arian's head as he approached, and he dove back under to swim toward the stilts and the strange staircase, which reached to the bottom of the pond.

He resurfaced under the shack, the wooden floor of the cabin above him creaking with steps. The sea witch was home. The stairs led to a trap door, and Arian knocked. The steps stopped, then came back in a crescendo, and the door swung open.

A man appeared in the opening. His young face was that of a

Puerto Rican native, but it was mixed with something else, though it was hard to see when the candlelight cast a halo around his head and shadows on his face. But his hair was dark and his skin a golden brown, and he wore a strange robe.

"Well, hello, hello, what do we have here? A curious little customer?" he said. "Come up, come up."

Arian pulled himself onto the stairs until his upper body was in the hut, his fin swaying in the water. The place was a madhouse. The walls were lined with vials containing hair, different powders and grotesquely shaped, flesh-colored items Arian had never seen before. There was a jar filled to the brim with human ears, an oversized, stuffed rodent covered in dried orchids and a whole shelf of chubby cotton-lined dolls, bits of straw sticking out. The walls were lined with bookshelves and painted symbols, most of which didn't mean anything to Arian. He recognized the five-pointed star and the crescent, but there were others too. One looked like two one-eyed fish chasing each other's tails, forming a circle. Others resembled complicated forms of human writing that even Fernando wouldn't be able to decipher. Amidst the overflowing shelves and scattered objects stood a cauldron, emitting a pungent smell and purple steam.

Arian had come to the right place.

The sea witch plopped to the floor, crossing his legs. "Name's Malik."

"Arian."

"Well, Arian, what brings you here? What loony, moody twist of fate made you seek out my services? No, don't say. Let me guess. You're not hunting for fortune as your purse is filled with gold." He pointed his chin at Zade's leather pouch. "Perhaps a sleeping potion? Your eyes are puffy."

"I need legs."

It would change his life. With legs instead of a fishtail, he could not only personally bring Fernando the gold and apologize, but it would also nullify the curse he was bearing. He would be able to live life as a human. Start working toward goals. What they would be, he wasn't sure—he'd have all the time in the world to explore that. And maybe, there was a chance Fernando didn't hate him. That they could have a go at what they had glimpsed together on the island.

Malik's eyebrows shot up to his hairline. "Mother of the forest, he wants legs." He broke out in giggles. "How long do you need legs for?"

How long? Arian's eyes widened. "Permanently, I hope."

"You hope. Well, then I have to tell you if I had the means to give you legs permanently, I'd be doing all sorts of things, and you and I wouldn't be sitting here. That's a no. But..."

Malik jumped to his feet and swept through his hut, inspecting his shelves, a couple of chests and a leather trunk reeking of mold. He didn't find what he was searching for. Scratching his head, he went back to his bookshelves and pulled at the leather-bound volumes, most of which were coming apart at the seams. Finally, he produced a single shard of a seashell. He looked at it with a longing appropriate for a long-lost spouse returned.

"I can give you legs for a day," Malik said slowly, studying the shard, "but it's going to cost you. I only have one of these."

A single day? Arian must have misheard. Surely the famous sea witch would be able to give him legs for longer than that.

"Don't look at me," Malik said. "It's the best I can do. If you compensate me accordingly."

"What's it going to cost me?"

"Hmm," Malik said and tilted his head. "How much gold do you have? Not enough in that little pouch of yours."

"And I need the gold for something else. Is there anything else I can offer you?"

"Lifelong servitude."

Arian blinked. He couldn't possibly mean what Arian thought he'd said. A day with legs in exchange for serving Malik for the rest of his life?

"I don't—"

"If you're not interested, please leave," Malik said, and turned his back as he walked back to his cauldron. "I have a lot of work to do, and this new recipe I'm trying requires my full attention."

"You can't ask for this," Arian said. "That's insane. I want legs for a single day."

"Yes, I heard. And legs for a day requires the only mothershell shard I have. Which I happen to need for something else. Something important to me."

Arian played with the pouch in his hands. Perhaps if he offered some of the gold? Malik shook his head.

"If you want legs, we'll need a gold coin to make the potion. But the mothershell shard is something that cannot be purchased with money. It's a powerful magical ingredient and hard to come by. Impossible to come by. No less than what I asked for will do."

"Is there nothing else?"

"What else can you offer? You said you can't spare the gold. It wouldn't be enough, anyway."

Arian did need the gold to give to Fernando; otherwise, it would expose that the main reason he'd come to see him was indeed pure selfishness. He did want the gold to go to Luis's family, though more importantly, he longed to visit Fernando. Have another chance.

But as Tarlis had said, Arian couldn't afford any illusions. Fernando didn't want to see him. He'd take the gold and shut the door in his face. Arian would return to the archipelago and die of boredom.

He had come so far. Turning back was not an option. Arian pictured handing the pouch full of gold back to Zade, telling him Malik had asked for too much. How shameful. And the mere thought of visiting Fernando was elating to the point it was irresistible.

Arian took in the interior of the hut one more time. It looked interesting. There was something to be learned and understood here. Books lined the walls.

"Will you teach me how to read and write?"

Malik smiled at his victory. "I don't see why not. It would make you more useful to me. Not right away as there are other priorities, but eventually."

"Then we have a deal."

"Good. Good. Let's make a potion."

Malik took a ridiculously oversized book, set it on his table and flipped through it. Not finding what he needed, he picked up another one, smaller but thicker. That didn't help either and he went through a few more until he found a set of loose sheets, squinting as he read them over. "This is it..."

He grabbed a thick, blood-red candle and set it on the floor. On top, he placed a three-legged contraption, which held a glass vile. Malik pulled out the vial and eyed it, then produced a hunting knife. Before he could react, Malik had cut Arian's arm. He flinched back, but Malik's grip was a vice.

"Hold still," Malik said as he let Arian's blood flow into the vile. "We need your blood for the potion."

"You could have told me."

"It's less painful when you aren't prepared. Just another moment, and we'll have enough... there." Malik pulled back, placed the vial over the flame and picked up a small jar. He dipped his finger into the opaque gel inside and smeared it over the cut on Arian's arm. The skin healed before his eyes.

"There. Wasn't so bad, was it?" He stalked over to the shelf that held small, powder-filled containers and pulled them out one by one. "Dried loganberry, pulverized badger paw, crushed tanna leaf..."

Malik poured various amounts of their contents into the vial. A dash of this, a pinch of that. When the cauldron in the other corner rumbled, Malik returned his attention to it for a moment, stirring it with a large wooden spoon. It didn't make the smell any better.

"What's that going to be when it's finished?" Arian asked.

"Wouldn't you like to know. Don't worry, you'll learn a thing or two when you work for me. Not tonight."

He walked back to the vial above the candle and regarded the mothershell shard. With a wistful look on his face, he dropped it in the vial. "This better be worth it," he mumbled.

Malik added a clear liquid to the mix and let it simmer while he watched sand pour through an hourglass. When all the sand had run through it twice, he picked up the vial and shook it, the shard clicking against the glass.

"I need your gold now," Malik said. "An escudo is enough. One of the small coins."

Arian opened the pouch and stuck his hand inside, pulling out a handful of coins. They all had different symbols on them, none of which meant anything to him. He picked out the smallest one and showed it to Malik. "One of these?"

"Perfect," Malik said, and took the coin, dropping it into the vial with a clang. "And last, but not least," he said as he pulled out a pair of dull scissors, cut off a toenail and added it to the concoction.

Arian gagged. "I'm supposed to drink that?"

"In a few hours when it's all dissolved. Not my fault witch's toenail is on the list of ingredients I need for this."

"It's disgusting."

"Not worse than the time I made myself a potion containing merman snot."

Arian recoiled. "Eww. I wouldn't drink that. How did you even get merman snot?"

Malik raised an eyebrow. "How did you know where I live?"

Realization dawned on Arian. Zade? The idea sounded so preposterous it was probably true.

"And now?"

"And now we wait," Malik said. "Why don't you tell me why you want legs so badly?"

Arian told him the story of how he'd lured in the most handsome man that had ever walked the Earth, how their time together had ended and why he needed to see him.

"Oh dear," Malik said. "Love gets you into all sorts of trouble."

"I didn't say I was in lo—"

"Oh, please," Malik said, and waved his hand. "You sold your life to see the man once more. Of course you're in love."

Arian chewed on the thought. Was he in love with Fernando? He didn't know. He had blurted it out in climax, but he had no reference point for the feeling. It was different from what he felt for his friends. Different and far more intense. He'd heard of men who drank a little rum, then a lot of rum until they drank all the rum, all the time. Addiction. He was addicted to Fernando. It was impossible to get enough of him. No one in their right mind would do what he was doing.

"I'm addicted to him," Arian said.

"That's how it feels. You cannot eat or sleep when they aren't there. You keep thinking you lost something, only you haven't, you just miss them. That's love."

Arian sank into thought and only half-listened to Malik's spiel of how his mother, daughter of a Puerto Rican native and a Chinese merchant, had fallen in love with his father who happened to be the son of an African slave from the Kingdom of Congo and a Spanish landowner, and how they'd discovered their magic together, then later taught their son. Arian couldn't listen to this when he had other things on his mind. He'd get the full story from Malik when he served him. They'd have all the time in the world.

Arian's mind was preoccupied with thoughts of Fernando. How would their meeting go? Maybe Fernando wasn't home, having departed days ago. Maybe he was there and refused to see him. Maybe Arian had misunderstood and Fernando's house wasn't in San Juan but elsewhere. A million ways for this to go wrong.

Periodically, Malik picked up the vial and shook it. When the gold and the shard had dissolved, he declared it finished.

"Before I forget..." Malik said, and picked up his scissors. Faster than Arian could move, he had cut off a strand of his hair. "For insurance purposes." He picked up one of the dolls and glued

Arian's hair to its head. Then he poured a small amount of the potion onto the doll. "This is a Voodoo doll. I have connected you to it, and whatever I do to it, you will feel."

Malik picked up a needle and pricked the doll. A stabbing pain drove through Arian's arm. He clutched it in panic, staring at Malik with the needle in his hand.

"I'll keep this since I've made you an expensive, rare potion, and need to be certain you won't run off. Or swim off in your case."

Arian's blood ran cold. A deal with the devil indeed. What was done, was done.

"Drink the potion at sunrise, and it will give you legs," Malik said. "You have one day and one night. By the time the sun rises again, your legs will return to their fishtail form. If I were you, I'd make sure to be back in the ocean by then. After that, I want you here by mid-morning, and you will begin your service."

"How will I find my way out of the mangrove forest and back in? You haven't signposted it well."

"I'll show you the way out and wait for you at the entrance when your time is up. Despite how you look at me, I'm not a monster. I won't make your service to me unnecessarily hard on you."

Malik corked up the vial and handed it to Arian.

"Meet me out at the pier. You can follow my boat."

Arian slid back into the water, and Malik shut the trap door above him. It was pitch black outside, or so it seemed until Arian's eyes adjusted to the darkness. He swam out from under the house and along the pier. The front door creaked, and Malik stepped outside, carrying a wrought-iron lantern. He climbed into his boat and set it down at the stern. The lamp's warm, yellow glow illuminated their way out of the forest.

From there the swim to San Juan was easy. Malik confirmed that Arian couldn't miss the town if he stuck close to the coast. And off he was.

Arian slept on a beach near San Juan throughout the small

hours of the night, pouch and vial clutched to his chest, jerking awake a few times, fearful either might be gone. But they were both there, Arian letting out a sigh of relief each time.

When the sun sent its first rays over the horizon, Arian was already hovering in the waters of San Juan. Wooden houses sat several yards back from the beach, forming a wry line.

Arian pulled up the vial and uncorked it. It did smell of blood, the scent dark and heavy in the fresh morning air. This would give him legs. Take him to Fernando. It would taste bitter, disgusting. But it would be worth it.

He poured the potion into his mouth, swallowing fast. The liquid was cool, salty and sour. It didn't taste as bad as he had feared. The moment it was all gone, he was retching. Determined to keep it all in, Arian clamped his lips shut. Cramps twisted his insides, and he dropped the vial. Good thing he had the strings of the pouch wrapped around his arm. Tingles ran down the length of his fishtail. And the pain set in.

Worried about making noise and waking the humans living in the huts, he pushed underwater. Good decision because the next second something was cutting his fishtail in two, right down the middle. He screamed in pain, air bubbles streaming out of his mouth. His whole world was an angry while-hot prison of agony.

But the pain was gone as quickly as it had come, and then Arian was treading water. With two legs, long and shapely. Perfect. His next scream was one of joy. Roaring out his victory over the broken curse, temporary as it might be, he backflipped again and again. He had done it. He was on the coast of San Juan with two human legs and one goal in mind.

He pushed up with all his might, breaking through the surface. Mad bliss thundered through his veins as he made for the shore. Swimming with legs was different from with a fishtail, and he wriggled and paddled them until he found a movement that worked.

Soon his feet found purchase in the soft, sandy ground underwater, and he walked out of the sea. It was easy until he was in the air up to his navel. He stumbled, catching himself at the last minute. The water was no longer deep enough to help him carry his weight. Arian switched to shuffling forward, but it buried his feet in the sand. In the end, he dropped to his knees and walked ashore that way.

It got more difficult once he was on land. How did humans balance themselves on two legs? They made it look so easy. Arian crawled first on his hands and knees, then hands and feet. Every time he tried to pull himself upright, he stumbled and fell, scraping his knees. This was not how he'd imagined his first steps.

But after a few more tries, he learned to stabilize his weight, balancing it equally between his legs. His eyes roamed over his new body. He liked his legs—and his cock. It was in proportion to his frame, a tad on the larger side. He wanted to run his hands over it, play with himself. The thought hadn't occurred to him until now. He'd only thought about getting legs, never anything else. Which was puzzling, considering he spent his days craving sex. He had been so focused on the legs, he hadn't thought about what other privileges they came with.

Was this Malik's doing? Arian had told him after all that he was coming after a lover.

His cock was tempting, but he couldn't touch himself here, not in front of all these houses where someone might come out at any point and see him. Speaking of which—he was stark naked. While this hadn't been a problem for Fernando on the island, it would be a problem for Arian in a human town.

He scanned the line of houses and spotted a rope stretched between two of them with clothes hanging on it. The people who owned them wouldn't be rich like Fernando. If he stole these clothes, it would hurt them. But he only needed them until the next morning. He'd borrow them for a day and bring them back, no harm done.

Arian took wobbly steps toward the clothesline, catching his fall a couple of times. He pulled a pair of breeches off the line and a white shirt.

Stepping into the breeches was a challenge. He fell over, dirtying up the white cotton. He winced. It would've been better had he been able to return the clothes somewhat clean. Arian leaned against the house for support and tried again. It worked. After that, pulling the shirt over his head was child's play.

Having fabric on his skin was the strangest sensation. Not uncomfortable, but it would require getting used to. The breeches pulled with every step. They were too tight, intended for a shorter person. Nothing he could do about it. His feet were bare, but there were no shoes to be found. Barefoot it was.

Which wasn't great. While the sand had been soft under the soles of his feet, grass and stones pricked and prodded at his skin with each step. What if he stepped on something sharp and cut himself? No wonder humans wore shoes everywhere.

Arian took the little path between the houses and stepped into the street. It was dead quiet in the early morning, not a soul outside. Best to be on his way. He followed the street to its end, keeping an eye out for where that wide road lined with trees leading to Fernando's house could be.

San Juan didn't take long to wake up once the sun was peeking over the horizon. The first human that saw Arian gave him a startled look. Arian looked down on himself to check if anything was amiss, but no. Was it the way he walked?

More and more people opened their front doors to the fresh morning air. Soon the sounds and smells of the human world assaulted Arian. There were hammering noises and swirling smoke. Children laughing and small animals squeaking.

Arian reached the outskirts of town where it was quieter. If he followed the invisible line around San Juan long enough, he'd have to find Fernando's house. But all he had was a single day. He didn't want to waste any more of it than he already had looking around town. So he worked up the courage to outright ask someone. He picked a man who was clearing away the dirt in front of his house and inquired if he knew in which direction Fernando lived.

"Fernando? You'll have to be more specific than that. More Fernandos here than leaves on a tree. What's his last name?"

Last name? Did humans have multiple names?

"Um... I don't know. He's rich and lives in a big house."

That earned him another bewildered stare, and then the man's eyes traveled to the gold-filled pouch. Arian pulled it behind his back.

"If you're talking about *señor* Santos Veracruz, he lives that way," the man said, pointing to the right. "Follow the road and take the third to the left. Then the next right and then left again. If you continue along that one to the end, you'll see a broad road that leads straight up to the manor."

Arian thanked the man and set off, hiding the gold under his shirt. It took him a while to get there, but when he saw it, he was sure. Tall, slender trees grew to either side of the road at whose end stood the most impressive manor in all of San Juan.

Unlike the houses so far, this was no wooden hut. Two stories tall, painted pristine white. The roof was slanted, forming a triangle over the protruding entrance of the manor where a double-winged door spoke of grandeur.

It was a house fit for a king.

Arian's heartbeat quickened. He hadn't thought this through. Fernando was a more important man than he had realized. The new knowledge hit him like a rock. He couldn't possibly walk up to this manor and knock. If anyone other than Fernando opened the door, he would be sent away. Though, he had the gold. If he showed whoever opened up the gold, they would at least consider him. But maybe he would embarrass Fernando. He had been stared at in the streets, so something had to be off with him. Though then again, the whole endeavor had been an exercise in selfishness. Arian had come this far, he might as well go through with it.

With shaky steps, he walked up the road to the grand house at its end. The last yards were the hardest, his legs heavy, his mind fuzzy. The faintest noise drifted from the house out to the front yard.

Someone was home and would open up, even if Fernando wasn't home. Arian could leave the gold with a trustworthy-looking person and give them a message for Fernando.

He knocked at the imposing door, the sound echoing through what must be an entrance hall on the other side. His heart in his mouth, he waited for someone to answer.

Chapter Thirteen

Fernando

"Excuse me, *Señor*," Ayah said as she stuck her head through the door to Fernando's study, "there's a young man outside wanting to see you."

Fernando furrowed his brow. He was not expecting anyone this early. There was the lunch meeting with Carlos, one of his business partners, but it wasn't noon yet. On the other hand, Carlos was infamously unreliable and Fernando wouldn't be surprised if he had mixed up the time of the meeting—although Carlos tended to be hours late, not early. He was the bane of Fernando's existence.

Or could it be someone with a message about the ball that evening? He was looking forward to it. Fernando's week had been tiring, and he wanted nothing more than a night full of fun and dance, perhaps a round of roulette.

"What's this about?" Fernando asked.

"Well, it's rather bizarre. He's... he's not wearing a lot of clothes, walks around barefoot. And he's hiding something beneath his shirt he wants to give to you."

Oh dear, it was one of the beggars that came occasionally. It burdened Fernando's conscience, but he didn't want them to loiter around his property or make coming to him a habit.

"Send him away," Fernando said. "Tell him to not come back."

"Yes, *Señor*," Ayah said, then hesitated. "Um, he asked me to tell you his name, said you knew him. What was it? Adrian or something?"

Fernando leaped to his feet. "Adrian? You mean Arian? Arian is here?"

Ayah barely had time to get out of the way before he pushed out the door and strode down the hallway toward the marble-clad entrance hall.

Could this really be Arian? Fernando must have misheard. When he'd open the front door, there would be a beggar expecting alms. A beggar named Adrian, a boy not right in his mind. Not a merman a mile inland. The idea was ridiculous.

Out in the hall, light streamed onto the white stone floor through the tall glass windows looking out to the backyard, but the front door was closed.

There'd be nothing behind it other than a tramp, waiting for Fernando to open his purse and hand out coin. Yet he was drawn to it like a magnet. Just the off chance that Arian had... what? Found someone to carry him to Fernando's house? Absurd. Ayah would have said something if a merman was in front of his house.

But he was already pushing the bolt back, twisting the doorknob. He might as well get it over with.

The door swung open, and Fernando froze in his tracks.

The strawberry blond hair, those impossibly blue eyes. That perfect face. And long, shapely legs clad in nothing but white, skin-tight breeches leaving little to the imagination. No fishtail. Also, no shoes, no stockings, the breeches by themselves leaving his calves exposed for the world to see. For Fernando to see. He gaped at Arian, who, unfamiliar with clothing conventions, had no idea how inappropriate, how indecent his attire was. He was half-naked with just an undershirt thrown on top. And it was hiked up as Arian was indeed clutching something underneath it.

All kinds of thoughts warred in Fernando's head. Warmth radiated through his body, all the irritation of the last days blown away.

Arian was here, he had come to see him, and he was wearing too little clothing. Fernando should run inside and order Ayah to fetch a *justacorps* and stockings to cover his calves. Why in the world was Arian showing his calves? He would have been better off tearing the arms off the shirt and stuffing them into the breeches for makeshift stockings rather than running around like this.

At the same time, Arian was wearing too much. Fernando wanted nothing more than to help Arian out of the rest of his clothes and see what was still hidden. The outline of his cock was visible, but Fernando lusted for the details. The color. The texture...

No. This wasn't the time for such thoughts. The house was full of people. Carlos was coming. That meant danger. Danger to whom? Arian because Fernando's staff might find out he was—had been—a merman? Or a danger to his staff because of what Arian might do?

Fernando had to handle the situation, and swiftly.

"Come in," he said and stepped aside. Fernando bolted the door as soon as Arian was inside. Arian who barely looked at him, fascinated with the floor.

"Ayah! Ayah!" Fernando yelled toward the hallway. The heavy footfall of his housekeeper echoed through the hall as she stormed in to heed his call. "Clear the house," he told her as he put a hand on her shoulder. "I want everybody gone. Get everyone off the premises, out of the garden. Send a courier to Carlos and tell him not to come. Make sure he stays away. Take money from the kitchen jar and get rooms at the inn."

His staff lived largely on-premises, and he had to get them away. No good would come of them being around a merman. Former merman. Whatever.

"For how long?" she asked.

"I'll be gone soon," Arian said in a small voice.

"Soon?" Fernando asked. Arian had just arrived. He was dangerous, but he should stay. Fernando wouldn't let him leave when he had just arrived. Irrespective of the fact that Fernando shouldn't have let him in the house, near his staff, near himself in the first place.

"By tomorrow morning," Arian said.

"Stay at the inn until after lunch tomorrow," Fernando told Ayah. "Do not come back today. In fact, hire a guard to watch the road leading up to the house."

"Yes, *Señor*," she said, and off she was.

The moment she was out of sight, Fernando's full attention refocused on Arian, who was still looking at the marble tiles instead of him. His bare feet must be getting cold. In a split-second decision, he took him to the drawing room. Here mahogany upholstery stood on a red carpet, intricate floral designs woven into the fabric. A chandelier hung from the stucco ceiling, portraits and mirrors lined the walls.

Fernando watched Ayah through the floor-to-ceiling windows looking out to the garden as she pulled the gardener away from tending to the bushes. He followed her, albeit in bewilderment. More bustling through the rooms, the hallways, then the heavy front door fell shut with a satisfying thud, and silence settled over the house. Alone at last.

There were many things Fernando could say, but he was unsure where to start. Arian was uncomfortably shifting from one foot to the other.

"It's good to see you," Fernando said.

Arian's shoulders relaxed, and he looked at him with those blue eyes. He was tall, Fernando realized with a start. Fernando merely had an inch or two on him.

"I'm glad I came," Arian said, voice shaking, though a small smile tugged at the corners of his lips.

"How did you get here? I mean, you have legs," Fernando said, gesturing at the miracle before him.

That sent Arian back into his shell. "I... I knew someone who could help me. It's temporary."

Of course. If mermen could get legs permanently, they would

have done so a long time ago. But even having legs for a short while couldn't have come for free; otherwise, it'd be more prevalent. Fernando was going to dig deeper, but then Arian pulled out a leather pouch from underneath his shirt. It clinked as Arian handled it and looked heavy too—it had to be full of coins.

"I'm sorry about how things ended with Luis," Arian said as he pulled at the strings of the purse. "Zade deeply regrets what happened. It was an accident, we didn't mean to cause any harm."

That's what this was about? And here he was, thinking Arian had wanted to see him. He should have known better. What had happened on the island was nothing more than a random encounter to Arian, it didn't hold deeper meaning. Not that it did for Fernando. Not at all.

"Zade wanted Luis's family to have this," Arian said, and held out the purse to Fernando, who took it automatically.

The inside glinted under the light falling in from the windows. The pouch was filled with escudos and doubloons. Fernando was appalled. How could Arian think this was okay?

"Arian, you cannot give someone blood money," he said, pushing the coins back into Arian's hands.

It was a ridiculously small amount compared to Luis's wealth. Good thing Arian had come to him, not Luis. It would have insulted Luis beyond measure.

Arian flinched back, bottom lip quivering. "I'm sorry." He cleared his throat. "Zade thought this was valuable to you. We don't have use for gold…"

Which made the gesture worse. But of course, Arian didn't know that, unfamiliar as he was with human customs. Fernando only had to look at what he was wearing to be reminded.

"Look, if it makes you feel better, I'll take it and give it to Luis pretending I miscalculated his share of our trade run and I owe him. He'll be happy about the extra gold."

"Luis is alive?" Arian asked.

Fernando blinked. "You thought he was dead?"

"Well, yes. He was unconscious when you left."

"He's alive. Not in the best shape, though he'll recover."

"Oh, okay. That's great news," Arian said, handing him back the purse. "Then I want you to give this to him in an acceptable way. We meant no offense. I thought the gold could help his wife and children had he passed away. I'm glad he's alive. Zade will be too—"

Arian abruptly stopped in his remark about Zade, his eyes widened, like he had just remembered something.

"What is it?"

"Nothing."

"This is about Zade having hurt someone before?" Fernando asked as he put the pouch between the golden clock and a vase on the side table.

It was a sore spot for Fernando. Why hadn't Arian told him things had gotten out of hand with him before, hurt someone, maybe killed them.

"What? No," Arian said, visibly taken aback.

"Why didn't you tell me about it? Why didn't you mention Zade was a risk?"

"I didn't know. I found out when you did. Most of the stories they tell about mermen are just that—stories. Based on one-offs or rare occurrences. They aren't a reflection of who we are. Zade is older than the rest of us, whatever happened back then was before Finn, Tarlis and I came to the archipelago. Which is no excuse, of course. I should have talked to Zade one day in before it all went wrong."

The tension seeped out of Fernando, and he relaxed against the wall. It had been an accident. Arian had been upfront with him. He should have trusted Arian to tell him the truth—he was honest and blunt with everything that crossed his mind. Fernando should have expected no less of him than being upfront.

"Then I'm sorry for having thought you less honest than you are," Fernando said. Although, there was one thing Arian hadn't been upfront about. And Fernando needed to know. "But I have one more question for you: how did you get legs?" Arian fidgeted, wrestling with the question. What on Earth had he done? A sense of foreboding overcame Fernando. "Arian?"

Arian mumbled something unintelligible.

"What?"

"I went to the sea witch in the mangrove forest," Arian said, eyes trained on the carpet. "If I wanted to bring the gold to you," he swallowed, "if I wanted to see you, I needed legs. I knew Malik was powerful. For the right price, I was sure he could give me legs."

There was so much to unpack. Arian had wanted to come to him. This wasn't just about Luis and the gold. Egregious relief hit Fernando. He should be ashamed for feeling that way. But there was something bothersome about what Arian had said.

Fernando pushed off the wall. "Arian, what did you give the sea witch?"

This time, Arian didn't look away but lifted his chin in defiance. "My life in servitude to him."

The world tilted. Fernando grabbed at the wall, finding purchase on the door frame. "Why? Why did you do that?"

"Because I needed to see you."

No. Not because of him. Arian had not thrown away his life for him. It couldn't be true. "Why?"

"It's not so bad. Otherwise, I would've spent my days dying of boredom at the beach. Malik is eccentric, but he's not a bad person. He even agreed to teach me how to read and write."

"*I* can teach you that."

Arian's face fell. "I wouldn't be here if I hadn't gone to him."

Fernando took a deep breath. "I know," he said, and his voice broke.

"We only have one day. I need to be back in the sea before sunrise tomorrow morning."

"Then we better make good use of it," Fernando said, and gathered Arian in his arms.

He buried his face in Arian's hair. It smelled of seawater and sunshine. Oh, and he liked how tall Arian was. A tilt of his head and he was kissing him. No bowing down like he had to when he kissed a woman. Arian's solid frame pressed into him as he tasted his lips. Soft and plump. How he'd missed them. Arian opened for him, and Fernando deepened the kiss. He was ravenous. His tongue stroked Arian's, and his entire body awoke. And there it was, Arian's rock-hard erection pushing against his own.

Chapter Fourteen

Arian

Kissing Fernando was like coming up for air after staying underwater for too long. Arian wrapped his arms around Fernando's neck, pulling him close, breathing him in.

It had been worth it. So, so worth it. Arian had bartered a life in servitude for a day with Fernando, and he'd do it all again. His boldness had paid off.

Fernando was kissing him, pushing into him, and Arian's cock flooded with blood. All his awareness sank into that one expanding organ as it hardened in his breeches. He bucked his hips. It caused him to brush up against Fernando's erection. They gasped at the contact, and Arian ground them together, his mind high on the pressure in his groin.

"Feels so good," he said against Fernando's lips.

"I missed kissing you."

"Me too. You taste amazing."

He licked into Fernando's mouth. Hands ran down his back, deeper and deeper, making him squirm in need. They moved to his ass, cupping him. Fernando hummed in approval at what he found.

Those large, callous hands slipped under his shirt, making him gasp at the skin-to-skin contact. They roamed up his spine, gathering fabric. Arian shivered in anticipation when Fernando lifted the shirt over his head and let it tumble to the floor.

"Now this," Fernando said as he dragged a finger across Arian's chest, his stomach, "I'm already familiar with. But I do wonder... what's down here." He captured Arian's bulge in his hand.

A pathetic little moan fell from Arian's lips. More of those followed when Fernando worked open the buttons. Arian's wildest dreams came true. The breeches were too tight to simply fall off, and Fernando sank to his knees as he pulled them down. They pooled around his ankles, and Arian, unsure on his feet, had to lean onto Fernando's shoulders as he stepped out of them.

Fernando's gaze was trained on his face the entire time. He wasn't looking at Arian's exposed crotch, his erect penis. Was he having second thoughts? Fernando had been fine with making out with him back on the island, but there, Arian had a fishtail. Now he didn't, and his body had become undeniably male.

"Are you okay with this?" Arian asked, making a gesture at his groin.

Fernando licked his lips. "Yes. More than okay. But I'm thinking... maybe I should step back."

Step back? Fernando was backtracking. Arian had pushed his luck too far.

Then velvety lips kissed his frenulum.

"I'd love to touch you, taste you," Fernando said. "But you haven't even touched yourself. Found out what you liked."

"What-What are you saying?" Fernando was not pulling back? What was he suggesting?

"I want to watch you."

"Watch me?"

"As you discover pleasure," Fernando said, then placed his hands on Arian's hips and stood.

"But I need you." There was no way Arian wanted to figure this out on his own. If what he enjoyed doing to other men also worked on his own body. If he responded to a fast hand and deft fingers. Fernando should be the one touching him.

"I'll be right there with you. Come," Fernando said, and guided Arian to the couch.

Red velvet stretched on the dark wood frame, the upholstery facing away from the windows but toward the baroque mirrors decorating the opposite wall. The fabric stroked Arian's butt as he sat down, Fernando next to him, resting one arm on the backrest behind Arian.

It should have been awkward, though with Fernando breathing in his ear, warmth radiating off him, Arian was nothing but at home. Gingerly he took his cock in hand and let his head fall onto Fernando's shoulder. The first stroke was tentative, and the skin of his cock sliding over his shaft sent a shiver of pleasure down his spine.

The cotton of Fernando's shirt brushed his sensitive skin, and Arian sank into the embrace. The vulnerability of sitting naked next to a fully clothed man had his cock hardening further until it was fully engorged, the skin on his glans stretched tight, shiny and purple. The first drop of precum welled up. With the next stroke, it grew to a glossy pearl. What would it taste like? Arian had tried other men's... He gathered it up with his finger and brought it to his mouth. It was sweet. Before he had time to appreciate it, Fernando kissed him, rolling his tongue over his.

"Hmm, I thought you'd taste good," Fernando said as he pulled back.

Arian flushed and closed his eyes, unable to look at their reflection in the mirror. His hand fell into a steady rhythm, and he swiped his thumb over the head on the upstroke. It was pleasurable, intense and everything Arian had wanted. His legs fell open as pressure built. It mounted, and every muscle trembled, hips jerking forward.

His other hand wandered to his balls, cupping them first, then lifting and weighing them, rolling them. A filthy little moan escaped him.

So this was the joy men experienced. Arian used to wonder

what it felt like to become erect, to blow your load. He couldn't wait to find out. He would be denied it again too soon and so he let the sensations grow and grow, taking his hand away when it got too much, never allowing himself to reach the edge.

"You're so beautiful," Fernando mumbled, kissing the top of his head. "You should look. Open your eyes."

Arian did, and there was no denying the picture they struck in the mirror was quite the scene. A pink blush had crept over his face and chest, his hair in disorder as he sat there, leaning against Fernando, lips parted, legs spread, cock in hand. Fernando moved in closer, resting his head on Arian's as they watched the mirror.

This time, Arian tracked every stroke of his hand, every flick of his thumb. And there was another sensation between his legs, an unexpected one. The potion had given him the anatomy of human men; cock, balls and anus, but one thing was decidedly different. His hole was not connected to his digestive tract, legs or no legs. And it was getting slick. Was this Malik's doing? If so, he must have had some crazy ideas about what Arian and Fernando would get up to. Fernando wouldn't be interested in anything that required Arian to have a hole, self-lubricating or not. Would he?

Feeling brave, since he was already naked in his arms, he told Fernando, watching his expression in the mirror as his eyes widened in surprise. But then Fernando's lips twitched, and he looked all too pleased by the news.

"Why do you look like that?" Arian asked.

"Like what?"

"Like someone gifted you a horse."

"Because it will make things easier later."

Arian gasped. The thought of Fernando anywhere near his hole had his stomach tightening. His hand flew over his cock in a blur. Fernando's attention was glued to his erection. Arian hissed.

"Getting close?" Fernando asked.

"Yeah."

A hand caught Arian's wrist and pulled it away.

"What—"

"I don't want you to come all over the furniture and the carpet. They were expensive," Fernando said with a twinkle in his eye.

He got off the couch and stepped between Arian's legs, then sank onto his knees. That sight alone was nearly enough to have Arian shoot all over the place and only a firm grip around the base of his cock prevented it.

"I'm not going to blow you," Fernando said, "this orgasm is all yours. But it would be a shame to let a drop of it go to waste."

When Arian dragged his hand back up his cock, he did it while gazing into Fernando's eyes. They were brown with flecks of gold and begging Arian to come. And Arian ached for it.

He ran his hand up and down his shaft and built a heavy rhythm. His stomach tightened, and his balls drew up to his body.

Fernando's mouth fell open, and his tongue darted out, covering his bottom lip. It was an obscene invitation. Arian shifted forward on the couch and buried a hand in Fernando's curls, the other holding onto his own cock with a firm grip.

Their reflection in the mirror was something else. Fernando kneeling fully clothed on the red carpet, Arian stark naked on the couch, trembling with need, chest rising and falling with his labored breathing.

Arian's insides throbbed with the urge to come. It wasn't his hand that did him in. It was the picture of Fernando waiting for him between his legs, tongue out, wet and shiny. Arian lined up with that glorious promise of a mouth. A few more strokes. His tip brushed Fernando's tongue. It was all he needed.

He gasped with the first powerful contraction. The force of his orgasm shot through him, blinding him for a second. Then he was back and watched as white ropes hit Fernando's tongue, over and over and over again as Arian's insides convulsed. Fernando's mouth was wide open, the tip of his tongue massaging Arian's frenulum. It drew the pleasure out of Arian to the last drop.

Fernando swallowed it all and licked his lips as Arian collapsed forward onto Fernando's shoulders. Strong hands grabbed Arian's waist, holding him up.

He took a moment, letting his pulse calm down, catching his breath. But he had to know. He dipped down and captured Fernando's mouth. Their tongues glided together, and Arian tasted himself, rich and salty. Fernando deepened the kiss, sharing the taste, and Arian shivered. That's when Fernando came up, and his warm arms enveloped him. Arian sank into it, all his muscles relaxing. He had never felt so safe.

Firm hands rubbed him all over, taking care of his post-orgasmic need to be touched, cared for, loved. They lay together in silence for a while, letting Arian descend from his high.

Fernando's arm slipped under his knees, the other wrapped around his torso. Arian let out a surprised yelp when Fernando picked him up from the couch.

"You're lighter like this," Fernando said as he carried him over to another velvet-covered piece of furniture, a divan. A couch without a backrest, as Arian had been told by a sailor he'd met years ago after a shipwreck where chunks of furniture had washed ashore. It would resemble a narrow bed were it not for the curved wooden rests on the long sides.

"Lighter?"

"Than with a fishtail," Fernando said and laid him down on the velvet upholstery. "Like this, I could've carried you around the entire island and not broken a sweat."

"You made it look easy when I did have the fishtail."

Fernando chuckled and climbed on top of him, growing serious. Arian looked up at him, seeking out his gaze as Fernando's weight came to rest on him. He reveled in the heaviness of it, in Fernando pinning him to the divan with his muscular body. There was no escape.

Then Fernando leaned down, bringing their faces together. The touch of firm lips coaxed Arian's open, ready for Fernando's heady taste. Arian poured his emotions into the kiss, how glad he was to be here, how much he wanted Fernando, unspoken words of affection and love.

Was it love that he felt? Malik had said so. Arian had confessed it himself when he was drunk on pleasure that last night on the island.

He dragged his tongue over Fernando's, slow and deliberate, conveying what he meant to him. Arian wanted to drown in him. Fernando kissed with restrained possessiveness, hard and pushy, but holding back from devouring him.

"I want to do everything with you," Arian said, which earned him another hard, eager kiss.

And when Fernando let go of his mouth, it was with reluctance. Arian chased after him, but Fernando held him down, his lips wandering to his neck. And he knew where Arian liked to be touched, for at the first sucking motion on his pulse point, Arian's eyes fluttered closed, and he bucked, Fernando's weight containing him.

After last time, he had no doubt Fernando would make this mind-blowing, even if he'd never been with a man before. Fernando traveled down his body, caressing every inch of him. When he reached Arian's hips, he sat up, straddling the slender divan. He pulled Arian's legs up and apart, resting them on his shoulders. Arian's face grew warm as he lay there, open and exposed to Fernando. He towered over him and Arian's pelvic muscles clenched at Fernando's power in this position.

Large hands roamed over Arian's legs, exploring their curves and angles. They roved from his thighs over his knees, along his shin and back across the sensitive skin of the underside. Arian shivered as Fernando approached his crotch. Would he cup his ass? Rub over his crotch? Arian wasn't sure what he wanted more. All of it, that was the answer.

"Your legs are stunning," Fernando said, and pressed a kiss to his ankle.

They better be, considering how expensive they were. But Arian didn't say that, instead he gave Fernando a smug smile. Which fell off his face when Fernando wet his lips, leaned forward and ran the tip of his tongue over Arian's glans. Arian cried out and nearly came off the divan. Where his own fingers had been pleasurable, Fernando's wet tongue was a slice of heaven.

"Do that again," Arian gasped.

When Fernando obliged him, Arian's eyes rolled back in his head. Like a flower in the sun, he bloomed under Fernando, muscles relaxing, limbs growing pliant and lithe. He opened up, his body readying itself to take him in. His hole was getting wetter by the minute. Something in there was screaming to be touched, desperate for prodding fingers, or even better, the thrusts of a thick, long cock. Arian licked his lips. Fernando had hinted at the possibility…

Fernando's tongue circled the corona of his glans as he was looking up at Arian, watching him pant and writhe. With the next lick, he was laving his slit, as if that could coax out precum. Except it did, and Arian gulped down air as they both watched the bead form. Fernando lapped it up and Arian entered paradise. Had he known, he would've paid Malik even more, no price too high for having Fernando take him apart like that. He'd die for it.

Arian wasn't prepared for Fernando to take his cockhead into his mouth. He screamed his affirmation, craving more, more, more of the glorious wetness. Fernando's tongue stroked his frenulum and Arian leaked into Fernando's mouth. He soared as that tongue caressed him all around. Had Fernando felt like this when their roles had been reversed? The ecstasy men got to experience exceeded his wildest dreams.

Fernando moved his head up and down, the wet heat sliding over Arian. When he took him in further, Arian let out a broken whine, his head falling back on the divan, strong hands restraining his hips. Fernando gagged around him and didn't let up, kept going until Arian was buried inside him to the root. His legs trembled as his cock twitched and throbbed against the back of Fernando's throat. He was in deep. All the way. Home.

And Fernando didn't move. When Arian lifted his head, Fernando's neck was straining, his eyes wet, leaking tears but holding him there, swallowing around him in an inverse image of what Arian had done to him on the island.

Seeing him like that was unbearable. Fernando couldn't hold his breath for endless minutes. Yet he held still, drowning Arian in sensations.

Arian loved him, this man who'd do anything for the ones he cared about. He never wanted to be anywhere else but in his mouth. This was where he belonged. With shaking fingers, he reached out, ran his hand through Fernando's curls and down his cheek, wiping away a tear caused by the effort of keeping Arian lodged deep inside him. Fernando answered the gesture by swirling his tongue over Arian's underside.

Sparks zapped at the base of Arian's cock, in his balls. He was ready. But before his orgasm could barrel down his spine and wreck him with convulsions, Fernando eased his thumb and forefinger between his mouth and the base of Arian's cock, closing around him. With his other hand, he went for Arian's balls, gently keeping them away from his body.

Arian hissed with frustrated arousal. He couldn't come like this. Fernando was doing what he had done to him first. Arian had toyed with him for hours before he'd let him come, whereas Fernando had already let him climax once and was just starving off his second orgasm. And Arian had forced him to come with those rings constricting his cock and balls. And this was the bill.

Fernando's face turned red from the effort, and he swallowed hard around Arian's sensitive cockhead. His climax was lurking, ready to spring on him given the chance. Fernando's hands didn't let up. Neither did his mouth, his constricting throat. Arian was left hanging in unsated lust, his entire being wound up in the pressing need to come, to let go, to convulse.

"Let me come," Arian said, caressing Fernando's hair, his face.

"Please. I need to. I need to come so badly."

But the look on Fernando's face was one of defiance. What had Arian said to him in the cave?

You will come despite it. If you want it so badly, you will come. I want you so desperate for orgasm nothing can hold you back.

And now it was coming back to bite him. Fernando was beating him at his own game. Fernando wasn't a man who left the bed owing his partner an orgasm. No, he dished them out, and you took them, your crotch spasming out of control the only thanks he wanted. And he was getting it.

I want you to overcome what's holding you back. I want you to look at me and fucking explode into contractions, splashing your cum against my lips because when I pleasure you, nothing else matters.

Fernando's face said it all, the ironclad determination to pay Arian back. His hand massaged Arian's sack as he rolled it in his palm. His tongue swept up and down Arian's underside. A finger pressed against Arian's perineum, pushing into something inside of him. Something responsive.

Arian lifted off the divan, then stiffened as a thrill chased down his spine. It shot into his balls and up through the constriction at the base of his cock, right into the glans cradled in the wet, hot paradise of Fernando's mouth. He fell back on the upholstery as his entire groin seized up in mind-numbing contractions. He came right down Fernando's throat, which was in constant movement as Fernando kept up with Arian's spurts, milking him. Arian shuddered as another wave of bone-deep tingles sped through him, making his cock twitch in orgasm. The waves kept coming for a long time, until they ebbed off, leaving Arian limp and relaxed.

Only then did Fernando pull off him. He dropped kisses on Arian's thighs, his stomach, stroking his sides as Arian floated down from the peak of lust. Arian reached out and petted Fernando's hair. This was it. There was nowhere else he'd rather be. Fernando rested his head on his torso, his hands continuing their calming strokes. It melted Arian. There was nothing he wouldn't do for Fernando.

"I could make you come all day," Fernando said after a while.

"And you wonder why I used to take sailors to play with them?" Past tense. There'd be no more men after Fernando. He'd be working for Malik, anyway.

"I can see the appeal." Fernando ran his fingertips over Arian's hip, his thigh. "I do wonder what our differences are. In anatomy, I mean."

Arian's cock stirred in response.

"See?" Fernando said. "You barely need a minute. Makes me wonder how many times in a row I can make you come."

That had Arian back to throbbing with need. How did Fernando do this? "You must be rock-hard yourself."

"Oh, trust me, I am. But you are something else," Fernando said, mouthing Arian's cock. "I wonder if there's a way to make you come so hard, you faint in satisfaction."

"That's what you like to do?"

"Sometimes."

Arian shouldn't have asked. It was an ugly reminder of Fernando's past—and future—with women. Women he'd have coming over and over and over again until they were putty in Fernando's hands. Arian had no doubt he could do it. And Fernando could do it to him too. Thinking about that sent precum trickling onto his stomach. Fernando lapped it up, licking him clean.

"So eager," Fernando said.

"Malik went the whole nine yards when he gave me legs. That's all I asked for. Like I ordered a donkey and got a racehorse."

"You said you were getting wet."

"Still am."

"Curious."

Fernando sat up and placed a couple of fingers on Arian's lips. He opened and brushed the tip of his tongue over the pads, then sucked the digits into his mouth like he would a cock. He licked them over, flicked between them, making sure they were nice and slick for what was to come. Fernando pulled them out, and Arian sent them a goodbye with one last kitten lick.

A single finger pad settled on his sphincter. He twitched, opening and closing, effectively kissing the tip and let out a low moan. He was more sensitive than he'd expected.

"Was that involuntary?" Fernando asked.

"The twitching? Yes."

"Hmm. And you are soaking wet."

Fernando circled his entrance in a slow motion, and it stirred Arian's hunger. He twitched again. Arian gave himself over to the sweeping circles. Fernando touching him there held meaning. His finger wasn't only tracing the nerve ends of his hole, but the core of his being. Arian yearned for that finger to dip inside of him, to probe him. He needed to be explored and mapped.

"You like that," Fernando said.

"So much."

Fernando added a second finger and rubbed them both over his winking ring of muscle. It wasn't meant to feel this good. And yet, it took him higher and higher.

When Fernando pulled away, he wanted to protest but held back. Because right then, Fernando lifted Arian's hips, and he had to prop himself up on his shoulders and arms before Fernando's tongue came down on him in a series of whirls. Arian was utterly powerless to the surge of desire it brought on him. He quivered as the broad, flattened tongue washed over him.

More precum beaded at his tip and soon spilled over, drawing wet streaks onto his stomach. With devilish tardiness, Fernando pushed his tongue inside Arian.

It set every last one of his cells on fire. A blurted curse was all he got out before orgasm took him by surprise. He squeezed Fernando's tongue, still wriggling inside him, massaging him to ever higher peaks. The thunder of it was deafening. His cock shot all over him, painting his stomach and chest, even his cheek, with white ropes. He was panting like a runner when Fernando eased him back down.

"Jesus Christ, what was that?" Fernando said with pride, confusion and friendly amusement warring in his features.

"I—I don't know. I'm not sure. I'm so sensitive in there."

"Yeah, I noticed," Fernando deadpanned, and went to lick Arian clean.

"Maybe... You know the human prostate and how it responds to touch?"

"I had a thorough lesson recently."

"I think my entire hole is like that."

Fernando's eyes widened, and he mumbled something intelligible, between a curse and a prayer, before he kissed the last bit of cum off Arian's cheek.

"And you know what's worse?" Arian asked. "We've created a monster. Because right now, my hole is virtually begging for more." For something that went deeper. That was thicker.

Without warning, Fernando pushed in a finger. Arian gasped. His entire channel stood to attention. He spasmed around the intrusion while Fernando kept still.

"How does that feel?" Fernando asked.

"Like it's about to make me come again."

"You can't be serious."

Arian's insides throbbed in answer. "Every bit of me is hyperaware of your finger. If you move it, I'll come."

Fernando gripped the base of his cock. "This should delay it for a bit."

Then he probed deeper. Arian arched off the divan, and only Fernando constricting around his root kept him from shooting his load all over again. Nothing had ever been this intense.

"You're incredibly tight," Fernando said. "I don't know how I'll—"

"It's fine. You push inside, and I'll take it."

"I don't want to hurt you."

"I don't care. You won't." Arian pulled him in for a messy kiss as Fernando fingered him. They were breathing into each other when Fernando pulled out only to add a second finger, fastening his hold on Arian's base.

"Try not to come."

The double intrusion had Arian gaping. His face contorted as he stared at Fernando, holding onto his curls with one hand, pulling with tamed force. Fernando spread his fingers, scissoring his soaking wet, twitching walls apart. Arian's existence narrowed to Fernando probing him. The epitome of ecstasy. And then Fernando crooked his fingers. Arian saw stars. He must have said something, made a sound, though he wasn't sure because the next thing Fernando said was, "So you do have a prostate too."

But his words were muted, as if said through a wall. Arian's insides pulsed in time with his heartbeat. Fernando prodded him, once, twice. It was too much, despite his grip around Arian's base. He tried to hold back, desperate to hold onto control.

"Stop or I'll—"

The next tap to his prostate did it. Against his attempts to keep his pelvic floor strained, it broke through, and he erupted in powerful contractions. They tore him apart as he convulsed around Fernando's fingers nudging his prostate. Which had him break out into new spasms, again and again, tingles flooding him from head to toe as his body twisted and bucked. Had Fernando been a weaker man, he wouldn't have been able to hold him down.

It took a while for the contractions to slow.

"You have no self-control," Fernando said with a wicked grin. "Can't hold your cum for two minutes."

He rubbed over him one more time, pulling a last contraction from Arian, and removed his fingers. They were wet and shiny, and Arian surged up, capturing them in his mouth. A strange combination of salty and sweet assaulted him. He cleaned Fernando diligently.

All the while his hunger for him was insatiable. Deep down, Arian knew there was one thing that would satisfy him to his core.

One thing that would leave him sated and blissed out, floating in bone-deep fulfillment.

He stole a glance downward at Fernando's crotch. Fully erect, his cock strained against his breeches. Precum had formed a small wet spot. Arian licked his lips. What Fernando could do to him... He would rip him in two. And Arian couldn't wait for it.

Fernando lifted his chin with a finger, forcing him to look up. He pressed his lips to Arian's in a kiss too chaste for what had passed between them. For what was going to happen.

He pulled back and cradled Arian's face, tucking a strand of hair behind his ear as he searched Arian's eyes.

"You don't know what you do to me," Fernando said.

"I could say the same," Arian said, and stole a quick kiss. He reached out and pulled Fernando's shirt from where it was tucked into his breeches. Fernando grabbed it and tugged it over his head, discarding it on the carpet while Arian worked the buttons of his breeches open.

With Fernando's clothes off, Arian explored his body, running his hands over broad shoulders, hard abs and down, down, down. Fernando's cock was long, thick and veiny and had taken on a dark red color, skin stretched tight over the engorged cockhead. Precum glistened as it pearled out of the slit. He had been waiting for so long, and Arian ached to shower him in pleasure. He spit in his palm and wrapped his fingers around Fernando, slicking him up. He pulsed in his hand.

Fernando peeled him off and guided him down on the divan. Arian spread his legs wide open, creating space for Fernando to lay between them. He grabbed the wooden frame behind his head and held on while Fernando positioned his cock. This was it. This was all of Arian's dreams coming true. He would be filled out, taken.

He let out a broken whine when Fernando's cock brushed against his tight ring. Fernando had loosened him up with his fingers, but his cock was far bigger, wider. Especially the fat head. How good it would feel inside of him... Arian pushed out, and

Fernando held onto his hip as he guided himself inside.

The wide crown penetrated him, stretching him open, and he gasped at the intrusion.

"Fuck, you're tight," Fernando bit out as he slowly pushed in.

All the while, Arian was blind with need. As Fernando entered, every inch of him rubbed new, untouched nerve ends, which came alive at the attention. Arian couldn't get enough. Every fiber of his being wanted Fernando to slide in deeper, to fill him completely.

Fernando stalled, fingers closed around the base of his cock. "Don't want it to end before it starts. You're so hot and wet, it's hard not to come. And you're gripping me so well. I don't want to lose control. Not before I make you feel so good you go insane."

Arian's eyelids fluttered. Fernando bent over him, fighting to control himself was a vision. Inch by inch, he eased in. It lit Arian up, the pressure against his sensitive inner walls nothing short of glorious.

One final push and Fernando was lodged balls deep inside of him. Tremors ran through Arian's hole and spread through his torso and into his limbs, down to his fingertips. Fernando was touching him everywhere he'd ever wanted to be touched. The feeling of fullness, of completion, overwhelmed his senses. This was what he had waited for all his life.

Shaking, he reached out to bring Fernando in for a kiss. Their lips moved together in tenderness, the urgency lost when they were where they had yearned to be. Their tongues met in an unhurried dance. Fernando pulled out an inch for a first small, slow thrust. It made Arian moan into Fernando's mouth.

"You make me feel so good," Arian whispered against his lips.

The next thrust was just as slow, and Arian basked in the sensations it brought to his hole. Fernando was panting, though not from the small movements of his hips but the restraint it cost him not to climax.

"You can come if you like," Arian said with another kiss. "I don't mind. The opposite, I love it when you come. I live for it."

Fernando took his hand, twining their fingers. "Not yet. I want to make this last. It's not only your first time."

Fernando never had anal sex before? He must have. But not with a man. The idea of sharing this with him blew Arian's heart open.

Fernando moved inside him in an unhasty rhythm, dragging out their lovemaking. That's what it was. Lovemaking. Arian undulated, massaging him all around. That Fernando hadn't come yet was a testament to his unbreakable determination.

Arian met his moves by rocking back onto him. Every time Fernando slid in, Arian dropped little moans and helpless whimpers. The world around them faded into oblivion. Nothing mattered except for their connection. And like their bodies were joined, Arian felt their souls fusing too. He wanted nothing more than to be one with Fernando.

Rolling his hips, Fernando brought him right up to the edge. And Arian's pelvic floor locked, not allowing him to let go yet. It sent him floating. He lost himself to the steady in and out that reached so deep it pleasured his very core.

Fernando whispered sweet nothings against his lips, brushing them together now and then. He went incoherent. With a groan, he rested his forehead on Arian's, keeping his hips still. His labored breathing was loud in the silent room. Then he changed the angle of his hips by a fraction and went back to long, deep thrusts.

From the first one, he nailed Arian's prostate, nudging it every time he filled his hole anew. Arian soared. The gentle pushes against his oversensitive love spot carried him to rapture. His hands in Fernando's sweaty curls, eyes locked, he broke out into deep, desperate moans. And when he thought this couldn't feel any better, Fernando plunged into his prostate and stayed. Pressure built. Arian's hole cinched closed, his inner muscles holding Fernando tight. He might have not been able to pull out anymore. Fernando bit his lower lip as they gazed at each other, their joint need increasing to the boiling point. Arian's insides swelled, expanding.

Disbelief was written all over Fernando's face. Despite Arian's vice grip on his cock, he managed to push in deeper, his cockhead pressuring Arian's prostate. It forced him over the edge into orgasm. The steady contact ripped a first, violent contraction from Arian. Then he exploded in a series of convulsions that tore him wide open. Triggered by the powerful muscles rippling over him, Fernando erupted inside of him, spurting against Arian's prostate. Arian screamed. He fisted Fernando's curls, crying out his release into his mouth as he writhed and spasmed under him, his own cock shooting between them, hitting their stomachs, their chests, flexing and unloading with every contraction. Hammering convulsions possessed him. They overcame him over and over again as he rocked back and forth on Fernando's cock, thrashing and moaning, entirely out of control. He couldn't see, blind with pleasure, just feeling, as he dug blunt fingernails into Fernando, his cock and hole pulsing in unison.

When the last of his contractions faded, his body went slack. Fernando collapsed on top of him as they both fought to catch their breath. With what strength Arian had left, he used to pet Fernando's hair, threading his fingers through it, kneading his scalp.

Fernando ran his thumb over the skin of Arian's chest in a soothing motion. His contentment was palpable.

Sated and happy, Arian slid into a nap. He woke when Fernando stirred. Wordlessly, they hugged, touching everywhere, skin-to-skin in that safe space where lust had faded and love remained.

Chapter Fifteen

Fernando

Fernando dressed Arian in some of his older clothes. Arian was about the same height as him, and back when Fernando had left university and first come to the New World, he had been less bulky. His clothes would end up being a little big on Arian, but not by much.

He rolled the delicate white stockings over Arian's calves and knees, then helped him into the royal blue breeches. Their golden buttons and borders caught the sunlight falling through the window of Fernando's dressing room. They were part of an exquisite ensemble, which included a matching waistcoat, which Fernando buttoned up over Arian's undershirt, and a stunning *justacorps*, a long coat reaching down to Arian's knees, dark blue with gorgeous, thick, golden brocade trimming all around.

The blue brought out Arian's eyes and, along with the gold, complimented his honey blond hair. Fernando tied his ruffled cravat and helped him into white leather shoes, wisely with minimal heel to avoid Arian stumbling in them, completing him as the perfect gentleman, ready for an audience with the King of Spain.

Fernando picked an outfit just as elegant for himself, choosing a muted brown ensemble with white flora trimming. Sometimes he enjoyed dressing to impress, especially when the opposite sex was to be floored with his appearance. Or the same sex, he supposed.

Arian was the picture of perfection and looking at him made Fernando twitch with the need to pull him close and take those clothes off again. He'd have to guard him tonight if he wanted to keep him to himself.

They struck quite the pair in the mirror: Arian golden elegance, Fernando warm darkness.

The sun was setting when they left the house. They'd spent the day lazing about in Fernando's drawing room where Arian asked him to tell him the *Iliad*. Fernando obliged him, recounting the tale of war and love. Later, they went for a walk in the countryside where Fernando led him past animal pastures and plantations. Arian soaked up everything like a sponge, eager to learn whatever he could. He asked questions about breeding animals and fertilizing the fields, and with every explanation Fernando gave, his mind expanded, curiosity never-ending.

But to experience the full scope of life in San Juan, there was no better way than attending one of the evening balls. And while Fernando couldn't attend the events of the nobility, he was a frequent guest of the festivities organized by other wealthy inhabitants of the town.

When Fernando and Arian arrived at the villa, the ball was in full swing. Chandeliers hung from the ceiling, overflowing with lit candles, and the strings played Scarlatti. The dance floor was crowded with people, some dancing, some engaged in animate conversation. A cluster of ladies chatted behind their fans, agitated gestures betraying their excitement.

"Fernando!" Carlos greeted him. He was another frequent guest of the San Juan ball scene. "What's going on with you? Didn't see you for a while, and then you bail on me for lunch."

It would have been a lunch meeting, not lunch, but Fernando swallowed his frustration with Carlos's careless deposition. After all, Fernando had canceled their plans today.

"I had an unexpected guest," Fernando said, thinking on his

feet as he not only had to explain the cancellation, but also Arian's presence at the ball. "May I present to you Arian... Arian Del Mar. An artist. Painter. Quite the protégé. My second cousin's brother-in-law."

"*Encantado*!" Carlos said, only now looking at Arian—doing a double-take. "My, my, Fernando, you have the ladies falling over themselves for you, but dare I say, you might have to contend yourself as second choice tonight." He took his hat off and bowed. "It is my pleasure, Arian."

"The pleasure is all mine," Arian responded as Fernando had instructed him, though with more uncertainty in his voice than a genuine answer allowed.

Carlos didn't notice. "It's wonderful when such fine young people join us. Are you staying permanently?"

"I'm afraid not."

"That's a shame, the ladies will be crying," Carlos said. "Well, and if the ladies bore you, I'd be more than happy to entertain you later tonight," he said with a gap-toothed grin.

"His entertainment is taken care of," Fernando ground out, stepping between Arian and Carlos. "If you'll excuse us."

He took Arian by the elbow and stirred him through the crowd, which took notice of Arian, whispers audible despite the attempts to hide them behind fans and the drifting music.

"... more beautiful than any woman."

"My god."

"Who is he?"

"Impoverished nobility, I bet."

"With that *justacorps*? Never. He's got more money than he knows what to do with if he's wearing that."

"But these aristocratic features... He has to be old blood from Castile."

Fernando pulled Arian to the dance floor. The crowd swept over it in pairs, dancing a minuet, slowly toward and away from their partner in spirals. Fernando and Arian were swarmed by a group of ladies. Faster than he could react, they got between them, always eager to find a partner for the minuet.

"Watch what I do!" was all Fernando could get in before he was pulled away for a dance. Arian's gait had stabilized over the day, but he was by no means a dancer. He wouldn't be able to watch the lady's feet, hidden under her lilac, floor-length ball gown. And the minuet was not a simple dance but an intricate series of complicated steps.

A blonde moved into stance before Fernando, and he had no choice but to fall into the minuet dance with her. Her baby blue gown swept the floor as they moved together. Fernando misstepped more than once as he kept his attention on Arian. And Arian wasn't doing well. He threw helpless glances at Fernando's feet, trying and failing to copy what he did. The lady in lilac didn't mind one bit as she beamed up at Arian, while he looked adorably helpless.

Fernando had to save him.

"Forgive me," he told the ladies as he bowed and moved away from the blonde, toward Arian, "my friend is from the provinces and has not learned to dance. Perhaps I should show him the steps before I return him to you."

Lilac Gown nodded, flashing her teeth in a grimace between a smile and baring her teeth at Fernando. God help him if she didn't get Arian back. Fernando bowed to her in excuse, then to Arian, as the dance required.

Starting with the right foot, he approached Arian with two minuet steps, then moved back in the same fashion.

"Mirror my steps," Fernando said, going deliberately slow, out of time with the music. Arian copied the moves, coming toward him.

Now that he could watch Fernando's feet, he learned with remarkable speed. He got the basic step quickly, and Fernando moved with him into the circling dance as they approached each other in an ever-tighter spiral. It was different to dance with him rather than the ladies. There was this incredible pull toward him as if an invisible band tied them together. Arian's eyes shone, his hair glowed golden in the candlelight.

Fernando showed him when to stretch his right arm out to touch hands and when they did, a spark lit up his soul. They circled, holding hands, and the pure joy in Arian's eyes made him want to pull him in instead of letting go as the dance dictated. He had never understood why the minuet was a courtship ritual. Not until now that he was moving with Arian. Fernando could have danced with him all night, approaching and retreating, a play of seduction and chastity.

"I've never been around so many humans," Arian said in a low voice when they were close.

"How do you feel about that?" Fernando asked.

"They smell funny," Arian snickered. Of course, he wasn't used to the boatloads of perfume some people showered in. "But I like being here. There's a world of opportunity. I can learn new things, meet people from different places."

Fernando's heart swelled. Too early, they had to separate again.

As soon as Arian was halfway competent in the minuet, Lilac Gown and the blonde cut in.

"I'm sure your friend will do fine on his own," the blonde said while Lilac Gown took Arian's hand and led him away.

It rubbed Fernando the wrong way, though there was little he could do short of causing a scene. He moved into position with the blonde, never letting Arian out of sight. The more Arian danced, the more graceful his movements became until he fit in with the rest of the dancers. If he stood out, it was due to his beauty. His hair flowed around his shoulders, and Fernando reveled in how good he looked in the three-piece.

Later when there were food and drink, Fernando sat next to Arian at the long, set table. He sank into conversation with the Creole investor next to him, who asked him countless questions about transatlantic trade and where to best put his money. Arian was quiet—it was smart of him to stay out of conversation lest he gave himself away, but Fernando didn't like the loneliness he radiated.

He snuck his hand under the table and placed it on Arian's thigh, the transgression hidden by the long, white tablecloth. Arian froze, but Fernando gave him a reassuring squeeze, and out of the corner of his eye he saw Arian's lips pull up. Arian's slender hand settled on top of his, and they interlaced their fingers. Warmth spread in Fernando's chest, and he found it harder and harder to follow the conversation with the Creole, his attention fixed on the patch of skin Arian kept stroking with his thumb.

When the first course was served, he quietly instructed Arian how to use and hold the cutlery. Arian laughed quietly, finding the rules of polite society ridiculous. He tried, nonetheless. Fernando hoped his excuse that Arian came from the countryside covered up the way he struggled with a knife and fork. Probably not, but why would anyone look at the cutlery Arian was holding when his angelic face was right there.

The urge to hold Arian became overwhelming. As soon as the plates were cleared away, they escaped under some pretext. The ball had been fun, but Fernando didn't want to waste another minute talking to someone other than Arian. Their time together was precious and short, and they took an open carriage back to Fernando's manor.

He led Arian to his bedroom, dominated by the dark mahogany four-poster bed. Fernando lit the oil lamps, their shine revealing pristine white sheets and crimson curtains.

Every night since the departure from the Culebra archipelago, he'd lain there, thinking of Arian, his divine features, the wet paradise of his mouth. He'd trembled with arousal, pulsing cock in hand, stroking himself to orgasm with Arian's name on his lips. Rinse and repeat when he woke up in the morning, cock leaking and straining against the sheets, begging to be coaxed to climax by long, delicate fingers.

Whatever happened tonight, Fernando would burn it into his memory. If this was all they got, he'd treasure every detail. Every word spoken, every gesture made. Fernando lit the final lamp as Arian dropped his *justacorps* on an armchair and unbuttoned his waistcoat. It fell to the side, followed by the cravat, and then he pulled his undershirt over his head, inch by inch revealing his slim waist, his firm chest, knowing full well Fernando was watching.

Fernando didn't want to wait anymore. He pulled at his clothes, discarding them in a heap.

"You sleep here?" Arian asked. "Not in the other room?"

Of course Arian wasn't familiar with human furnishing habits. Had he assumed Fernando slept on the divan? Quite possible. Fernando had never taken the privileges he'd earned for granted, but Arian reminded him of how different their lives were. How different Fernando's life was from what he'd grown up with.

"I sleep here," Fernando said, pointing at the bed.

Arian inspected it. "Looks comfortable."

Seeing Arian crawl onto it on all fours, naked ass in the air, limbs sinking into the downiness, stirred Fernando's most basic instincts. He freed his cock from the constraints of his breeches and joined Arian on the sheets, rolling him over and climbing on top of him.

Arian stretched, twisting under him in the sheets. "It *is* comfortable."

Fernando traced the line of his cheekbone, his jawline, then ran his fingers over Arian's peachy lips. He deserved a comfortable bed. With distaste, he thought of Arian sleeping on the hard stone of the cave, the coarse sand of the beach. It was all Arian knew. Fernando longed to shower him in luxuries. The finest clothes, the softest sheets. He'd spare no expense to offer Arian the best. What if Arian stayed? He dismissed the thought as soon as it popped into his mind. If Arian owed a witch powerful enough to give him legs, he better make good on his part of the deal. Never mind how much Fernando disliked the idea.

Arian's fingers trailed over his sides, down to his hips. He gripped Fernando, and in a flash, he had flipped them over. Arian grinned, hair falling over his face in a veil. He was slimmer than Fernando, but it was moments like these that his underlying strength became obvious. Bending down, he got close enough to kiss, but instead, his tongue darted out and licked Fernando's lips. Fernando surged up, claiming Arian's mouth. Arian met him with vigor, pushing him back down into the pillows with gentle force. Fernando's cock pulsed at the display of dominance. Arian in charge was just as hot as pliable Arian.

Fernando's legs fell open, accommodating Arian as he settled between them. He smelled of the sea, of sand in the sun.

When Arian nibbled at his jaw, Fernando smoothed his hands over his hair, his shoulders, his back, as low as he could reach. He wanted to touch him everywhere. Arian's skin was hot silk, and Fernando bucked up into him, rubbing his erection into his abs.

"So impatient." Arian wandered down to his neck to suck at the erogenous zone there. A drop of precum fell onto Fernando. Arian's movements smeared the wetness over him. He loved it.

"And look who's leaking already."

"Every drop I spill is for you. Because of you." Arian grazed his teeth over his neck. "I was made for you. My cock was made for you."

Fernando's heart skipped a beat. Because it was true. "And I breathe for you. I want to live for you."

"And you come for me." Arian drew his nipple into his mouth. It made Fernando's cock twitch.

"Yes."

Arian raised his head. "You are the singular reason why I've ever orgasmed. Never forget that. I owe you everything."

Fernando started to say something, but Arian was back to licking and thumbing his nibbles. Fernando moaned, growing harder with every flick and twist. He arched into it, his cock seeking friction against Arian's velvety skin.

Arian wasn't having any of it. With one wet kiss to Fernando's stomach, he moved between his thighs, leaving his cock hanging in the air as it throbbed for attention.

"Turn around, and get on your hands and knees," Arian said.

There was only one reason he'd ask for this.

"I should be the one spoiling you," Fernando said.

Arian raised an eyebrow and gave him a reprehensive look. It was stern enough to make Fernando comply. He didn't want to argue, not tonight. Not ever, had there been a future for them.

The mattress dipped under his shifting weight. Fernando ordered himself to relax. He hung his head and spread his legs. Hands cupped his cheeks, kneading the firm muscles. His fingers curled in the sheets.

Arian pulled his cheeks apart, opening him up. Fernando had never been this vulnerable with anyone else. This was for Arian, and Arian alone. The fact that they weren't doing this with him tied up in a cave but in his bed carried more meaning than he was ready to think about.

He gasped at the first touch of that heavenly tongue against his pucker. Warm and wet, it danced over him, slicking up his hole. He clenched at the thought of it. Arian's tongue washed over him, teasing all tension out of him. When his ring of muscle yielded in the smallest way, Arian pushed in.

Fernando threw his head back. How could he have forgotten how good Arian tending to his hole felt? Arian wriggled inside, licking and massaging his tender inner walls. How much he craved that touch. His cock jerked, precum pooling at the tip. Another lick and he was dripping onto the sheets in a long clear thread. He would do anything to hump his pillow, but Arian would never let him. Fernando's pleasure belonged to him. He'd give back later, give back tenfold, make Arian melt into putty in his hands, under his tongue, his cock.

He exhaled sharply when Arian pushed deeper again. Fernando bit down on his lip, lest he moaned like a whore. Though, wasn't that what he was? A whore for those talented lips, those deft fingers?

Arian withdrew and spit on his hole. Before the thick merman saliva could slide down to his balls and flow onto the bed, Arian pushed it into his entrance with a finger. Yesyesyesyesyes. That finger. He involuntarily squeezed it as it entered him. Arian moved in and out, granting him the barest stretch. Fernando prayed for him to crook his finger, to touch him where he needed it the most. But Arian didn't. He pulled out.

When two finger pads circled his rim, Fernando couldn't suppress a whine of anticipation and desire. By now, he knew the game and pushed out. Arian didn't take the invitation. But fuck, he needed those fingers inside him.

"Please," he begged.

Arian rubbed his fingertips up and down his twitching hole. "Please what?"

Fernando was past shame, he wanted this more than he wanted his dignity. "Please finger me."

He pushed out, and this time, he was rewarded with two digits pressing into his entrance, and he groaned in relief as they slid past the resistance. He tightened around them as they dove deeper. Arian buried them to the hilt inside his anus. Fernando sighed, at home with Arian dilating him so good. He felt every movement the digits made, withdrawing and returning in maddening slowness.

On the next stroke, they nudged his prostate. Fernando groaned as his pleasure center snapped to attention. He wanted more. But Arian avoided touching it, rubbing sweet circles all around it, but never probing him there, no matter how much he needed it.

For how long would Arian play with him until he rubbed his prostate again? It drove him crazy. He was swollen and sensitive, begging for Arian's attention. Fernando pushed back against his fingers, hoping Arian would take the hint.

"What do you want?" Arian asked.

Fernando bit his lip. He wanted to take Arian to unimaginable heights. But right now, his body was screaming for one thing and one thing only. His desire warred with the need to overwhelm Arian with ecstasy. His arms trembled. If he let Arian do this, he'd make it good for him afterward. His head dropped as he gave in to lust.

"I want you to massage my prostate."

Arian withdrew his fingers. What?

Fernando looked back at him. Arian petted his hip, avoiding his gaze.

"What if I massage it with my cock?" Arian said, staring at the sheets.

That had Fernando turn over and sit. The idea hadn't even occurred to him. Sure, he'd had Arian's fingers in him, the plug... But the notion of getting fucked by another man was nothing he'd considered. He wasn't considering it now—was he?

Fernando had offered Arian his throat to fuck without hesitation. He'd wanted Arian's cock in there, craved it. His ass was a different story. But Arian's cock was right in front of him. It was a beautiful cock, long and thick, but not too thick. Proportionate. Perfect. A pearl of precum threatening to spill crowned the bulbous head. It was broader, wider than Arian's fingers. Having it hammer his prostate would blow his mind, no doubt. Fernando's cock drooled precum onto his stomach.

"Sorry, I shouldn't have asked," Arian said, fumbling with the sheets. "Forget about it." He forced a smile onto his face, and Fernando's heart broke.

"Come here," he said, and lay back, opening his legs, waving for Arian to crawl into his lap.

Arian followed him down hesitantly but then lay his head on Fernando's chest. "I'll let you take me instead," Arian said, warmth returning to his voice as Fernando stroked his head.

"I didn't say no. You surprised me, that's all. I hadn't considered we had this option."

"We don't have to do it. It was just a thought."

But did Fernando want to? Did he want to get fucked into the mattress by this gorgeous angel of a man, all golden hair and sapphire eyes? The man who'd sold his life to be with him for one more day? Have that magnificent length dive into him, fill him, prod his prostate?

His cock, throbbing and leaking between them, already knew the answer.

"It could be a first time for us both," Fernando said.

Arian lifted his head. "Yeah."

"And I do want to give this to you. Only you." He cupped Arian's cheek. "There are many things I'd only do with you."

Arian surged up and kissed him, hard and desperate. Fernando met him with zeal, pouring all his desire into the kiss.

"I want to know how you feel inside of me," Fernando said.

"I want to feel how tight you are."

"Then take me."

For a moment, Arian didn't move. Then he sat back on his heels and slicked up his cock. How would it fit inside of Fernando? Arian was big enough to make him worry. But he had stretched him. And Arian had taken his own, even thicker cock. Men did this all the time. Heck, he'd done it to women. It'd be fine.

Yet he tensed up when Arian's cockhead nudged his rim.

"Relax," Arian said, soothing one hand over his thigh. "Push out for me, babe."

He did and despite the resistance his body was offering, Arian pushed into and past his tight ring. It trembled when his hole swallowed Arian's mushroom head. The stretch was intense, a burning sensation as Arian opened him.

Arian waited for him to adjust before he moved in deeper. Inch by inch, he slipped into his narrow hole. Fernando had never felt so full. He melted into the pressure, and when he gave way, Arian pushed in balls deep. His smooth cock was the best thing Fernando had had inside him. Better than the vibrating plug, Arian's slick tongue, even his talented fingers. Because Arian's cock pulsed with need, it was thick and heavy and alive. Arian's eyes dilated. He had to be so crammed inside of him.

He placed a kiss on the heel of Fernando's hand. "I'm going to fuck you now."

Arian dragged his cock out until only the head remained inside him. Then his hips snapped forward and dove back in. Nailing Fernando's prostate.

It tore a surprised cry from him. His insides quivered, his prostate pleading for another thrust like that. And he got it. Arian plunged into his love spot, again and again, moaning every time he bottomed out. Fernando lost his mind. Brutal pleasure contorted Arian's face. Had he known how Arian would react to this, he would have offered up his hole sooner.

Arian went wild. He lost all semblance of rhythm and thrust blindly, hips jerking, ceaselessly pounding his swollen prostate. It had them crying out in unison, Fernando clutching Arian's hips.

"You're so fucking tight," Arian said. "Grabbing me so good."

Fernando squeezed around him on purpose, and Arian gasped, eyes snapping open. He rolled his hips and hit Fernando spot on.

"Fuuuuck...," Arian whined. "I wanna come so deep inside you."

Fernando yanked him down for a bruising kiss. He rocked back against Arian, increasing the force of his assault.

"Then fucking come," Fernando said, slamming his hips toward him, meeting him knock for knock.

"You..."

"Don't worry about me. I want you to blow your load."

Arian trembled, fighting for control. "No. Ride me. Sit on my fucking cock and ride me. Need you in control."

Fernando didn't have to be told twice. Anything to make Arian's night. He held onto Arian's hips as he pulled out and climbed on top of him, Arian's luminous hair fanning out on the white pillow.

Settling onto his cock was a whole other experience. He held Arian up to his hole, sinking down the tiniest bit. It was easier with his anus already stretched open. Gravity helped as he seated himself on Arian. The delicious feeling of fullness returned, and he exhaled in appreciation.

Fernando rolled his hips, setting his hands on Arian's pecs, massaging them. The angle was different like this. Moving up and down, he found his prostate. He moaned as he impaled himself on Arian's cock again and again. It had Arian writhing under him. Fernando thumbed his nipples.

"Fuck yourself on me," Arian moaned. "Want to see you lose it."

Fernando lifted his hips and dove back down. His cock and balls slapped Arian's abs with every thrust. The more he let go, the more pleasure he took, the louder Arian groaned, the harder he thrashed. The sight alone could make Fernando come, never mind he hit his prostate with every move, massaging himself on Arian. Tingles traveled down his spine, into his balls, his cock. And that bulbous cockhead rubbing his pleasure center was going to push him over the edge any moment. He wriggled against it, his mouth dropping open at the intensity spike.

Arian slapped his hands onto his ass, sending ripples through his inner muscles. Fernando held onto his climax by sheer force of will. No way he'd let himself come before Arian.

"I'm close," Fernando said. "Can't hold back much longer. Your cock feels too good."

"Don't hold back. I wanna come with you squeezing all around me."

"Fuck!" Fernando slammed down hard.

Arian took his cock in hand, stroking him rapidly. Fernando's head fell back. With every upstroke, Arian flicked his thumb over his cockhead. No matter what Arian said, he wanted to hold on. Make sure he took care of Arian first.

"Come all over me," Arian said, and Fernando's good intentions fizzled out. Arian's hand moved in a blur.

Fernando's entire world narrowed to the cock grinding into his prostate and the hand flying over him. His orgasm came barreling down on him. There was no holding back. The first contraction of his anus around Arian's cock struck Fernando like lightning.

"Yes!" Arian roared.

Cum shot out of Fernando, splashing onto Arian's chest and face. His hole spasmed out of control. Arian's powerful spurts of cum hit his insides, drenching his hole. Fernando rode him like a galloping horse, fast and merciless. He let out a deep growl at the sight of Arian quaking in orgasm beneath him. There were no words for the rapture soaring in him at making Arian fly apart. He rocked his hips past the point where his own contractions ebbed off. Only when Arian dropped back on the mattress with a satisfied sigh did Fernando allow himself to collapse.

He nuzzled Arian's face as their heart rates slowed. This was the single best thing he'd ever done. Giddy, he licked his sperm off Arian.

"Why are you grinning like that?" Arian asked.

"Because you're in my bed, and I can feel your cum leaking out of my ass."

Arian laughed and pressed a kiss to his forehead. "I liked coming in your ass."

"Yeah. Me too."

He gathered Arian in his arms and held him tightly. Never wanted to let him go. Where was his usual need to get away after the deed was done? Nowhere to be found. He buried his nose in Arian's hair and inhaled his scent. If every night could be like this. He'd make Arian come two, three times before he'd give in to his desires and come. Inside him, on him, it didn't matter. He just wanted to see Arian blissed-out and sated.

Sex had never incited these feelings. He'd enjoyed it, but he'd never wanted anyone to linger afterward. And while the women he'd met at balls and through friends had been friendly and often attractive, he had a hard time picturing life at their side.

Fernando desperately wanted someone to share his life with. The joys and sorrows of living in San Juan, of traveling the seas, of having breakfast and going to dances and running a business. And no matter how much he wanted Arian to stick around, it couldn't be.

He held Arian closer, ran his fingers over his golden skin, rested his chin on his head. This was his happy place.

Chapter Sixteen

Arian

Fernando's breathing was so deep and even, Arian thought he'd fallen asleep. But when he peeked up, a huge, closed-lip smile was plastered onto Fernando's face, making him look like a cat basking in the sun. As Fernando felt him move, he squinted at him, lips stretching even wider. He pulled Arian closer, and they exchanged a lazy kiss.

Arian never wanted to leave. This was where he was meant to be, where he belonged. No part of him wanted to go back to Malik. Or even Culebra. But he had no choice. Malik had the Voodoo doll and wasn't afraid to use it if Arian didn't show. Or he'd hunt him down and hurt Fernando too. Yet Arian's eyes stung at the thought of leaving.

No matter how unfair it was, all he could do was make the hours they had left unforgettable. Burn them into his memory, into Fernando's. So that one day, when Fernando was married to a woman and had a bunch of kids, he'd sometimes think of him, of their time together, short as it had been. How selfish of him. But that was how he felt.

"I love you," Arian said, voice heavy with emotion.

Fernando kissed his jaw. "And I love you."

"I wish I didn't have to leave."

"Then stay." Fernando tucked Arian's hair behind his ear, cupping his face. "But you can't, can you?"

"No."

Sadness flickered across Fernando's features.

"I want to be yours," Arian said.

"You are," Fernando said and rolled on top of him.

Arian loved nothing more than Fernando's heavy weight pressing him into the mattress. The need to be taken, to be owned, swirled through him. The thought of being Fernando's made him rock-hard. Lust boiled in his veins. Arian bucked up against him. He ran his hand through Fernando's hair, fisting his curls.

"Prove it," Arian said through gritted teeth. "Make me yours."

A deep shadow settled over Fernando's face. "What are you asking for?"

"For you to take me. To fuck me so hard, I forget my name. So hard I can't walk tomorrow and be glad to have the damn fishtail back."

Fernando clenched his jaw. "You don't want that."

"Oh, I do. That and more. I want you to break me. To leave me bruised and battered so when I leave, I can still feel you. Feel you for days. If this is all we have, I want you to own me. I want you to use me like I'm your fucking whore. Because I am."

"And what about what I want?"

"You don't want to lay your claim on me?" Arian asked, raising his eyebrows.

"I do."

"Then do it. Fuck me within an inch of my life if you will. I am yours. I did this for you. I got legs for you. A cock. This only exists for you. So take it. Take me."

Fernando's eyes darkened. "Do you know what I want?" he asked, his breath quickening. "I want that stupid witch to keep his hands to himself. If I ever hear his cock got anywhere near you…"

"It's not like that. I'll work for him, nothing more."

"I know. I don't care," Fernando said, gripping his jaw with bruising force. "You're mine. Tell him that."

"Yes," Arian said, as much in response to Fernando's words as to his iron grip.

Faster than he could process it, Fernando flipped him on his stomach, his face landing in the pillows. Fernando yanked his hips into the air. Hell to the yes. Wetness seeped out of his hole.

A smack hit his ass, so hard his eyes watered, but no sound left his lips. Arian loved the sting of it, loved it because it was Fernando's doing. He'd take anything Fernando was willing to give him. If he got a knife to cut him open, Arian would let him do that too.

Another smack to the other cheek, more forceful.

"Who do you belong to?" Fernando asked.

"You."

Smack. "I can't hear you."

"YOU."

"That's right. Don't you ever forget that."

Arian would do anything Fernando asked him to do. He held onto the pillows, hiding his heated face in them. They muffled his shocked cry when Fernando bit his ass, hard enough to leave a mark.

"Perhaps," Fernando said, suddenly close to his ear, "I should take revenge on the man who locked me in chains in a cave? Stimulate you until you're out of your mind but never let you come? Or the opposite... make you come so often, you beg me to stop."

"I'd never ask you to stop," Arian said. There was no defiance in voice, only obedience.

Fernando shoved two fingers into his hole. Arian gasped in surprise, head snapping up, back arching. The shock of it was so great, his inner muscles tensed up, getting ready to shoot. The intrusion burned, but Rough Fernando was what he needed.

When Fernando's fingers slid out and back in, they sent sparks through his sensitive hole. Every nerve ending stood to attention, relishing the contact. More responsive than any human, Fernando had brought Arian to the edge of orgasm with two moves.

"I'm close," Arian whimpered. His groin strained further at the admission, barely holding it together.

"I want you to come on my command."

Arian's head dropped as he shook with lust. Fernando's words… that's what he wanted. For Fernando to control him, own his orgasm. That's how it was meant to be when he was the reason Arian had experienced one at all.

"Yes," Arian said.

Fernando moved his fingers in and out once again. Arian held back. His hole was singing with lechery, his balls climbed up, ready to unload. How long would he be able to contain his climax? Not long at all. If Fernando moved again, he'd be in trouble. Arian's legs shook as he fought to control his body.

In and out. It was too much. He cinched tight around Fernando's digits. Heat rushed over him as he clamped his pelvic floor down, on the brink of breaking into convulsions. He kept still as sweat formed on his brow, the strain unbearable. No chance of keeping his body from coming if Fernando moved.

Fernando petted his hip. "You're doing well. I can feel how much this takes you. You got a death grip on my fingers. I can't wait for when you do that to my cock."

Arian panted. Fernando dirty talking wasn't helping. His face in the pillows, Arian balled his hands into fists as his inner muscled threatened to give in.

"Come," Fernando said, thrusting his fingers into his hole.

Arian detonated. He cried out as he squeezed and released Fernando's digits in rhythmic compression. Cum shot across the sheets, soaking them. He bit the pillow as spasms wrecked him. When they slowed down, Fernando slammed his fingers inside him a couple more times, and Arian blew again, his cock unloading, his walls convulsing. Tears of ecstasy streaked his cheeks.

"Thankyouthankyouthankyou," Arian mumbled as he came down from his peak.

"I didn't allow you to come the second time."

Oh, shit.

Before Arian could as much as apologize, Fernando curled his fingers over Arian's prostate. It hit him like a whip. He tried to tense his muscles, but it was no use.

"I can't—" was all he bit out before he erupted again, shaking and quivering as he contracted around Fernando. All he hoped for was that Fernando saw that every time he came, it was to honor him. Goosebumps covered his skin when tingling convulsions took over his whole body. His entire being pulsed through the orgasm. He crashed from the high with a shout, a final contraction milking the last out of him.

Fernando let out a dark laugh. "Seriously?" A smack hit Arian's ass, hard enough to leave a bruise. "You have no control, slut."

"I'm your slut."

"That you are. Let's see how far we can take this."

"What—"

Fernando curled his fingers over Arian's prostate in a come-hither gesture. Once. Twice. By the third time Arian was coming dry, helplessly orgasming under Fernando's ministrations. Everything his merman body had denied him was served to him in abundance in his human form. And Fernando kept giving him more and more. How could Arian not love him when Fernando was giving him the one thing he'd wanted all his life and never thought he could have? How could he not love Fernando when he was owning his body, making him come over and over and over again until he had nothing left to give, and yet Fernando would still draw more out of him?

Fernando fingered him relentlessly. Arian shook and convulsed, his mind growing fuzzy by the sixth or seventh orgasm. The world muted to muffled noise, as if underwater. His legs gave in, but never mind, he was already on a cushy surface. What, he could not remember. All that existed was his needy, throbbing hole and his oversensitive bundle of nerves deep inside it, against which something warm and loving nudged. Two fingers. They rubbed sweet circles over him, making him cramp up deliciously. They massaged ever new highs out of him. And when unconsciousness crept toward him, they hammered him, jolting him back to life with new, all-encompassing contractions.

Arian didn't know when one orgasm ended and the next started. It was like an ocean washing against the shore. Sometimes, the waves were smaller, sometimes bigger. Sometimes, they were tsunamis shaking the world. But they never stopped.

Was he dead and in paradise? If so, those glorious, rapturous convulsions would continue through all of eternity. It was all he wanted.

"What you feel right there," a distant, divine voice said, "what you feel in your prostate, how good that feels, that's how much I love you."

Arian sobbed. Love. It pulsed through him, it vibrated against his pleasure center, through his hole, his entire body. And for the first time in his life, he was worthy of love. Because if something so great gave it to him, it couldn't be wrong.

Eventually, it retreated from his insides. He wanted to protest, but only a croak came out. His throat was sore as if he'd been screaming on the top of his lungs for a long time. Had he?

Smoothing motions caressed his back. Whoever was touching him was trembling too, with need or exhaustion.

Minutes passed, maybe more, he couldn't tell. Someone left and came back, a door creaking, footsteps on the wooden floor. Then he was being turned on his back and given water. Arian looked up and saw a figure resembling a dark angel. He wasn't sure, he could barely move. But *he* was beautiful.

"You're out of it," the dark angel said amused, running his knuckles over Arian's cheek. "I'd be too, had I come non-stop for that long."

He set the glass aside and shifted on the... on the bed, Arian realized, the water revitalizing him.

"But I'm not done with you," the angel—Fernando!—said. "I am going to ruin you. Ruin you for anyone else."

"You already have," Arian said languidly.

Fernando kissed him, a gentle brush of his lips, soft and warm. "You asked for rough sex. To be owned. I will take you, and you will put up a fight. I want you to fight like you mean it. In the cave, you told me if I was crying, kicking and screaming, you'd let me go. You can do all that, and it won't help you. You know how you can stop me? Tell me you want to go to Malik, and I will throw you out of my house right that second."

"You're stronger than me. And you've worn me out."

"That, my love," Fernando said with another transient kiss, "is the point. I've fingered the life out of you. And now I'm going to fight and fuck you to heaven."

Arian stared at him. He was fatigued and fucked out, but one look at Fernando's rock-hard cock, veins pulsing angrily after being denied for too long, Arian's length rose. For Fernando. Only for him.

And Arian wanted this. They were onto their final hours together and what better way to spend them than reaffirming they belonged together. That he was Fernando's, no matter who he'd sold his life to. There was only one man who owned his body and soul, all else be damned.

Fernando let him rest for a while longer. He rubbed Arian's skin, fed him an orange he'd fetched.

Eventually, he leaned over to the nightstand and fished something out of the drawer. A steel ring, two inches in diameter. A cock ring. Arian went hot and cold. Cold because Fernando had likely used it with someone else in the past. Hot because of the possibilities that came with it.

"What?" Fernando asked. "You're not the only one with a chest full of toys, albeit mine are not enchanted. Put it on me, so I don't come the first time your greedy hole clenches around me."

"You're very confident you're going to get inside me in the first place if I fight you in earnest."

Fernando said nothing, instead held the cock ring out to Arian.

He took it and slid it onto him. Arian hadn't thought it possible, but Fernando's cock grew even bigger, the head turning a shiny dark purple like it was ready to bust. For how long had he been hard? If it was Arian, he'd fight as well to get to sink his overstimulated, unfucked cock into someone.

He licked his lips. Fernando must be aroused beyond measure. He'd worked Arian for ages, denying himself the pleasure he was giving him. Fernando would fight him hard, he'd grab him and hold him down. Own him. Own his hole. This was going to be good.

"Run," Fernando said with a devilish grin, and it whipped the smirk off Arian's face.

He scrambled to get off the bed, headfirst toward the floor. Arian hit the bedside carpet and struggled to his feet, fatigued. He made it all of two strides before Fernando tackled him to the floor. Strong arms wrapped around him, he kicked out. Fernando didn't even react when he hit his shin. He picked him up, indifferent to how much Arian was struggling. Fernando carried him over to the bed where he dropped him unceremoniously.

As soon as he hit the sheets, Arian sought purchase and leaped forward, but Fernando snatched his ankle before he could get off the bed. Arian kicked behind him, hitting Fernando. It got him nowhere. Fernando grabbed his other calf and pulled him across the bed, dragging his cock over the sheets. The thrill of the fight had made him rock-hard.

Arian's heart hammered against his rib cage as he twisted to fight back. Useless. Fernando's powerful legs dropped onto his, immobilizing them. Fuck, yes. Arian reared up. He wouldn't make this easy. But Fernando was stronger, moved faster. He trapped him under his heavy body, catching Arian's wrists. He pinned them in front of Arian's face with a single hand. Arian's cock oozed precum onto the sheets.

"That's all you got, hmm?" Fernando said into his ear, erection pressing into Arian's crack. "You had ropes and chains to hold me in the cave. I don't need those. I'll fuck you holding you down myself."

Slickness seeped out of Arian's hole. His cock twitched in time with his heartbeat.

Pathetic. Fernando had overwhelmed him effortlessly. Arian bucked, thrashed, yet Fernando held him without even breaking a sweat. He could wait for Arian to exhaust himself and then claim his hole at his leisure. Try as he might, there was no escape from Fernando, and Arian went slack, catching his breath.

A large hand came around and covered his mouth. "Spit into my palm or I'll fuck you dry," Fernando said, voice dangerously low.

Fuck me within an inch of my life, Arian had told him. Had he bitten off more than he could chew?

He did as he was told, then listened to the slick sounds of Fernando lubing himself up.

His fat cockhead pushed into his rim, demanding entrance. "Be a good little whore and push out."

Arian obeyed and cried out when Fernando dove all the way into him in one fell swoop. Buried balls deep in his hole, Arian trembled around him.

"You're massaging me so good," Fernando growled. "Best fuck of my life. You don't know how much you would make in a whorehouse. You'd clean out all of San Juan, and they'd still come back begging for more."

Fernando's hands traveled up the length of Arian's arm to where he held his hands captive. He cupped the backs of Arian's hands, interlacing his fingers with Arian's.

"Imagine the queues," Fernando said, his thumbs stroking Arian's. "Even if you charged them an arm and a leg to fuck your sweet little holes. But that will never happen. I own you. Your holes are mine. Nobody else will fuck you. You open up for me and me alone."

Fernando pulled out of him, only to slam back in. A deep burn prickled across Arian's inner walls as they were ripped apart. The pain was exquisite. It mixed with the delight of friction, creating an intoxicating mix. Fernando stayed inside of him, let it build.

Arian panted. His hole shrunk, gripping Fernando like a vice.

"Fuck, you're so tight. Fucking gorgeous little whore."

Fernando tore back against the resistance and pistoned into Arian's ever-tightening insides. Arian gaped, hands squeezing Fernando's fingers. His wet hole throbbed with love for Fernando's cock. Not much longer and Arian would be coming again, no matter how long he'd climaxed for earlier.

"So good," Arian whined, dropping all pretense. "Don't stop."

Fernando fucked him violently. The solid mahogany frame of the bed rattled and creaked. Fernando rubbed through Arian's entire hyperalert hole. There was one more thing he needed.

"Please," Arian said.

"Please what?"

"Please... my prostate." Fernando had been purposefully avoiding it, Arian had no other explanation for why else he wouldn't be nailing it. "Take me back to that place. That place where you make me come and come and come without end."

"You wanna be coming all around me?" Fernando panted, keeping his mad pace. "Squeezing my cock non-stop while I let you orgasm for half an hour straight? You're going to turn me into a beast."

Fernando pulled out until only his cockhead was lodged inside Arian. He tilted his hips, changing the angle. And took it home. He drilled into Arian's prostate. It seized, turning Arian into a mindless, babbling mess. He undulated around Fernando, and came with brutal force.

"Oh, god," Fernando groaned. His rhythm faltered for less than a second.

Arian convulsed, screaming in ecstasy. His cock squirted cum all over him, all over the sheets, jerking rapidly. The hammering against Arian's pleasure center never stopped. Instead of ebbing off, his contractions intensified. Growing harder, faster.

"Fuck me, fuck me, FUCK ME!" Arian roared as he shuddered

with it, his entire body a pulsing heap of rapture.

Fernando didn't let him down, thrusting into him with a vengeance. "Wanna come so hard inside you."

"D-Do it," Arian moaned.

"Not before you lose your fucking mind."

The next wave built, surged and crested, then crashed into Arian with a force that tore him to shreds. He imploded. Floated.

Reduced to his love spot, he was blind and deaf. Nothing mattered except the devastating, vibrating ecstasy and that glorious cock causing it. Arian spasmed around it. The spongy head plunged into his core over and over again. His body loved Fernando's.

The next time Fernando hit home, burying himself in Arian's prostate, Arian cinched shut. Unable to pull out, Fernando's forehead dropped to Arian's back.

With the constant pressure on his prostate, Arian never stopped coming. His tight hole contracted around Fernando.

"Can't move," Fernando panted, his hands clenching around Arian's. He rocked his hips.

The pressure on Arian shifted, and he moaned. Incapable of all else, Fernando rocked into him, catching his breath.

"Do you feel me rub against your prostate?" His voice was far away.

"Y-Yes..."

"How does it feel?"

"F-Feels s-so good." Understatement of the century.

"Then let me make love to you this way," Fernando said, rolling his hips.

The movement was tiny, but Fernando was stroking his very soul. Arian floated, trapped under Fernando, trapped in a paradise where small nudges brought divine convulsions onto him. With every one of them, his world expanded and shrank, expanded and shrank, centered on the place where their most sensitive parts connected.

Fernando quivered. He rubbed his cockhead into Arian's

prostate. "You're my heaven," Fernando whispered. "Wet. Hot. And so very tight." Arian spasmed. "I'm moments away from coming."

Arian cried out at the next small slide over his core. Raw and open, every minuscule movement sent him flying into another round of pulsations. He loved it. He loved Fernando. Loved the man who took him to ever new highs.

"Fuck, babe," Fernando said. "I feel it all, feel you come so hard every time I shift."

Rubbing. Arian exploding.

Fernando gripped their joined hands. "Can't hold back. I'm done. This one's gonna make us both come."

He pushed into Arian by a fraction, nuzzling his glans into Arian's love spot. That, along with Fernando's words, shoved Arian into oblivion. He pulsed violently, and Fernando splashed against him in hot, fast bursts, triggering wave after wave of orgasmic contractions. Arian sobbed in release, at the love and care Fernando was giving him. Moments later, he blacked out.

When he came to it, he was lying on his side, Fernando spooning him, arms wrapped around his torso, keeping him close and safe. Fernando was his home.

Arian cried silently, as for Fernando not to notice. He wanted to get taken by Fernando on a nightly basis for the rest of his life. Instead, he had to work for a crazy witch. But he'd had this night. Fernando had made the trade more than worth it.

At least with the fishtail, no one else would have him. He'd always be Fernando's. He had fucked him so thoroughly, Arian's insatiable desire wouldn't return for days. And when it did, he'd be clenching up, thinking of Fernando.

Even his deal with Malik out of the picture, there was no future with Fernando. Arian wouldn't have had legs in the first place to come here. His fishtail would be back by morning, and he had to return to the water. Humans and mermen couldn't live in the same places. He needed to be in the sea, Fernando on land. There was no solution for them.

He failed to suppress the next sob, his shoulders heaving.

"Hey, hey," Fernando said, holding him closer, soothing his thumbs over his skin. "I'm here. You're here." He kissed his head.

Arian allowed his tears to flow freely. "It's not fair. How is it fair that we cannot be together? How does the world allow us to fall in love but deny us more?" He clutched at Fernando's arms.

"You're everything to me. I'll always remember you. I love you." Fernando's voice broke on the last words.

"I love you too." Arian turned and kissed him. It was bittersweet.

Fernando wiped Arian's tears away, his own eyes shiny, lids heavy with exhaustion. Arian snuggled up to him. They stayed like this for a long time until their breathing evened out, and Arian's eyes closed.

"Promise me you'll wake me up before you leave in the morning," Fernando said sleepily. "I want to bring you to the shore and kiss you goodbye."

"Of course," Arian mumbled as he drifted away.

It was still dark outside when he woke. Fernando was fast asleep. He looked so peaceful, his arm lying across Arian's waist.

Arian couldn't wake him. He'd embarrass himself by sobbing his eyes out when he said goodbye. So instead, he pressed the lightest kiss to Fernando's lips, then extracted himself from under his arm.

His hands shook as he dressed in the clothes he'd stolen the day before. For a long moment, he regarded Fernando's sleeping form, committing his face to memory. He swallowed his looming tears and tiptoed out of the room, sneaking out the house before the sun kissed the horizon.

Chapter Seventeen

Fernando

Awareness seeped into Fernando. The fog of sleep cleared, and he started. Something was wrong. His eyes flew open. He was alone. Where was Arian? He turned in bed. No Arian. Fernando jolted out of his sleepiness as cold lightning struck his chest.

"Arian?" Fernando sat up. "Arian?"

He wasn't there. Not in his bedroom anyway. Perhaps he'd gone to the kitchen to get some water. He wouldn't have left without saying goodbye. Fernando got up and slipped into a silk dressing gown. He was fastening it around his waist with shaking hands as he stormed out of his bedroom.

"ARIAN!"

His call echoed through the empty house. No answer. Dread crept up on him. What if Arian had left? Fernando checked every room. What if something had happened to him? He could have gone outside to see the garden, fallen and injured his leg. What if someone had broken into the house and kidnapped him? That was ridiculous of course. Fernando refused to face the alternative. Panic mounted. The sun was already up.

When he had checked the last corner of the house, a storage cupboard on the second floor, it became undeniable. Arian was gone. Arian had left. This wasn't fair. He had counted on seeing him one more time, kissing him, holding him close before he had to let go forever. Why had Arian done this to him? Bereft of his last hour with Arian, he punched the hallway wall. Sharp, satisfying pain shot up his arm. A welcome distraction.

The fucking bastard had left, just like that. Fernando had nothing. He stomped back into his bed chamber and banged the door closed. Breathing heavily, he leaned against it. Pain and anger raged in him, fighting for dominance. He was a mess. So was the bed. The sheets were rumpled, even torn in places. Fernando didn't know if he wanted to tear them off the bed and burn them or sink back into them and cry his eyes out.

The suddenness of Arian's departure was unbearable. It ripped into Fernando, leaving behind an empty, hollow space. How could Arian do this to him?

Fernando hadn't been exactly happy when he'd come home after the island. Now it was worse. Because he'd been granted another glimpse at what life could be like with Arian. If things were different. How happy he would have been, had he been able to live with Arian, read him books, spend his nights pleasuring him. He would have taken Arian to heaven every day for the rest of his life.

Part of him was angry with Arian, wanted to hate him for leaving without saying goodbye. For robbing him of their final moments together. But it would only serve as a wall between Fernando and the truth: he had never felt so lonely. Arian had filled the hole in his heart Fernando had never succeeded to stuff with the company of women.

He slumped into his armchair, looking out to the garden and wished he was out at sea, the slow sway of a ship in the waves of the ocean calming him. There was no calm here. His mind alternated between racing panic and ice-cold emptiness.

How was he going to live without Arian? The man who had signed his life away to be with him for a single day. Fernando's hands balled into fists. He had run away from the island in fear and worry for Luis. That had caused Arian to follow him, regardless of the consequences. So stupid, so courageous.

Fernando had experienced something precious, and it was gone. He'd never love again. He'd tried and tried in the past, and nothing came from it. And then Arian had swept in and conquered his heart.

He sat in his chair, unmoving. Hours later, the front door opened. Voices in the entrance hall, steps in the hallway. His staff had returned from their stay at the inn. Yet Fernando remained frozen in his chair. He couldn't face the world.

The house filled with life, and eventually, there was a knock on his door. Tired, he called for them to come in and turned in his chair. It was Ayah. An expression of shock flashed over her face at the ruined sheets, evidence of Fernando's wild night. She wouldn't have to guess with whom. Fernando didn't care. She was smart and loyal enough to keep quiet about it, and she liked him too. Ayah wouldn't talk.

"May I...," she started.

"Yes," Fernando said, "clean the room."

He didn't move from his chair but turned back to face the garden. Ayah busied herself, her shoes clacking against the wooden floor, sheets rustling.

Time seemed to stand still and speed up simultaneously. The following days passed in a gray cloud. Fernando distracted himself. He met with his lawyer, with business partners, hosted a gala at his house. Drowning himself in the company of others took his mind off Arian, off the pain. But it was nothing more than an insufficient bandage for the wound gaping in his heart.

He avoided seeing Luis and the others, not wanting to be reminded of their time in the archipelago. It was best if he forgot all about it.

Then his lust, which had been buried under the agony of the separation, came back with a vengeance. He didn't want to feel it, but it was there. An insatiable hunger for Arian caught him when he lay in bed. The bed they had fucked in. Though the sheets had long been replaced, Fernando's mind played tricks on him, and he smelled Arian when he climbed into bed as if his essence had seeped into the room.

In the beginning, he resisted, but soon he gave in, stroking himself with a guilty conscience because while he was taking care of business, nobody was taking care of Arian. Arian, who suffered under the burden of a lust he couldn't relieve. Fernando buried his face in his pillows, inhaling deeply. He thought of no one but Arian whenever he touched himself. Nothing excited him but a passing thought about the merman would leave him rock-hard in his breeches. Strawberry blond hair fanning out on his pillows. Cerulean blue eyes looking up at him through dark, long lashes.

Most pathetic of it all, Fernando missed his company. Arian had raptly listened to his rendition of the *Iliad*, keen to learn more. Ambition, not unlike Fernando's, was slumbering in him.

What was Arian doing? What did his life with Malik look like? Was he happy?

Days turned into weeks. Fernando had to return to normal life. What happened with Arian was a fling that was in the past. He had to look ahead. Make plans. A voyage back to Boston in spring, then across the Atlantic in summer. None of it excited Fernando. He should be busy procuring sugar and rum for the trip up north. Instead, when he pulled out the map, he stared wistfully at the Culebra archipelago. Sometimes, hours went by during which he did nothing but get lost in memories.

One day, he snapped, angry at himself. This wasn't his life, sitting around moping. No, he'd take matters into his own hands. And what better way to get over an unfortunate relationship than to find a sustainable one. If he tried hard enough, he'd find a suitable woman to love and marry. Then he could put the insane affair with Arian behind him. He only liked women that way, after all.

In the end, he responded to Isabella's letter. He'd left the lady waiting for too long, and in his reply, he apologized, citing his busy life as an excuse.

She happily agreed to meet him at his earliest convenience.

And what better place to meet up than at the upcoming ball hosted at Carlos's villa. That evening, Fernando stalked through his dressing room, picking out an ensemble to wear. His gaze fell on the dark blue three-piece with the golden brocade Arian had worn to the ball. Fernando ran his fingers over the fabric, the softness of the velvet, the coarse brocade. What he wouldn't give to see Arian in it again.

He tore his hand away from the *justacorps* as if burned. No more lingering in the past. Fernando chose a forest green ensemble with subtle bronze trimming, perfect for a night out.

A carriage brought him to Carlos's manor. It was a similar affair to what he had attended with Arian. Gentlemen in wigs and *justacorps*, ladies in ruffled gowns. Drinks were served from behind a long baroque table while candles glowing on chandeliers, their light reflected in the mirrors lining the wall.

Isabella spotted him immediately. She rushed over in her light pink gown, which clashed grotesquely with her auburn hair, tripping over her own feet.

"It's good to see you," she said in her high-pitched voice, curtsying to him. An overpowering smell of flowery perfume wafted around her as if she had taken a bath in it.

Fernando responded with a slight bow. "My pleasure." Lie.

"It's been a long time. You've missed the cockfighting competition last month."

Fernando recoiled. He'd never visited one of those vulgar events, which had two riled-up animals fight each other to the death for sport.

"It was quite the show," Isabella continued, oblivious. "Won three escudos with my wagers."

Fernando rubbed his temple. Isabella gave him the space to greet the other attendants of the ball but lurked nearby. Fernando dragged it out, not wanting to be roped into a dance with her. Social norms dictated he'd have to ask her. She'd told him her father was one of the landowners to the west of San Juan, and it was best to stay in everyone's good graces and not offend them by publicly denying their daughter the opportunity of a dance.

Yet he dreaded it, wishing he could shake her off somehow. Everything about her was wrong. Her hair color was off and her skin too pale, the pitch of her voice earache inducing.

"Would you like to dance?" Fernando asked her when he could no longer avoid it.

She squealed in delight. "I'd love to."

The strings played and guests chatted in the background as he guided her to the dance floor. They bowed to each other, then fell into the minuet step. Isabella floated through the dance, skilled and in perfect harmony with the music. Yet watching her brought Fernando no joy. Arian hadn't had her skill, but more grace.

Fernando and Isabella approached each other with the airy steps of the minuet. Isabella wasn't ugly, and Fernando searched for the pull toward her, the desire to be closer, but it wasn't there. If anything, there was a vague repulsion and an urge to get away.

The spiral of the dance tightened, and he reached for her hand for the next part. It was cold and clammy, unlike Arian's warm skin. Fernando's posture stiffened with her so close. It was wrong, she shouldn't be near him. When he lifted their hands for her to turn under his arm, he wished himself far away. Her pirouette was flawless but uninspired. Arian had been eager to learn anything new, his eyes sparkling with every discovery. What would make Isabella sparkle? And would Fernando care?

They drifted apart in spirals, Fernando glad for three feet of distance between them. Isabella was eager, moving in with enthusiasm in the next round, but Fernando ended the dance at the first opportunity when Carlos spotted him from across the floor, waved and strutted over.

"Good to have you here, my friend," he said, the smell of rum accompanying him. "And you've met the lovely Isabella. Great to see you two together." He looked back and forth between them as if missing something. "Tell me, Fernando, where's your friend?"

Arian. Fernando blinked, the reminder cutting into his soul like a knife. "He... he departed."

"No!" Carlos exclaimed. "Already? Such a shame. Handsome young lad. You should have seen him, Isabella, you wouldn't even look at Fernando when he's around."

Fernando's hands curled into fists. Carlos wasn't allowed to talk about Arian like he was a piece of meat.

"I doubt it," Isabella said, and inexplicably, it made Fernando even angrier. Was she questioning Arian's beauty? He had to calm down. She hadn't even met Arian. What was wrong with him?

"Anyway," Carlos said. "How's the apothecary going? I haven't seen your father in ages."

Apothecary? Wasn't her father supposed to be a landowner? Maybe Fernando had misunderstood her. But shock widened Isabella's eyes, and they darted between Carlos and him as she flushed bright red. There was no misunderstanding. She had either lied or stretched the truth until it was so thin it ripped. Had she meant her family house had a backyard when she'd said "landowner"? Fernando snorted. She was a social climber. Though her father's apothecary must be doing well, looking at the fine silk of her gown, the heavy silver of the jewelry hanging from her neck, her ears. Or perhaps it was all paid for with borrowed money. Then she had double reason to marry wealth.

Arian would've never lied to impress him. He was honest and blunt, blurting out his thoughts without shame or consideration. He wore his heart on his sleeve, confessing his love when he felt it, instead of waiting for a good moment.

Isabella stirred the conversation into more comfortable waters for her. And talked about the slave her father had acquired.

"Your father bought a slave?" Fernando asked. After Arian had opened his eyes to how wrong it was, the idea appalled him.

"Yes," she said, flashing her teeth, "and she's doing a good job around the house. Taking care of the younger ones, cooking and cleaning."

"You could employ somebody to do that," Fernando said.

Isabella sucked in air as if to speak but cut herself off.

"Too expensive these days," Carlos said, and Isabella let out a breath.

A social climber indeed.

Around them, the ball moved on, dancing couples swaying over the floor. It would be enjoyable with the right company. Fernando loved get-togethers, meeting people. And he wanted someone at his side to enjoy it with. Not Isabella though.

She and Carlos decided they should all get food. When she took Fernando's hand, irritation flooded him. Her hand was all wrong in his, too small, the fingers short and fleshy. They found seats at the long dining table where light dishes were being served. It reminded Fernando of the night at the ball with Arian. How different it had been. He had sought out Arian's hand under the table, holding him, touching him in the small ways he could get away with in public.

Fernando pulled out of Isabella's hold as soon as he could without causing offense. He shook his head when she sat next to him. Her perfume overdose was giving him a headache.

She talked and talked and talked with Carlos, all the while trying to rope him into the conversation. He was glad for the plate of mussels in front of him. It wasn't a good excuse to avoid her mind-numbing talk, but whatever. He should get out of here sooner rather than later.

"What have you been up to, Fernando?" Carlos forced him back into their chat. "Haven't seen you much lately."

Fernando pressed his lips together, controlling his face. He didn't want to offend them by rolling his eyes. "I've been preparing for a couple more trade runs. There's a lot to do."

"And when you're not working?" Isabella asked with interest.

"Reading Homer." It was true. Since Arian had left, he'd pulled out the *Odyssey* again and again, rereading the passage about the sirens. And the *Iliad* with its two tragic love stories. Fernando found it fitting.

"Hoe-what?" Isabella asked.

"Homer," Fernando said. "He was a writer of epic poetry in ancient Greece."

"Huh?"

Fernando went on to explain, but by the second sentence, her eyes glossed over. She wasn't interested. Arian had soaked it all up. Had listened and asked for more, keen to hear stories of foreign lands, the adventures of a sailor and the tragic love of two men.

Fernando ended the evening early, like the night he had ducked away with Arian after one course of the meal but for different reasons. Now he wasn't escaping to a night of pleasure, he was escaping from another minute of Isabella's shrill voice and narrow mind.

The following week, he went to a gala and met a blonde. She was nice, but nothing about her enticed him. Too short, too round, too soft. Friendly, but brainless. The next woman he met was older, approaching thirty, but she wasn't right either. Too bitter about life, too preoccupied with bad-mouthing people she barely knew.

Fernando looked to men, but none sparked his interest. Even if they were attractive, led an interesting life, there was always something missing.

He didn't go to a whorehouse either. The idea of sleeping with someone who wasn't Arian revolted him. That was new. Fernando had had a reliable sex drive his entire life, but it was gone. Well, not gone. At night when he sank into his sheets, memories of Arian flooded him, and he couldn't help himself but wring an unsatisfying climax out of his body.

Fernando buried himself in his business, and while it provided a distraction, it didn't fulfill him. A vital piece of his life was missing. A companion. Someone to love and treasure. No matter how many women he met, he always had something to complain about. None of them were Arian.

One night, fed up with polite society and its pretentiousness, he walked down to the harbor and entered one of the sailors' taverns to get a strong drink and rough but honest company. The smell of spilled beer and deep-fried, rancid fish hit him as he stepped through the door. It reminded him of a ship's mess. He felt right at home.

And there, at a table all by himself, crumbled over a glass of rum, sat Darin. Fernando debated whether he should talk to him or find a dark corner to sulk in with a large bottle. But he preferred company, so he pulled out a stool opposite him, its legs scraping over the floor. Darin peeked up through his fringe.

"Fancy seeing you here," he drawled, his English accent thick.

"And you," Fernando replied in English.

"Huh? Didn't know you spoke English. Only heard you talk in Spanish and French."

And Portuguese, but Fernando wasn't going to make a point of it. "Guess it never came up."

"What brings you here?" Darin said, and took a swig of his rum.

"Same as you, I suppose."

"Yeah," Darin said. "It's been crazy, you know. Feels like I never left the island." He'd had a bit to drink but didn't slur his words. He wasn't drunk. Good. Fernando had deliberately used English so they wouldn't be understood by the rowdy tavern crowd around them in case a drunk Darin mentioned the mermen. He wasn't interested in recounting the story in front of a curious crowd who'd ask if they heard them talking about that.

Fernando ordered a bottle of rum from the keeper. If they were going to have this conversation, he needed more than one drink.

"Part of me wants to go back," Darin said as the keeper sat the rum and a glass down on the table. "I mean what happened to Luis sucks, but they're not all like that. Your merman seemed nice. Mine's a bomb. Luis and Kristian got the short end of the stick."

Luis maybe, although he'd had fun up to a certain point. But Kristian? Fernando saw through him. Kristian had loved every minute with his merman, whether he admitted it or not.

"Speaking of which," Darin continued, "I saw Kristian the other day. He's raging mad. Says he wants to 'hunt that bitch down and fuck him up.'"

Kristian was a hopeless case. It'd take ages for him to admit he liked Tarlis.

"Have you seen Luis lately?" Fernando asked. He'd brought him the mermen's pouch of gold a few weeks ago under a pretext but hadn't visited him since.

"Last week. He'll be fine. Weak in the legs, but he's getting better. I'm not."

"You're not what?"

"I'm not getting better. I dream of that bloody island every night." Darin blushed. "Of Finn."

So Fernando wasn't alone in his lingering infatuation with a merman. "Yeah. I feel you."

Darin swirled the rum in his glass. "You don't know how often I sit and think about getting a boat to go back to Culebrita. It wouldn't even cost that much. It's damn tempting."

"So why don't you?"

"Why don't you?"

"*Touché.*"

Fernando would never tell him he'd seen Arian since. Arian had made an incredible sacrifice. He didn't want to give Darin any ideas. The past was the past.

"I need to move on." Fernando took a sip. "You need to move on. They lured us in, and it was meant to be a bit of fun for them. We were never meant to get involved emotionally. It was a physical thing, and it's done."

"That's what you're telling yourself," Darin said. "The rum's telling me something else."

Okay, Darin was drunker than he seemed. "What's the rum telling you?"

Chapter Eighteen

Arian

Bleary-eyed, Arian heaved himself through the trapdoor and splashed the octopus onto the wooden floor of Malik's cabin. Malik rushed over, cursing under his breath as he grabbed the live animal and added it to his steaming cauldron. Today, it was emitting dark blue vapor for a change. The smell wasn't too bad, though that changed minutes after the octopus landed in the pot. The cauldron whizzed, then with a *pop*, it bounced into the air before smacking back down, spilling half its contents.

Maybe this potion would finally be right. By now, Arian must have caught Malik one of every octopus species in the world. The Caribbean reef octopus hadn't been right for the potion and neither had the Atlantic pygmy, nor the deep sea octopus. Malik had added them to the various iterations of his concoctions and all of them—or so Malik said—had failed. Arian had no clue what he was trying to achieve, and Malik wouldn't answer his questions. So much for teaching him. But whatever potion he was working on, it was more complicated than giving a merman legs for a day.

Malik hadn't made good on the promise to teach him how to read. He sent Arian on one quest after the other, each crazier than the one before. The octopuses were the tip of the iceberg. Arian had gotten him Aztec gold from a sunken ship, which he had to look for over weeks before he found it, all types of seashells and even a lock of his hair. The latter, Arian had been reluctant about and had only given it to Malik after ample assurances he wouldn't make another Voodoo doll.

One day, he managed to get Malik another shard of mothershell, like the one he had used for the potion that had given Arian legs. He had to dive to the bottom of the ocean to get one and nearly drowned in the process. When Malik saw the shard, he pressed a sloppy kiss to Arian's cheek, which Arian whipped off in disgust while Malik danced through his shack, fist curled around the precious item.

But whatever potion Malik was trying to brew, it never worked.

Arian was exhausted. Malik's quests were endless, and so was Arian's suffering. Though that wasn't Malik's fault. Arian missed Fernando more than ever. When he saw a ship in the distance, he was thrown back to when he had lured Fernando in. Palm trees and coconuts reminded him of Fernando's retelling of the *Odyssey*. Every beach, every wave brought on a memory. It was inescapable.

Sleep eluded him most nights. He lay awake among the mangrove roots, half hoping a crocodile snatched him. In the early hours of the morning, he passed out from exhaustion, only to be woken a couple of hours later by the shrieking parrots inhabiting the forest.

He didn't eat much either. His appetite had vanished when he left San Juan. Malik gave him potions to sustain him during his search for the obscure item of the day. Arian struggled to force them down.

"You know, little one," Malik said as he wiped away the puddle Arian's latest catch had left on the floor with a dirt-stained rag, "you don't have to flaunt your disgruntlement. I get you're not happy. I get you miss your fancy man, but don't blame me. I did my part."

Malik was right. But more than once, Arian had thought about going back to San Juan, to watch the harbor, see if Fernando was there among the docks getting ready for his next voyage. It was a horrible idea, but Arian would have gone had Malik not kept him busy with his odd requests.

"Give me a day to go to San Juan," Arian said, requesting what he had wanted all along.

"To do what?" Malik asked as he tossed the rag in the corner and returned to his cauldron to clean up the spilled potion with an even rattier cloth. "There's no more canoodling for you, buttercup. What's a visit gonna do for you?"

"I want to see him."

"You mean you want to waste a day of *my* time on the off-chance prince charming rocks up at the harbor. No."

"He might be there. Fernando owns ships, of course he'll come to the harbor sooner or later."

"And if he does?" Malik asked, and picked up a humongous wooden spoon to stir the blue, bubbling concoction. "You set your pretty eyes on him, he smiles at you, if that. Maybe you talk, and then he's gone again, and you are back to square one. Nah, nah, nah. You need to get over this man. The sooner, the better, if you ask me."

Malik didn't understand the compulsion. The all-encompassing need to see Fernando. Be in his presence. Breathe the same air. Touch, kiss... It consumed every minute of every day. The urge was overwhelming. Even if it was a bad idea and wouldn't lead anywhere.

"I want to see him so badly. It hurts to be away from him."

"I know. But where is it going to get you? Nowhere. You don't even know if he's in Puerto Rico. Maybe your lover boy has sailed away again, off to new shores, new adventures, new..."

"Don't say it," Arian spat.

Malik stirred his rumbling cauldron. Then he turned to his shelves and picked out a cobalt blue powder. He added it to the cauldron and the potion *giggled*. The malodorous smell vanished, replaced by a sweet and spicy scent. Had the octopus worked for once? Malik pulled out the mothershell shard Arian had fetched him and eyed it indecisively. He shrugged and dropped it in the cauldron. The emerging steam sparkled. Something was working.

"What I'm saying is that it's been weeks," Malik said. "The man's moved on. And so should you. If he loved you, don't you think he'd found his way here by now? Don't you think he would have come after you? He hasn't, and that's all you need to know."

Malik was right. And Arian hated him all the more for it.

Chapter Nineteen

Fernando

"The rum," Darin said, "is telling me to do what the bloody hell my heart wants me to do. Which is to say, 'screw everything, I'm going back to him.'"

Fernando exhaled. He understood the sentiment. He'd thought the separation would get easier with time. It was getting worse. It robbed him of his joy, turned his days gray and his nights restless. Most days, he was in a foul mood, clenching his jaw as to not yell at his servants over nothing.

"And you know what," Darin continued, "maybe I will. There's no bloody point pretending I'm happy like this." He sniffed, eyed his glass and downed the rest of his rum before helping himself to another serving from Fernando's bottle.

No, there was no point pretending either of them were happy. Fernando had tried everything. He met women and found them unattractive no matter how pretty they were. He buried himself in work, and it turned out to be dull and uninspiring. Looking at the half-empty bottle of rum between them on the table, it was clear where this was headed next. And Fernando couldn't let it go there.

There was one cure. But how? And then what?

Fernando took a sip, poured himself more rum. "One way to fix it."

"Yeah. I want to be with him. Wish I knew how to make it work."

"So do I."

This couldn't be how it ended. He was unhappy, and Arian was enslaved to a sea witch for the rest of his life. Fernando refused to accept it. He had told himself to move on, tried to put the past behind him, and it led him to a shabby tavern at the port with a head full of sorrows and rum in his glass to drown them in.

"I have a confession to make," Darin said after another swig of rum. "This wasn't the first time I ran into mermen. I know Finn."

"What?"

"I used to be a pirate," Darin said, and fiddled with his glass. "Sorry. Our ship got lured in, like *The Haste*. Spent a day with Finn, then we got away. But ever since, he's been the reason for every one of my wet dreams."

Fernando pushed back on his stool. "Did you know there were mermen around Culebra?"

"No. I met Finn elsewhere. I was okay after the first time. But now, after spending more time with him, it's killing me."

It explained why Darin and Finn had seemed close from the beginning.

"Why didn't you say something?"

"Dunno." Darin fiddled with the hem of his shirt. "Didn't wanna blazon out that I like to get blown by a merman. I'm sure you understand."

He did, far too well.

They sat in the tavern for hours. Fernando's wheels turned. Darin's state was a wake-up call. Fernando had gone to the tavern to get drunk. Darin had been doing exactly that for however long. Fernando didn't want to end up like that. He would if nothing changed. The status quo was unbearable. And so with rum in his hand and Darin for company, a plan formed.

If he hated his life, the way Arian had, he might as well squander what he had to get what he wanted. That's what Arian had done for him. It was about time Fernando returned the favor.

Over the following days, he planned and plotted. He went over his books, visited his lawyer. Some of his assets were easy to hide, others impossible. The result was far from ideal, but it'd do.

Fernando packed his bags, moving his personal belongings into trunks and chests. He assembled a crew, finalized the purchases he'd been working on for weeks and boarded the *Liberty*, his private galleon. A typical merchant ship, she was a Spanish design, sluggish due to her sheer bulk, but an excellent choice for transporting large amounts of cargo. Equipped with seventy-four cannons, her stupendous firepower was that of a warship. With three decks and four masts, she was among the largest ships in the Caribbean. Perfect for long journeys.

The crew had been the most difficult part. The average galleon needed at least fifty staff to be operated, but a behemoth like the *Liberty* required a couple of hundred crew at a minimum. Fernando had paid an arm and a leg to hire men on short notice and then doubled their salary when he told them what they were going to do.

The smaller problem was finding out where the sea witch lived and asking around town with perseverance had gotten Fernando the information. It took the *Liberty* a couple of hours to get to the mangrove forest. From there, Fernando proceeded alone in a rowboat. He instructed his crew to let him down in the boat and wait for him, no matter how long he took. They had agreed, bewildered but too obedient to question their new boss.

Fernando rowed the boat toward the marker at the entrance of the mangrove forest. Map in his lap, he stirred the boat into the maze of twisting roots and hanging branches. Birds shrieked and chirped in the treetops as Fernando passed under them through the forest's water channels.

He found Malik's rotting shack at the end of a channel, leading to a wider water basin. Murky and putrid. Fernando wrinkled his nose. Arian had swum through this? Unthinkable. Fernando's fists clutched the paddles.

His boat darted across the water toward the decaying pier. Would it hold his weight? He grabbed his rope and swung it over one of the piles, pulling the boat toward the pier. Fernando braced himself on the pile and leaped onto the boardwalk. He strode over to the shack, back straight, head held high. Arian would not stay here for another hour, let alone a day.

Fernando rapped against the ramshackle door. A scared bird shot out of the trees. The hut rumbled, someone cursed as if they'd stubbed their toe. Then the front door swung open.

A young man of native—or Asian?—descent came into view. Fernando wasn't sure what he'd expected, but not a young man with the world's most rumpled dark brown hair, wearing a royal blue nightshirt.

"Well, hello," the man said. "Look what the cat's dragged in."

"I'm looking for Malik," Fernando said.

"Yeah, I figured. That'd be me. And you must be lover boy. Finally made it here."

Fernando took in the absurd inside of the shack. "You don't have a cat."

"Let me guess, you're looking for a certain merman?" Malik asked and scratched his chin. "Blood piss blond..."

Fernando's facial expression stopped him, and Malik didn't say any more unflattering things. Which was best for his health. Ironclad self-control kept Fernando from picking him up by the throat and slamming him into the rotting wall. This was no company for someone as precious as Arian.

If he wanted to negotiate with the bastard, he had to keep his cool. Fernando scanned the interior of the hut. Overflowing shelves. Books, vials, jars and pots. A cauldron bubbled blue and emitted a vanilla scent so strong, it put every bakery to shame. Was it Fernando's imagination or did the steam rising from the pot sparkle?

"I've come for Arian," Fernando said.

"Well," Malik said and turned around, walking back into the shack, "he isn't here."

Fernando followed him inside. The scent grew stronger and mixed with the smell of decaying wood. "Where is he, and when will he be back?"

"Ah, wouldn't you like to know…"

Malik's games led nowhere. Better for Fernando to cut straight to the chase. "I've come to negotiate his release from his contract with you."

"Have you now?" Malik pulled a couple of books from his shelves and placed them on his table. "Unfortunately, the contract is not for sale."

"It will be for the right price."

"You overestimate my interest in gold."

"Who said anything about gold?"

"You're not even going to offer coin?" Malik paused. He had given himself away. "Anyway, not for sale."

Fernando smirked. This was familiar territory. Malik feigning disinterest. Offer and counteroffer. He didn't make his fortune negotiating like a greenhorn.

They went back and forth for half an hour. Fernando would insist he'd pay for Arian's freedom, and Malik rejected. They weren't getting anywhere. Fernando would have to change tactics.

A knock… against the hut's floor? Fernando's eye traveled over the planks. Malik was looking everywhere but. There! A trapdoor. Fernando didn't wait for Malik. He shot forward, heart pounding, and ripped back the wooden cover. Malik stumbled after him, too late. Either way, he wouldn't have had the strength to hold Fernando back.

Arian's momentum carried him up onto the shack's floor from where he blinked up at Fernando. It took a second for Arian's disbelief to dissipate into a glowing smile. "Fernando!"

Fernando swept him up from the ignoble floor and into his arms.

"Why are you here?" Arian asked, his hand roaming over Fernando's face, his neck, his shoulders, while the other was curled around an object Fernando couldn't see.

Fernando pressed their foreheads together. His heart sang. Bliss flooded his veins. "I came for you."

"You always *come* for me," Arian whispered against his lips.

Fernando huffed a laugh. "That too." And with that, he pressed his mouth to Arian's, possessive but quick. No need to give Malik a show.

He turned his head away from Arian and faced Malik. With his foot, he pulled a stool from under the table and sat down, Arian on his lap. Holding Arian in his arms had his heart overflowing with joy. He hadn't been this elated in weeks. Not since Arian had come to him.

"So your supposed prince charming showed," Malik said to Arian. "It changes nothing."

Arian uncurled his fist and slapped something on the table. A shard of a seashell. It must have belonged to an enormous clam, judging by how far the growth lines were apart.

Malik snatched it up, eyes twinkling in the dim light of the shack.

"I got you what you wanted," Arian said.

Fernando cataloged the information. The shard was valuable to Malik. The fact that Arian had brought it to him could either strengthen Fernando's position as Malik had what he wanted, but it could also weaken it because he needed more. Malik backed away and stowed the shard in a jar.

"Arian stays with me," Malik said.

"Name your price for his freedom."

Arian stared at him, eyes wide. "What are you doing? Don't—"

Fernando interlaced their fingers. He squeezed Arian's hand and leaned in to whisper in his ear. "I'm not leaving without you." His arm around Arian's waist tightened, and Arian shifted closer, pressing his body against his chest.

But Fernando had to control himself. Too much affection would drive the price up.

"You want to negotiate for him like for cattle?" Malik asked, raising an eyebrow.

"Don't put words in my mouth," Fernando said.

"Just wondering." Malik occupied himself with the books he had pulled out. He flipped through them, searching for something. "As I said, his contract is not for sale."

"Then why are you looking through your ledger?" Fernando asked.

Caught, Malik slammed the books shut. Fernando smirked. He had eight years' experience negotiating with everyone from Mexico to Spain. Malik would not beat him at this game.

"I'm not going to pay for him. I pay for his freedom," Fernando said.

"Semantics," Malik replied. "Why would you want to pay 'for his freedom' anyway, hmm? It's not like you two can have a life together."

"That's not for you to decide," Fernando said.

"Aw, is that what you want? You realize he doesn't have legs, yeah? Can't walk around town with your pretty boy. He doesn't have a cock either, no hole for you to fuck."

Fernando's vision turned red. Malik was not speaking about Arian like that. Arian, who paled, face pulled tight in a grimace of pain. Malik violated all rules of propriety. Why? Arian hadn't told Fernando much about Malik, but what he had said hadn't made Malik sound crude.

Malik was willing to sell. But then why did he say those awful things? What had he said? *And you must be lover boy. Finally made it here.* Malik knew of his relationship with Arian. That Arian had wanted to be with Fernando so much, he signed his life away for a single day together. Arian's descriptions of Malik had been friendly. Did Malik like Arian as a friend? Who wouldn't like Arian? There was an obvious conclusion. If Malik saw a friend in Arian, he wanted to protect him. *Finally made it here.* Malik had expected Fernando to show up. And he hadn't. Instead, he'd tried to date three different women. Fernando wanted to beat his stupidity out of himself. Malik was looking out for Arian. He was worried Fernando didn't truly care about him because he had taken too damn long to show up. Everyone in Puerto Rico knew Fernando was a wealthy merchant, and Malik might have speculated on this exact outcome. That Fernando would turn up and ask to buy out his contract.

"If you think I love Arian one bit less because he has a fishtail, then you don't know the first thing about me," Fernando said. "You are insulting him and me."

"And how will you live together?" Malik asked. "Seems rather difficult. I have no potion to give you legs, Arian."

"That's none of your concern," Fernando said. "I'll make it work. It doesn't matter if our lives will be unusual. I will provide a comfortable environment for Arian." He'd made everything work in his life. He wasn't going to give up on the love of his life because of logistics.

"He isn't a woman either," Malik said.

Fernando hated talking about Arian like he wasn't there. Had Malik no manners? He kissed Arian's cheek. "I don't care about that. I love you the way you are. It doesn't matter what that makes me. You matter."

"No more Mister I-Don't-Like-Men?" Arian asked.

"No more. It's laughable at this point." Fernando returned his attention to Malik. "I will ask one more time: what do you want from me to release him free and clear?"

That pacified Malik. "Well, everything you own, of course."

Arian straightened in alarm. Fernando ran his fingers over his skin to calm him. It was fine, there was a way. Arian had never seen him negotiate.

"Don't be ridiculous," Fernando said.

"Your potion is finished," Arian chipped in. "The one you needed all the things for that you couldn't get without a merman. Sunken Aztec gold. Shard of mothershell. Twenty kinds of octopus. Until one made your concoction *sparkle*. Don't tell me it isn't finished. I know it is. You'll add the last shard I got you, and that will be it, whatever you're brewing there. Am I right?"

Fernando beamed with pride at Arian's cleverness. Arian, with his curious and alert mind, had deciphered what was going on with what Malik was doing. Not in detail, but enough to understand how far Malik had come along. Fernando rewarded him with another kiss to his cheek. Arian was pure joy.

"Then the contract shouldn't cost that much to dissolve," Fernando said.

"You two are unbelievable," Malik said, flopping back in his chair. "No, it doesn't work like that. I asked for a lifetime of servitude in exchange for the potion. If I let you go, I need to be paid properly. Fernando, I want your ships, your gold, your land and your house."

"You want my *house*?" Fernando asked, voice ringing with shock.

"And your ships, gold and land."

"I can pay you in gold," Fernando said. "But you're not getting any of the rest."

"Then we've come to an impasse."

"Ten thousand gold doubloons." It was an obscene amount of money. A single doubloon could feed a family for a month. This was why most people didn't own doubloons, they had the lighter, lower value gold escudos and silver reales. For Fernando, it was go big or go home.

"No." Malik was an idiot to turn down the offer. Ten thousand doubloons and he'd live in luxury until the end of his days. It'd buy him anything he wanted. "I want your gold, ships, land *and* house."

"You want me naked."

"No," Malik said. "Arian wants you naked. I'll just get you there."

"Fine," Fernando said. "Ten thousand doubloons, two ships and my land."

"Don't do this!" Arian said, panicking. "It's not worth it. Please, don't."

"Babe," Fernando whispered so that Malik couldn't hear, "it's just money."

"You don't get it," Malik said. "I want it all."

Fernando gritted his teeth. He'd seen this coming. With reluctance, he said, "Ten thousand doubloons, my land and all my ships except the one I came in on. I get to keep my house."

"Fernando, no!" Arian said.

The villa in San Juan had become Fernando's home. It was a safe place to rest his head after a long journey. He'd overseen the construction of the place, furnished it to his taste. It wasn't just any old manor, it was his home, a piece of his soul.

"I've always fancied living in San Juan," Malik said. "Throw in the house and we have a deal."

Fernando exhaled. "Fine."

"No!" Arian said.

"Deal," Malik said.

They shook on it. Fernando had asked his lawyer to prepare the papers, and he filled in the blanks with a quill provided by Malik. He signed when Malik neutralized Arian's Voodoo doll. Fernando fantasized about killing Malik on the spot when he realized what kind of hold he'd had over Arian. He clenched his jaw and with more force than necessary slapped the papers onto Malik's table.

"There," Fernando said. "Take my gold, my ships, my house. Go to my lawyer in San Juan, and he'll finalize the transfer with you. It'll be a cushy transition. I hope you're happy."

He got up, and without sparing Malik another glance, he bridal style carried Arian out of the undignified shack. The boards of the pier creaked under his heavy steps. It was done. Fernando glowed with happiness, despite what he'd signed away. It was all worth it. Arian was free, which was all that mattered. He sat him down in the boat.

"I can swim," Arian said. "You don't have to—"

"And you don't have to swim through that murky brew. You

deserve better." Fernando climbed into the boat and rowed them away from Malik's hut.

Arian fidgeted. His eyes were glassy, his hands shook. "I'm sorry. You shouldn't have given him all this. I'm not—"

"You're worth it," Fernando said. "I can rebuild. Money can be replaced. I came from nothing and made a fortune. It can be repeated."

The boat took them out of the mangrove forest and to the *Liberty*. Good thing he'd warned the crew and paid them double. They had reluctantly agreed to have a merman join them after Fernando guaranteed their safety. Didn't mean they weren't shaking with fear when they saw Arian on the boat.

Fernando had to ask him the real question. It made him more nervous than the negotiation with Malik. "We can talk about the details later, but would you like to come on board with me? I've set it up for you in case you wanted…"

"I'd love to," Arian said, and squeezed his knee. "I don't know how we can make it work, but I'll follow you everywhere I can. And a few places I can't, too."

Fernando gave the crew the signal to bring the boat back up. They eyed Arian with unveiled curiosity. Some apprehensive, some with too much hunger in their gaze for Fernando's liking. When the boat hit the deck, they backed away. Fernando climbed out and picked up Arian. Under the watchful eyes of the crew, he carried him to his private quarters. It didn't matter what the crew thought. He'd told them what was coming, they'd agreed to it, and he'd paid them handsomely. Nobody would've been surprised to see him with another man. It happened plenty at sea. But a merman? They'd have to get used to it.

In his cabin, nailed to the floor and mounted to a wall, stood a hammock-shaped wooden bathtub. It was wide and filled with fresh water, rose petals floating on top. He bent to sit Arian down in it.

"For me?" Arian asked disbelievingly.

"Yes," Fernando said. "Everything for you." He'd commissioned the piece as a rush order. The carpenter had labored over it day and night and outdone himself. It was an excellent piece, smooth and perfectly molded to accommodate a merman's body. Comfortable for Arian to sleep in while keeping his fishtail in the water, which the crew was instructed to change a couple of times a day.

"Thank you," Arian said, and took his hand, kissing his knuckles. "This is amazing."

Fernando melted. "I have no words for how happy I am to have you here."

Arian's face darkened with pain and regret falling over it. Oh, no. Fernando had been too forward. This was too much, too soon. He should have let Arian slide into the ocean. Of course, he felt trapped in a bathtub in his cabin, helpless and unable to go anywhere without human assistance. He should have thought of this.

"I'm sorry," Arian said.

"Don't be. It's okay. I can let you back out. You can swim beside the ship if you like."

"What? No. I'm just…" Arian looked down and nervously flicked his fishtail in the water. "You did too much for me. I'll never be able to repay you."

"You don't have to repay me," Fernando said, and cupped his cheek.

"Malik took everything."

Fernando laughed. "Almost."

"What do you mean?"

"I still have this ship and my remaining two thousand doubloons." Fernando pointed at the chests lining the opposite wall. "Plus I have a villa in Spain he doesn't know about. Malik made bank today, but he didn't take everything. This ship is loaded to the brim with cargo. We're heading up north and will return with different cargo and more gold. I lost a lot today, but not all." He leaned in and kissed Arian's lips. "I'd have given him everything down to my last shirt if that's what it would've taken. I instructed my lawyer that it might come to that. He was appalled, but I was prepared. No cost is too high for this."

Arian grabbed his collar and pulled him in for a kiss. Fernando gave in to the sweet slide of lips, to Arian's probing tongue. He let him in, tasted him. There was no greater bliss than the wet heat of his mouth, the soft hands working his shirt open, stripping off his jacket.

With his clothes off, Fernando climbed into the tub and straddled Arian.

"Rest on top of me," Arian said. Fernando was worried about crushing him, but Arian pulled him down. "I love feeling your weight."

Fernando sank against him and captured Arian's lips. There was no more powerful aphrodisiac. He rutted into Arian, feeling him after long weeks of separation. His slick lower half fit perfectly between Fernando's legs. He pressed his erection against Arian's abdomen, shivering at the delicious friction.

"How do you feel about me not having legs?" Arian asked. "No cock, no hole for you to push into…"

"But you do have a hole for me to push into," Fernando said, and licked into his mouth.

"I meant…"

"I know what you meant. There'll be no cock-to-ass for either of us. It doesn't matter. I'll make you feel good regardless. Make you come. You'll make me come. We have lips, tongues, hands. There'll be toys for both of us. The idea that only penetration counts as sex is something repressed Catholics came up with to excuse all the other kinky shit they were doing. Don't think of me like that."

Arian reached up and wrapped his arms around Fernando's neck, pulling him down. "I don't."

"Then let's have fun," Fernando said against his lips. "You know the trick. Breathe deeply, all the way down to where I'm rubbing into you. Moan when you breathe out. I want the crew to know what's happening in here. That you're mine."

"That you can make a fucking merman come."

"That too." He kissed the corners of Arian's mouth, then slipped down to his neck. Lips and teeth closed around his pulse point. Fernando licked and sucked in time with Arian's moans. The tub would need a change of water more than twice a day.

His hand found Arian's nipple. The moans grew in urgency.

"Over time, I'll teach you how to come on command, so when I order it, you come in three seconds flat," Fernando said. Arian whimpered. "There'll be constant release for you. No more frustration. Just coming, coming, coming. Every hour if you want to."

He flicked and twisted Arian's nipple, making him arch under him. His pulse hammered against Fernando's tongue. With weeks since their last encounter and scorching hot memories to fuel their lust, they were on a hairline trigger.

Fernando slid down and took Arian's other nipple between his lips, gently biting it. Arian thrashed, spilling water over the sides.

"How…"

"How are you so close to coming already?" Fernando asked. "Your body knows what I've done to you before. That I can and will do it again. I make good on my promises, and your body recognizes that. It becomes a self-fulfilling prophecy."

His own balls were full and heavy. Wanting Arian to have it all when he was back in his arms, he'd refrained from jerking himself off the last couple of days. Now he barely contained his need, pulsing and throbbing against Arian.

Arian's hands ran down his body. They slid over the small of his back and onto his ass, kneading him. With one swift roll of his hips, Arian had their positions reversed. It sent half the bathwater flying. Fernando's cabin would have to get cleaned a lot more frequently on this journey.

"I thought you wanted me on top," Fernando said.

"Changed my mind."

"Naughty," Fernando said, and slapped his butt.

Arian squirmed. Fernando reached between them and placed his hand over Arian's lower abdomen, Arian's weight pressing him into his fingers. He rubbed gently and dished out another sharp smack. Arian's yelp turned into a moan. He wriggled against Fernando, who bit his lip as the slick up and down motion between his legs almost sent him over the edge.

No way he'd come before Arian. He fought for control and landed another slap. Arian cried out in pleasure, pressing his forehead to Fernando's shoulder.

Fernando wrapped his legs around Arian's lower half, immobilizing him. The next smack was so hard, Fernando felt it reverberate through Arian into his own cock and balls. Arian's breathing was deep and fast. His pulse raced. He was close.

"You're mine," Fernando said, hitting him again and again. "Do you know how I feel about you?"

"Yes."

"Say it," Fernando demanded. Arian was the type to question his worthiness. That had to be wiped out once and for all. He hit his ass when there was no response. "Say it!"

"You love me."

Fernando felt Arian's involuntary contraction against his crotch. "I love you." *Smack.* "You're mine." *Smack.* "You will obey." *Smack.*

"I will."

Fernando slapped his butt one more time, then pulled him flush against his chest, tucking his head under his chin, while their groins pressed together. "Come for me, baby."

Arian stilled and went rigid. He quivered in Fernando's arms and screamed his orgasm as his pulsing contractions throbbed against Fernando's cock. Slick and hot and convulsing, it was more than Fernando could handle. He growled, and Arian slid over him. His insides pulled taut, his focus narrowing on the spot where his twitching cock was trapped between their bodies. It straightened, and with fast, hard contractions, Fernando shot his cum between them. His groin seized endlessly, every wave a celebration of his reunion with Arian.

When the contractions eased off, he pecked Arian's head and stroked his hair. He'd rather be a beggar and be with Arian than have all the money in the world and face it without him.

Arian placed a kiss on his chest before snuggling back in. "So this is how it's going to be? I get to live in your cabin and travel the world with you?"

"If you want to, yes. Though, there's more onboard for you," Fernando said, trailing his fingertips over Arian's shoulder.

"Like what?"

"I'll read books to you. In fact, I'll teach you to read and write. And there are more bathtubs for you around the ship. I don't want you to be stuck. I've had one installed on deck, one in the mess... And of course, you should swim too. Don't feel tied to the ship."

"Thank you," Arian said, kissing him. "You do too much for me. I want to earn my keep. Is there any way I can do work on the ship?"

"Curious that you ask. I'd love to hire you as crew. I have a unique job opportunity for you, which will save me a lot of money in the long run."

"Yeah?"

"When we washed up in the Culebra archipelago, our ship was being chased by pirates. Over the years, my ships have been boarded by pirates more than once. Lost a lot of gold to the bastards. I wonder what they would do when they suddenly saw a merman between their ship and ours."

Arian snickered.

His unique skill set came into full play days later, when a pirate ship spotted the sluggish *Liberty* and made straight for it. A galleon, the *Liberty* was slow and cumbersome and had no chance getting away from a sloop, a pirate's favorite ship—fast and agile with a shallow draft. The *Liberty*'s cannons were useful, though unable to defend against frontal attacks or those to the stern.

But with the ship's newest crew member, handling the threat

was child's play.

Out at the balustrade, Arian jumped from Fernando's arms fifteen yards down into the water and fluked toward the pirates. Fernando followed him with the long glass. He could have sworn the entire pirate ship jumped in fear when they caught view of Arian's azure fishtail leaping through the sea. Fernando had never seen a ship turn so fast.

Epilogue

Arian

Two years later

The opening exhibition was an enormous success. The painting merman, the pools and connecting waterways in the largest villa the New World had ever seen—it drew a crowd. Arian sat on a ledge just under the surface of the pool and watched the richest Puerto Ricans float through the house on small canoes. The event was so exclusive and unique, it had even drawn the nobility.

After learning how to read and write, Arian had taken an interest in painting. He loved sea and island landscapes, but what made his work stand out were his underwater sceneries. Colorful coral reefs, decaying sunken ships, variegated schools of fish. Those were the things humans would never get to see, and the amount of gold such a painting could fetch was staggering.

Fernando had rebuilt his trade empire with vigor, and Arian helped however he could. With gold back in his pockets, Fernando drew plans for a gargantuan residence. A single-story villa of epic proportions, every room split between a normal setup and a pool. The broad hallways, too, were divided into a walkway and a water channel, allowing both humans and merman alike to move around the house. Large, open windows carried in fresh air and reduced moisture while servants worked on the never-ending task to change the water.

Arian had wanted to contribute to the expense of building such a lavish home. Fernando told him not to worry about it, more than happy to pay for everything. But Arian insisted. His art had found favor among the Puerto Rican upper crust and thus the idea of an exhibition was born. Never in his life had he imagined the violent bidding war that followed.

The pools and waterways were large enough for small canoes to maneuver, the on-the-water element adding another layer of excitement to the exhibition. They could have stuck the paintings on the walls, but where was the fun in that? Instead, they were sitting a few feet back from the pool edges on the low easels Arian had used for painting.

The guests were dressed to the nines. Ladies fought to get into the canoes with their wide dresses and fans while men had it easier with their three pieces. They all had wet butts in the end.

Fernando had stayed in a canoe for most of the evening, talking to guests while his lawyer took bids. As the affair was winding down, Fernando slipped out of his jacket and into the water. With powerful strokes, he swam over to Arian and onto the ledge.

"It's impressive," Fernando said. "The shark painting fetched two hundred doubloons. They love you."

A lady in a pink gown was quarreling with an elderly, wig-wearing gentleman over a painting depicting a merman tail drifting through clear blue water, his upper body hidden outside the picture's frame.

"I had fun," Arian said. "We should do this again."

"Absolutely." Fernando's eyes sparkled.

"I have some ideas. I want to work on more merman paintings. Maybe portray a merman and a human together."

"They'll eat it up."

Arian's integration into human life had not been seamless. Fernando's building plans for the villa had been celebrated for their innovation—until people found out a merman was going to be living there. It had taken Fernando a lot of cajoling the locals to get them to accept Arian. They had in the end, with reluctance, but once they got to know him, Arian made friends.

Fernando leaned in, his breath hot against Arian's ear. When they were in public, that meant one thing. Arian's breathing hitched as he clenched up inside and shivered with need. That had never changed. Fernando satisfied him bone-deep, but that didn't mean his body wasn't ready to come again a couple of hours later. Good thing Fernando could make him come on command whenever necessary. It kept him sane.

"I'm proud of you," Fernando whispered. "Your work is outstanding. Look at them. They're fighting over the last pieces."

The lady in pink hit the gentleman across the arm with her fan.

Fernando's warm, wet tongue traced the outer shell of Arian's ear. "I could order you to come, but we'll have more fun if we wait."

"You're cruel," Arian laughed.

"You like it. Anyway, I stopped by Malik's the other day."

Arian's eyes went wide, his heart rate shot through the roof. "Oh, god."

Despite what Malik had said two years ago, he was now able to provide them with more of the leg-giving potion. Not regularly, but he was producing it, the quantities increasing over time. The price had gone down too, from a life in servitude to a few doubloons. Far more expensive than what an ordinary person could afford, who had no use for the potion anyway. Mermen on the other hand... all of a sudden gold did have value to them, and there were rumors of sunken ship raids as mermen fought to get coin.

If Fernando had gone to Malik, it meant he'd bought a vial of the potion. And consequently, Arian was going to get ripped in two later that evening. He licked his lips. Or he'd fuck Fernando into oblivion. Who was he kidding? This was no either-or situation.

"Oh, yes," Fernando said. "And I figured out how he gets all the mothershell shards for the potion."

"Pray tell."

"He turned himself into his own kind of deep sea diver. Did you ever wonder why he required you to get all those different octopuses for his potion?"

"You don't mean…"

"I do. Malik got tentacles. The potion that gives you legs is invertible. It was what he was working on two years ago. And he let you go with me because with your help he'd gotten the ingredients he needed to make a potion that gave him merfolk abilities. So he could get more mothershell and what else he needed himself."

Arian gulped. What Fernando said had implications. "Do you think he never intended to keep me as a servant for the rest of my life? That he had simply wanted to keep me until his potion worked? And then he saw you and the opportunity to get rich…"

"It's possible. We'll never know. I should be angry at him for it. Considering his potion means I get to fuck your brains out tonight, I don't care. You coming for half an hour straight is worth any price."

Arian clenched up inside. He couldn't wait for the last guests to finally leave. Fernando would take him to heaven.

Thank you for reading *Escaping the Merman*!
Would you like to see more of Fernando and Arian? I've got good news for you! There's a FREE mini-prequel short story available to my newsletter subscribers. It's called *Merman Dreams Are Wet*; **grab it here**: aramisjordan.com/signup

Reviews are important as they help me stay ahead of the Amazon algorithm and are great social proof. If you enjoyed *Escaping the Merman*, **please consider leaving a review on Amazon**.

And don't forget to join my private Facebook group, *Aramis Jordan's Adonis Jungle*: facebook.com/groups/aramisjordan

Thank you & see you soon!

Much love,
Aramis Jordan

Read the sequel

Hunting the Merman
Cursed Mermen Book 2
An MM Enemies to Lovers Romance
(Kristian & Tarlis)

Available at Amazon

A brooding captain seeking revenge.
A gorgeous merman who takes as good as he gives.

Captain Kristian Andersen isn't ready when beautiful merman Tarlis lures in his ship and lets him experience his deepest desires. But when the dark myths about mermen turn out to be true, Kristian escapes, and the need for vengeance consumes him.

Tarlis knows he's made a mortal enemy, but he didn't think Kristian would hunt him to the ends of the Earth to exact his revenge. SoonTarlis realizes he didn't anticipate half the plans Kristian has for him.

Kristian is going to teach Tarlis a lesson he'll never forget.

Coming Soon

Stealing the Merman
Cursed Mermen Book 3
An MMM Romance
(Darin, Finn & Conall)

Release Day: 26 January 2022

Darin
A pirate looking for his own found family.

Conall
An infamous pirate captain who's sworn off love.

Finn
A cursed merman who yearns for what he can't have—pleasure.

When they meet, sparks fly. But having grown up in an orphanage, Darin is insecure. Conall was betrayed by the woman he loved, and he has locked his heart away. Finn has no means to break the curse and be with the men he loves.

And there's a dark secret lurking in the shadows.

Printed in Great Britain
by Amazon